GIDEON
VERSUS THE GODS OF
Cool

BY STEPHEN GASHLER

For information, or to order additional copies, please contact:

Beacon Publishing Group
P.O. Box 41573 Charleston, S.C. 29423
800.817.8480| beaconpublishinggroup.com

Publisher's catalog available by request.

ISBN-13: 978-1-949472-83-7

ISBN-10: 1-949472-83-3

Published in 2019. Printed in the USA.

First Edition. New York, NY 10001

For the old gang.

THE GRAY LADY

A scary woman is watching me.

No sooner does Gideon have this realization than he drops his twelve pound dumbbells on the bleachers, the sound clattering through the gym. Down on the floor, basketballs stop bouncing, shoes stop scuffing, and all heads look up.

Coach Griffith pulls a slimy whistle from his mouth, shouting, "Gideon, if you're not going to lift weights, then come down and join the game."

Gideon raises the collar of his trench coat, picks up the dumbbells, and resumes his pumping. "My doctor said I shouldn't." His eyes gravitate to the oblong window on the other side of the gym, where the woman was watching him.

She's gone.

Coach Griffith, plump, tired, and in need of a shave, rolls his eyes, then places the whistle back into his mouth. At his command, the chaos resumes: balls pound, bodies collide, sweat trickles.

Where did she go? Gideon runs his hands through his unkempt hair, studying the strange window above the bleachers, but it's dark and opaque, with no sign of the gray-haired woman. Did he imagine her?

Down below, the ball flies from one set of hands to the next, so long as the owners of the hands are wearing red jerseys. More than one blue jersey runs, jumps, and lunges, only to find himself crashing onto the hard, wood floor, humiliated and in pain.

What matters is that Gideon is safe … or at least he thought he was. Something about being spied on by a phantom authority figure has a way of disturbing one's inner sanctum. The mere memory of the woman's soulless eyes and stern expression gives Gideon chills. Perhaps he imagined her. But then, why would his brain conjure up something so creepy?

What's in that room, anyway? It's strange how he never noticed the long window before, which is apparently part of some mysterious office above the bleachers. Supposing the woman was real, what teacher or administrator has nothing better to do with their time than spy on boys' P.E.?

And there it is again, that unmistakable feeling of being watched. Though Gideon is loath to enter the killing field below, suddenly he'd rather be anywhere than alone on the bleachers.

What am I afraid of? He hasn't done anything wrong. Except, of course, for forging doctors notes … for the last two months. And he probably wasn't supposed to be wearing a trench coat to school. Then there were those many times he sluffed math …

Relax, Gideon. Either he's been reading too many science fiction and fantasy novels, and the woman was a product of an over-stimulated imagination, or she was probably just a janitor, who happened to glance in his direction before turning off the light. Surely the gaze meant nothing at all.

So why is his heart rate increasing? Gideon unzips his bag and pulls out his ear buds. There's nothing so frightening or horrible that Vivaldi's *Four Seasons* can't soothe. The senseless noise of the gym gives way to graceful strings, order, and harmony. The fury of the barbaric brute is quelled by gentility. The dark specters of authority figures vanish. Gideon can breathe again. Soon gym will be over, school will be out, and he'll have survived another day. He'll escape to his happy place of bright pixels and virtual reality, where life is a game and no one can tell him what to do.

Gideon Greenwich is a nerd; he was born a nerd, and he will die a nerd. He, of course, has no patience for sports, so when he finds himself watching the players below, it has nothing to do with jealousy or admiration, only an attempt to ease his troubled mind with the amusing pursuits of jocks.

Down below, a blond-haired gladiator pounds the ball against the floor. A red jersey sticks to his perfect physique as his brown eyes, determined and somewhat savage, scan the court. He makes his way through the defense … but there is no defense. No one dares stand in his way.

Doug Rock is a jock. As the seventh son of a football coach — so Gideon's heard — Doug was born a jock, and he will die a jock. At last, Doug throws the dripping ball to his teammate, Kyle Slater.

Kyle was also born into the jock dynasty. His father, an ex-convict, cage fighter, and hockey star, set a world record for the most fouls in the NHL … or so the rumors say. Regardless of the veracity of his reputation, Kyle's very presence elicits fear. His face pink, his mouth foaming, he plows through anyone who dares stand in his way … which, again, is no one.

Kyle jumps, shoots, and scores. Doug gives Kyle a congratulatory slap on the back, and Kyle returns the gesture. Thus having exhibited the acceptable limits of manly affection, the soaking athletes straighten their shoulders and return to their places.

Coach Griffith shouts, "Red team: one-hundred-eleven. Blue team: five."

At the center of the court, in a blue jersey, stands someone Gideon can relate to: two-hundred-fifty pounds of Dwight Farnsworth, a fellow nerd. Dwight wipes the sweat from his forehead, then finding his fingers sweaty, wipes them on his jersey, which is already saturated with sweaty finger marks. Resenting the very existences of sweat and jerseys, Dwight glances at the clock, that great god to whom even public school must bend a knee. It's one-forty-five. Class will be over in five minutes. Five more minutes of agony.

Gideon also watches the clock. The distractions are failing, the violins doing nothing. His heart is beating faster, and his eyes won't leave the dark, oblong window. He knows what he saw. Someone *was* watching him, and somehow, though it makes no sense, that someone knows the secrets of his teenage heart. He has to get out of the gym.

Uh-oh. Couch Griffith is shouting at him.

Gideon takes out his earbuds. "What?"

"Put those darn things away and get back to work!"

Gideon does as he's told, soon taking out his anxiety on the iron dumbbells. He curls all twenty-four pounds, watching his biceps contract and relax. He's got absolutely nothing on Doug Rock.

The clock is at one-forty-six. Four more minutes of agony.

The window is still dark.

Gideon closes his eyes and tries to clear his mind, but how can one hear the hum of the universe while bombarded by the mind-numbing racket of basketball? The mere concept of the sport — running back and forth yet going nowhere, bouncing a ball for no reason, stuffing it in baskets only for it to fall out again — is an exercise in futility, the epitome of busywork; no wonder it's so popular in public schools.

Still the window is dark.

Gideon looks up at the metal ceiling of the gym and imagines what's above it, beyond the steel frames and lead pipes, beyond the sentinels of the great machine that traps him. He projects his mind into that shining world where there are no teachers and no books, just wonderful things like spaceships, dragons, and attractive girls with swords.

He opens one eye. It's one-forty-seven, and the window is dark. Class will be over in three minutes. But he can't wait that long.

He studies the wall behind him. The railing of the balcony above is within reach. With a small jump, he could pull himself up and over, then slip away on the next level. With so many eye witnesses below, it's a risky endeavor, but then, class *is* almost over.

Why is his heart beating so fast? He sets down the weights, puts on his bag, stands up, and leaps. He grabs onto the top bar and executes the daring escape. A moment later, he's crouching in the darkness of the balcony. Heart pounding, breathing heavily, he looks down at the court, but no one has noticed.

Victory! The glowing exit sign is only a few steps away, and with the clock at one-forty-eight, he's bought himself two precious minutes of freedom. Perhaps to play it safe, or perhaps as a final attempt

to prove to himself that he's not crazy, he glances at the oblong window.

The room on the other side is no longer dark, and staring at him
is a woman in a gray skirt suit. Her hair is short, her glasses rectangular, and her eyes unmistakably stern.

Gideon runs.

MS. PRIMPLE

With the gym safe behind him, Gideon slips into one of the school hallways. He still has the feeling that he's being watched, but there's nothing around him but lockers and doors.

"There you are, Gideon."

Gideon whips around, his heart jolting. He's calmed by the familiar sight of his friend, Wanda Biggles.

Wanda has thick glasses, unkempt hair, and a faded *Pokémon* t-shirt over a girth that almost rivals Dwight Farnsworth's.

Wanda studies his face. "Are you okay?"

Gideon checks the other end of the hallway. Seeing no teachers in sight, he puts on his sunglasses. They go nicely with the trench coat, plus they shield his eyes from authority figures. "Wanda, you know that long window in the gym … the one above the bleachers?"

"What about it?"

"What *is* that place?"

Wanda shrugs. "Some administrative office, I think."

"But how do you get up there?"

"Why do you care?"

"I don't. I was just wondering."

Dwight Farnsworth, red and soaked from head to toe, steps out of the boys' locker room. His eyes go straight to Gideon. "You bum."

Thankfully, the sunglasses also mask shamed eyes. "My doctor —"

"You don't have to lie to *us*."

Gideon sighs. "I happen to believe that P.E. is cruel and unusual, okay?"

Dwight tries in vain to wipe the sweat from his forehead. "We all do, but at least I'm man enough to face it."

"Hey, Dwight, have you ever seen a teacher at this school with short, gray hair?"

"Changing the subject, I see."

"She has these rectangular glasses, and she looks kind of ... scary. You know?"

Dwight and Wanda just stare at him.

Gideon stuffs his hands into his trench coat. "We'd better get to class."

Sixth period: *Fashion Merchandising.*

Gideon and Dwight are the only boys in the classroom full of girls, who are less than inclusive. Though Wanda is technically a girl, she doesn't fit in any better. Together they sit in the back row, content to sit out the last period of the day in a mindless, throw-away class.

As the bell rings and the chatter dies down, the teacher, Ms. Primple, saunters to the front of the room, her hips rotating with each step. She's wearing her usual high heels, leather pants, and to-day a frilly blouse with leopard spots.

"Good afternoon, girls." She smiles, her lips covered in bright rouge. Then she glances at the back row. "I mean ... *class.*" She forces another smile and twiddles her blond hair.

Gideon has to make a concentrated effort not to stare at her. He's often caught Dwight doing the same.

"Before we get to your midterm presentations," Ms. Primple continues, "I'd like you to pull out your observation journals." She grabs a stack of magazines and begins to hand them out. One is tossed onto Gideon's desk. *Vainglory Magazine.* The cover features an evil-looking woman with a flat hairline and a skimpy dress. Gideon flips through the pages and sees more of the same. With a groan, he pulls out a pen and notebook and begins to write:

Today's observation: On page 17, a woman is wearing a

green and orange dress that conveniently flaunts her breasts and belly button. *She's lying on top of what looks like a kitchen counter. She has short red hair, and her painted nails are long and freaky. I'm too young to know for certain, but I'm pretty sure the expression on her face of suffering euphoria has something to do with sex.*

At the desk in front of him, Joan Cooper, one of the cheerleaders, says, "Oh … my … gosh."

Gideon peers forward to see what's so exciting. In Joan's magazine is a black and white photo of a muscular man in tight, thin shorts. With a dripping, wet body and a towel flung over his shoulder, the man stares at the camera with a look that seems to say *"I want to kill you."*

Joan shows the picture to her cheerleader friends, who likewise gush over it. Gideon thinks there's something unnatural about teenage girls gawking over pictures of nameless men in their underwear, though as always, he keeps his thoughts to himself.

At the front of the classroom, Ms. Primple is filing her red nails. "All right, class, put your journals away and pass forward the magazines. Like it or not, it's time for your midterm presentations. Who's first?"

A hand shoots up from Cynthia McDaniels … the beautiful Cynthia McDaniels.

Ms. Primple nods her head, and Cynthia takes her place at the front of the classroom; Gideon holds no reservations in staring.

Cynthia moves a lock of brown hair out of her face before reading from her pink binder. "For my research project, I studied the corset. Though in modern times, the corset has fallen out of fashion, for hundreds of years, it was viewed as mandatory for the well-dressed woman. By constricting the abdomen and forcing belly fat to compress, the corset made women appear skinnier and thus more attractive."

Cynthia is also a cheerleader. Gideon, of course, knows that she's way out of his league, but of all the impossible fantasies he likes to entertain, none are more alluring than the thought of her as his girlfriend.

"The corset's firm construction from whale bones made it virtually impossible to see tucks and rolls. Though the pressure of corsets caused many women to die from internal injuries, we must ask ourselves, what is the price we're willing to pay to look good? This, my friends, is a question you must answer for yourselves. Thank you."

The class applauds, and Cynthia takes her seat.

Ms. Primple looks up from her nails. "I had to ask myself that question when I was shopping yesterday. Would I rather have one-hundred-eighty-nine dollars or high heels that burn a mark on men's corneas?" She shows off her bright red high heels, and the girls voice their awe.

The time is two-twenty, only thirty more minutes until freedom.

Before Ms. Primple can call for the next presenter, the door opens, and a woman walks into the classroom: flannel skirt suit, short gray hair, rectangular glasses.

Gideon freezes. Suddenly he can hear his own heartbeat as the woman scans the room, her eyes stopping on him.

"Please excuse me," she says to Ms. Primple, her voice as cold as her appearance, "but I must meet with one of your students, Mister Gideon Greenwich."

INTERVIEW

Gideon follows the gray lady. The only sound in the empty hallways are their footsteps and the throbbing in his ears. They pass a picture on the wall. He's seen it before, but he's never noticed the details. It's of a beautiful sunset. In the foreground, a riding cowboy is cracking a whip at a herd of cattle. Filling the bottom of the frame is the word "Discipline."

The gray lady stops at a door that reads "Staff Only." Gideon knows this is the teachers' lounge. He's caught glimpses of many a teacher walking in and out, and the wonderful things within. Pizza, brownies, all sorts of fine delicacies that never made their way into the cafeteria.

The gray lady opens the door, revealing a narrow staircase … a dark staircase.

"But —" Gideon begins.

The gray lady scowls at him.

Gideon holds his peace, though his skin crawls at the weird mystery. Maybe the teachers' lounge was moved.

They ascend the stairs. At the top is a long hallway that leads to a single door. The gray lady pulls out a jangling ring that must have a hundred keys on it. She unlocks the door and reveals a small office.

"Enter," she orders.

Gideon obeys.

Florescent tubes buzz overhead. There are no pictures on the walls. On the left side of the office is the oblong window that faces the gym.

The gray lady closes the door and takes a seat behind a well-organized desk.

The only thing of interest in the room is a small bronze statue of a man on the desk. Etched in the metal are sunglasses, baggy pants, and chained necklaces. The figure looks like a rap star. Almost as perplexing are the small candles surrounding it, burnt at the wicks.

"Sit," the gray lady orders.

Gideon sits. He points to the statue. "Who did you confiscate that from?"

"That does not concern you."

"Am I in trouble?"

"We'll get to that."

The gray lady wheels her chair to a filing cabinet. She opens a drawer and pulls out a folder. "Here we are … Gideon Greenwich. Let's see here …" She thumbs through papers. "Quail Run Elementary school, second grade, Ms. Wordsworth's class. Quote …"

> *Gideon shows promise. He's one of the best readers in the class. But I can't get him to pay attention during math. He spends class time doodling on the back of his worksheets.*

The gray lady shakes her head.

Amazed and insulted, Gideon says, "That was almost … nine years ago."

The gray lady cocks her eyebrows. "So you *can* count. Very impressive for a sixteen-year-old." She pulls out another paper. "Fabelton Middle School … Mr. Roberts's class."

> *Gideon is really struggling with math. He never pays attention in class. I can't get him to stop drawing.*

Gideon says, "I didn't know I was being tracked all this time."

The gray lady laughs. "Well of course you were."

"For your information, I've never failed a single math class."

"Yes, you seem to do alright on the tests, but your classwork and homework scores are deplorable." She pulls out another paper. "Eastward High School. Ms. Penelope."

> *Gideon never does his homework. I don't know why he comes*

to class. His mind is always somewhere else.

Gideon throws up his arms. "What does it matter, so long as I pass the tests?"

"Mr. Greenwich, if school was about passing tests, we'd all be out of a job. You're here because you need to learn character, discipline, and life skills. Without us, you're like an untamed horse. If you're to be of any use to society, you must first be broken."

"I don't need to be babysat."

Shooting him a sharp glance, the gray lady continues down her list. "Ms. Fitzwater."

> *Gideon seems fascinated by ancient world history, but I can't get him to turn anything in. He just draws on every assignment.*

"Coach Griffith."

> *Gideon almost never participates in P.E. He pretends he has a medical condition.*

"Ms. Primple."

> *I don't know why Gideon and Dwight are taking Fashion Merchandising. They clearly have no interest in the subject. Maybe they thought it would be an easy A, or maybe they just like being surrounded by girls. While Dwight at least tries to participate, all Gideon does is draw pictures of weird things like dragons and spaceships. He makes the girls uncomfortable.*

The gray lady sets down the papers. "Mister Greenwich, I'm concerned about your education."

"Are you my new counselor?"

"No."

"Then who are you?"

"That does not concern you."

"You're *stalking* me. I at least deserve to know who you are."

"We do not *stalk*. We *track*."

"*We?*"

"We … administrators."

"If you're a school administrator, then why have I never seen you before?"

"Oh, I've been around. Are you sure you've never seen me?"

Gideon hesitates. There *is* something familiar about her, uncomfortably familiar. "I …"

"I work for the district, so I have many schools to visit; thus, you won't see me very often. And do you always address adults like such? No wonder you're at high risk."

"High risk?"

"Everything about you is a red flag — your questionable clothes, your seclusive tendencies, your poor academic record, your rude demeanor … for which I demand an apology."

The room falls silent.

At last, Gideon says, "I didn't do anything."

The gray lady folds her arms. "We do not talk back to adults. You will apologize when I tell you to."

"For what?"

"Have it your way. I'll call your parents." The gray lady pulls out a phone.

"Okay … I'm … sorry."

She glares at him. Then her face softens. "No, I'm sorry. I know I come across as stern, but believe me, my only objective is to help you achieve your highest potential. I want to be your friend, Mister Greenwich."

"But you haven't even told me who you are."

The gray lady extends a friendly hand. "Norma."

Gideon stares at her hand before taking it.

"Now," Norma continues, "as for your rehabilitation —"

"My what?"

"Your correction … your reprogramming. The first thing we need from you is a change of attire. Trench coats are for mobsters."

"But —"

"And those sunglasses … out of the question. I know you have them in your pocket. So go on, hand them over."

"I won't wear them in school anymore."

"Of course you won't; I'm confiscating them."

"But they're mine."

"Not anymore." She extends her hand. "How would you like to go home and tell your parents that you've been expelled?"

"What? Why?"

"Pleading ignorance won't get you anywhere, Mister Greenwich. I haven't told you everything I know about you, such as how you dismissed yourself early from your P.E. class today."

"It was going to end in two minutes!"

"Your conduct was unacceptable."

"It's no reason to expel me!"

"I can expel you with or without a reason."

"I want to talk to the principal."

"Mr. Bruce works for *me*. But if you're so eager to throw away your future, we can go down to his office right now and have him sign the paperwork. Is that what you want?" She slides back her chair.

Gideon doesn't budge.

"The glasses, Mister Greenwich."

Gideon hands over the sunglasses.

"And the trench coat."

"It's my *dad's*."

"It's against our dress code, and you know it. If your father wants his coat back, he can come and talk to me."

"But it's *cold* outside."

"I'm going to count to three. One …"

Gideon takes off his coat, feeling exposed in his white t-shirt. He hands it over.

"Now if we can stop playing these games, we'll both get out of here sooner. Next on the list, you need a change of friends."

"You can't tell me —"

"Shut up. That fat boy and homely girl have no motivation in life. If you continue to waste your time with them, you're destined for mediocrity. What you need are friends with drive, like Douglas Rock."

"Doug Rock? He's like the captain of the football team."

"He's everything that you're not. As soon as school's out, I want you to make him your friend."

"But —"

"I know, Mister Greenwich, making new friends is against your bigoted high school principles. Grow up. It's time to transcend your comfort zone and learn the lost art of small talk. No matter how many years of your life you've invested in hating everyone who wasn't part of your clique, you *will* make Douglas your friend. Which brings me to your next to-do, your lack of hobbies."

"I have plenty of —"

"Video games don't count. What you need is physical activity, challenge, discipline. You will be joining the football team."

"The football —"

"Now I know what you're thinking: you have no talent, no coordination … naturally. Lucky for you, the team has an open admissions policy. Of course, you'll never play in a game, but that's beside the point."

Gideon is at a loss.

The gray lady closes the folder and puts it back into the filing cabinet. "I believe that's all. You may go."

Gideon wastes no time in going to the door.

"Oh, and I'd like to follow up with you tomorrow. Same time. If you're not here by two-fifteen, believe me, I'll find you."

DOUG ROCK

Gideon doesn't go back to Fashion Merchandising. Instead he sits alone on a bench in the commons area. He stares up at the clock on the wall. Twenty more minutes to enjoy his unadulterated existence, twenty more minutes until he must do the unthinkable.

His grim meditation is spoiled by overpowering noise. Taking seats at another part of the commons is the *goth* clique. Their hair is died black, their skin pasty white, their clothes a mess of chains, skulls, and what appear to be satanic symbols. As if their appearance isn't loud enough, they announce their presence with a booming stereo system.

Gideon imagines it takes a guitar to make that noise, though it certainly doesn't sound *musical*. If not for the agonized scream of a human voice — or something that resembles a human — the sound would be indistinguishable from radio static. Meanwhile the adherents to this bizarre noise look on in reverence.

Gideon wouldn't mind them if they didn't force *everyone* to submit their minds to their hellish droning. As is, the relentless noise beats upon him like crashing waves. There's something alive in that sound, a demonic creature trying to pound its way into his skull.

And why not? Horrible or not, the sound *is* catchy. It moves his body. So why not just submit to it like the goths?

No, there's no time for this. Gideon must focus on his plan of attack. But his reeling mind proves incapable of coherent thought. His knotted stomach will allow no relief.

The bell rings. Doors open, and chattering students fill the commons. When Dwight and Wanda find Gideon, he can't look them in the eyes.

A concerned Wanda asks, "What happened?"

"I'm glad you asked," Gideon fumes. "That woman's insane!"

"What did she do to you?"

"She said she's going to expel me unless I …" He glances at the opposite side of the commons.

Doug Rock, the captain of the football team, is surrounded by an entourage of burly jocks and attractive girls. They're heading for the front doors.

Gideon continues, "I don't even have time to explain. I … I have to go talk to Doug Rock." He turns to Dwight. "Will you come with me?"

Dwight is amazed. "Seriously?"

"Why would I joke about this?"

"I have never been able to figure you out."

"It's messed up, but I've got to do it. Please man, don't make me go alone."

"You abandoned *me* in P.E."

"That's different."

"What are you going to say?"

"I don't know."

In the distance, Doug Rock and his friends are almost to the doors.

Gideon, fighting a swarm of butterflies in his stomach, hollers, "Hey, Doug!"

Everyone in Doug's group stops. Doug looks around. "Who said my name?" It sounds more like a challenge than a question.

All throughout the commons, the chatter dies down. For a moment, the only sound is the goths' music.

Gideon raises a guilty hand. Then, feeling beyond sheepish, he jogs across the commons.

Doug Rock studies him. "Who are you?"

Before Gideon can answer, Kyle Slater — a meat-headed jock Gideon has loathed since elementary school — says, "Dude, it's mafia boy. You know, from P.E."

Doug Rock's face lights up. "Oh, mafia boy! What happened to your trench coat?"

Kyle Slater says, "No coat? What would your doctor say?"

There are a few snorts of laughter.

Gideon, feeling the weight of the crowd, says in a small voice, "I want to join the football team."

This time the group erupts with laughter. Only Doug doesn't laugh. Instead, he continues to study Gideon's face. "Are you serious?"

Gideon looks down at his shoes. "Yes. What do I gotta do?"

As the group realizes that Gideon is, in fact, serious, the formerly jeering faces mirror Doug's confusion.

"Okay," Doug says at last. "Cool. Um … Coach McPherson would be the guy to talk to."

"Okay. Cool."

"Speaking of which, we'd better get to practice."

Kyle Slater says, "We'll see you around, mafia boy."

The laughter resumes as the group passes through the front doors.

A moment later, Dwight walks up to Gideon. "What the heck?"

Gideon says, "If I get expelled, my parents will kill me."

"Yeah, but … the *football* team? You don't even know *how* to play football. The *jocks* will kill you."

"Either way I'm dead. Want to join me?"

"Heck no."

Wanda approaches them. "Gideon, what's gotten into you?"

Gideon shakes his head. "It's not me, it's the gray lady. She's ruining my life."

Dwight laughs. "She's just a counselor."

"She's *not* a counselor. She says the principal works for *her*. And you know that room we thought was the teachers' lounge? It's really a staircase to her office. She's some supreme ruler of evil. And the weirdest part is she has this statue of a rapper guy, and there's no way she likes rap music."

"Listen to me," says Dwight, "you're a nerd. You watch anime and play *Magic* cards. Your distorted sense of reality is messing with your mind. But whatever she told you, you can't just up and become a jock. It's not even possible. You lack the muscle mass. You have no will power."

Wanda adds, "Even if it were possible, it's like you're betraying us."

Gideon is losing his patience. "I told you, I have no choice! I hate this even more than you do."

Dwight says, "Who said I hate this? I think it's hilarious. I'm just trying to save you from an untimely death."

"Then come with me."

Dwight smiles. "This is karma, man. Who am I to interfere?"

With a sigh, Gideon turns away from his "friends" and heads for the front doors.

"Be careful!" Wanda hollers, a little too much emotion in her voice.

Gideon rolls his eyes. *It's not like I'm going off to war.*

Not exactly.

FOOTBALL

First is the harsh sound of a whistle, then there's a cacophony of grunts. *Whistle ... grunt ... whistle ... grunt.* The strange chant fills the air, echoing off the school, ascending to heaven. Though gruff, the sounds are so orderly, they're almost reverent. Gideon wonders if this is what ancient warriors sounded like as they petitioned their manly deities, Thor, Mars, or other gods of war. Whatever the sounds mean, Gideon follows them to their dreadful source, walking as slowly as he dares.

Soon he stands at the end zone of the football field. At the twenty yard line, a row of tackling dummies stretches across the field. Each padded dummy, extending from a metal bar, serves to tantalize a football player, who, running in place, glares at it through his practice helmet. Coach McPherson blows his whistle, and the football players slam their bodies against the poor dummies. As if this accomplished something, the football players then resume running in place until the next whistle.

Gideon is amazed to have discovered something even more insane than basketball.

More than one football player cranes his neck to get a look at Gideon. Even Coach McPherson stares at him while blowing his whistle.

With no helmet, no pads, and no dignity, Gideon might as well be standing in his underwear.

At last, the exercise is over, and Coach McPherson sends the football players running around the field.

Gideon takes the opportunity to approach the coach. "Hi," he says.

"What's up?" Coach McPherson replies. He might be a nice guy, though with his eyes concealed behind reflective sunglasses, it's hard to say.

"I want to join the team." Gideon expects a belittling glare or a cruel laugh. He hopes with all his heart that, whatever the reason, the coach will turn him down.

"All right. You'll have to fill out some forms and pay your fees, but we can take care of that later. Since you're here, I guess you can start running."

Gideon's heart sinks. "Great." He starts to run, wondering what's happening to his life. Taking the rightmost lane of the track, he makes sure there's plenty of room for others to pass.

It doesn't take long for the team to catch up. The ground rumbles beneath their heavy footsteps.

From a passing helmet, Kyle Slater shouts, "Welcome aboard, mafia boy!" Kyle then administers a painful slap to Gideon's back. And like clockwork, one football player after another does the same.

Soon the stampede passes, leaving Gideon trailing far behind. His breath is short, his legs aching, his lungs burning. This is cruel and unusual. If only he had the sense to forge a doctor's note. Or would the gray lady find out about that?

How am I going to survive this?

One player, however, slows down to jog at Gideon's pace. He extends a dark arm.

Gideon attempts to take the guy's hand. Instead, his own arm is seized, and he's pulled in for an embrace.

"*Aloha ke akua,*" the guy says with a Hawaiian accent.

Gideon is quick to pull away. "What does that mean?"

"It means God is love."

"Okay …"

"I'm Bula."

"Gideon."

"You are my brother. Welcome to the team." Bula then sprints ahead, catching up with the others. It's nice to know that not everyone wants to hurt Gideon.

The excruciating run is only the beginning. Next, the team is forced to line up and perform fifty jumping jacks, forty pushups, thirty sit ups, twenty mountain crawlers, ten burpies, and a myriad of painful stretches. As tears form in Gideon's eyes, the coach finally blows his whistle, and the team relaxes on the grass.

Can they hear his pounding heart?

The assistant coach talks about what players have been promoted to first and second strings, how they're going to prepare for the upcoming game, and why the Westward High Beavers are going to be ripped in half. Coach McPherson then reads a motivational speech about cowboys, which, he explains, love to eat beavers. Gideon didn't know this.

He considers it one of heaven's tender mercies when Coach McPherson asks him to stand aside and observe the remainder of the practice. "Just until we get you some gear," he explains.

Gideon plops onto a comfortable patch of grass on the sidelines. There, observing an occasional ant or butterfly, his mind checks out, and it's back to his happy place. Finally he can focus on what matters: how he's going to get back at the gray lady for this.

When the sun is far in the West, and the Autumn sky is dimming, the team comes together for a closing hurrah. Gideon, keeping his distance, raises the customary fist and shouts with the others, "Go cowboys!" Then he slips away as fast as possible.

But he doesn't get far before receiving another slap to the back.

Doug Rock takes off his helmet, revealing his handsome face and flowing hair. "All right, Mafia Boy, I guess you're one of us now."

"My name is Gideon."

Kyle Slater joins the conversation. "No way, Doug. To become one of us, he'll have to be properly initiated. What do you say we invite him to our little get-together at the park tomorrow night?"

Doug's eyes widen. "With the Westward guys?"

"Yeah. It will be a perfect chance to prove himself."

For whatever reason, Doug laughs at the idea. Then, turning to Gideon, he straightens up. "All right, Maf — *Gideon* … mind if I call you Gid? It would be pretty cool if you join us at Riverside Park tomorrow night. We could use some extra help. And it will definitely give you a chance to prove yourself. That is … if you're man enough."

Gideon forces a smile. "Of course."

TEACHER'S LOUNGE

Gideon douses his sweaty body in a tub of steaming, hot water. Would Cynthia McDaniels hear of his joining the team? Indulging in a fantasy, he imagines her gaping at his tight-fitting pads. If only he could find a way to get some gear while remaining exempt from actual practice.

Wanda's right: this *is* like betrayal, to himself more than anyone. His calling isn't to achieve physical excellence. He's a gamer, a comic book connoisseur, a fan of fantasy, science fiction, and all things … imaginary. He never intended to do something with his *body*.

From first period till fifth period, all he can think about is the gray lady.

Who *is* the gray lady?

Before he knows it, it's P.E., and once again he's without a doctor's note.

His tortured thoughts are interrupted by another slap to the back.

Doug Rock says, "Now that you're one of the boys, you'd better join *our* team." Though Kyle Slater is holding back a smile, Doug looks sincere enough.

"Okay," says Gideon. And before long he's wearing a red jersey, standing across from Dwight.

Dwight stares at him with a look of betrayal.

Gideon shrugs. Though he fumbles with every dribble and misses every shot, and though he can't block an opponent to save his life, at least it's not as bad as football practice. In fact, he feels like a knight in training, imagining that Cynthia would love him more because of it.

But what is he thinking? If he enjoys himself, that's a win for the gray lady. He must hold on to his righteous indignation. He must not be broken. Soon, one way or another, he'll set things straight and return to his rightful place of physical inactivity. After all, it's the mind that counts. He'll find another way to impress Cynthia.

Between periods, he says to Dwight and Wanda, "I'm going to put this woman in her place."

Wanda, with her usual worried eyes, asks, "What are you going to say?"

Gideon pats his bulging pocket. "I've written a speech. I'm going to quote the opening lines of the Declaration of Independence and tell her that she has no right to meddle with my life. She'll probably say something like, *'Let's go talk to the principal.'* And then when she takes me to Mr. Bruce, I'll say, 'If you don't let me quit the football team, I'm going to call up the *Daily Messenger* and *Eye-Witness News* and pass out fliers until everyone knows that Eastward High is forcing a helpless minor to endure physical abuse."

Dwight laughs. "This is too good."

While his friends head for Fashion Merchandising, Gideon begins his lonely walk to the gray lady's office. Despite the confidence he exhibited in front of his friends, the mere thought of her impending reality fills him with butterflies.

He passes the picture of the cowboy and arrives at the "Staff Only" door. Entire minutes go by before, at last, he turns the knob.

Rather than a stairway, he sees a room with green carpet, a kitchenette, a long table, and vending machines.

Mr. Henegar, the old chemistry teacher, looks up from his lunch. "May I help you?" he asks.

Feeling lightheaded, Gideon answers, "Yeah, I'm looking for … Norma."

"Norma?" Mr. Henegar rubs his bristly chin. "Norma who?"

"I … don't know. She's some kind of administrator. I thought her office was right here, but I guess …" Again Gideon glances at the picture of the cowboy. There's no other door in the hallway. This *has* to be the right place.

Mr. Henegar shakes his head. "There's no one on the staff named Norma."

"I think she's new."

"Then you should check the front office. This is the teacher's lounge."

Gideon nods as the door slips from his fingers and swings shut. *Staff Only.*

"But …" he says aloud. Tortured by confusion, he opens the door again.

There's Mr. Henegar.

Gideon closes the door. Suddenly he has the feeling of being watched, just as he was at the top of the bleachers. He has to get away.

He's still catching his breath when he enters Fashion Merchandising, interrupting Patricia Berman's report on leotards. As soon as he takes his seat, he pulls out pen and paper, and writes:

The gray lady is a witch!

Seeing that Dwight is fast asleep, he folds up the paper and tosses it onto Wanda's desk.

Wanda reads the note, then thoughtfully pens her response before passing the note back. It reads:

Meaning she flies around on a broomstick?

Gideon replies:

Her office was gone! I was there just yesterday, but now it's the teachers' lounge. And Mr. Henegar tells me that no one named Norma works at the school. It's like she has the power to alter reality.

Wanda replies:

Neat!

Gideon replies:

Why do you think she stood me up?

Wanda replies:

Maybe you've already learned too much about her dark secret, so she's trying to make you think you're crazy.

Gideon replies:

That makes perfect sense. Only I'm not exactly sure what her dark secret is.

Wanda replies:

Maybe she's trying to enslave the minds of the student body!

Gideon replies:

And how, exactly, would she do that?

Wanda replies:

Easy enough. She's already enslaved your mind.

Gideon replies:

What???

Wanda replies:

You do whatever she asks, because you're terrified of her. If that's not slavery, I don't know what is.

Gideon replies:

I am not terrified of her. I'm just trying to make the best of the situation.

Wanda replies:

> *Maybe she's using the teachers to fill our minds with propaganda.*

Gideon replies:

> *Only if she's controlling their minds too. The teachers don't even know she exists!*

Wanda replies:

> *Except for Ms. Primple. She totally saw the gray lady. Maybe she's a witch too!*

Gideon is about to pen his reply when the note is whisked off his desk by the red claws of Ms. Primple.

After examining the note with amusement, Ms. Primple asks, "Would you like me to read your love note to Wanda?"

Just about everyone laughs at the idea of a love note to Wanda.

Wanda, edging on melodrama, replies, "No, please."

Of course, Cynthia McDaniels is watching.

Ms. Primple's amused expression turns to concern. She reads the note more carefully, then, suddenly, stuffs it into her pocket. In her eyes is the fire of the gray lady. "Gideon, I would like to meet with you after class." Then she regains her sweet composure. "Would that be all right with you?"

Thankfully, Gideon has an excuse … a *real* excuse. "Actually, I have football practice after class." Suddenly he doesn't mind that Cynthia is listening.

Ms. Primple leans forward, her big brown eyes gazing into Gideon's. "It will only take a few minutes. I promise."

She's so attractive. Gideon is powerless to defy. "Okay."

WITCH

The bell rings. The students go their ways. But not until every other student has left the room does Ms. Primple turn her attention to Gideon. He's mentally rehearsed his protestations a dozen times. But as soon as she fixes her brown eyes on him, he loses all defenses.

"Quite the comical note," she says.

"It was just a joke."

"Do you think fashion is a joke?"

" … No."

"I just received a message from Norma. She apologizes for missing your meeting. She had to attend to some urgent business out of town."

"Wait … you *know* Norma?"

"Superintendent Norma Cummings."

"Superintendent? So the principal *does* work for her."

"She's over all of us. Though she doesn't come to the school very often, so she must have had a pretty serious reason to meet with you."

"Why me? I'm not a bad student."

Ms. Primple glares at him. "It's not unheard of for district representatives to become involved with student disciplinary issues. They do so to set an example for the administration. I believe she took special interest in you, because she was an eye witness of your … delinquent activity."

"Does the whole faculty know?"

"She explained the situation in her message."

"I left *two minutes* early."

"You chose the wrong place to pull a stunt. Didn't you know the executive office overlooks the gym?"

"About that. I tried to go to her office, but it was gone."

"Gone?"

"I know I went to the right place. It's the hallway with only one door, you know, with the picture of the cowboy." *Why is she smiling at me like that?*

"You know our school mascot is the *cowboy*, right?"

"Right." At least he thinks he knew that …

"There's got to be at least twenty or thirty cowboy pictures in the halls. And I can think of four or five halls with only one door. Are you *sure* you went to the right place?"

Gideon looks at his shoes. As comforting as it was to believe that the forces of evil and laws of physics were combined against him, the depressing truth begins to stare him in the face.

"You probably took the second hallway after the main office, the one that leads to the teacher's lounge. It's an honest mistake. It looks just like the third hallway."

Gideon nods.

"One more thing. I'm concerned about your grade. Tomorrow's the last day to present your report. So far you haven't contributed much in class, so I'll be expecting something … snazzy. Can you do snazzy, Gideon?"

Gideon nods.

"Well, you'd better get to football practice."

"Right."

"Oh, and I'd prefer if you and Wanda would stop referring to me as a witch. I'm not that bad, am I?"

"It was really just a joke."

"Gideon …" She speaks his name so delicately.

He looks up.

"I'm not laughing." She gazes into his eyes.

"I'm sorry."

"You can go now."

"Right."

Gideon enters the commons, where Dwight and Wanda sit waiting for him.

"Somebody's blushing!" says Dwight.

Gideon resents the existence of that phrase; whether or not it's true, it inevitably *becomes* true.

"What, did she kiss you?" Dwight continues.

"Back off," says Gideon.

"And what's all this about love notes with Wanda?"

Wanda says, "I told you we're just friends."

Is Wanda blushing as well? *We* are *just friends, right?* Eager to change the subject, Gideon says, "The gray lady works for the district. I guess I'm in bigger trouble than I thought."

The three of them pass through the front doors and follow their usual path to Gideon's house for after-school-bumming. As they walk, Gideon closes his eyes. He feels the warm, afternoon sun. It's relieving to know that there is, in fact, a free world beyond the reach of the school system's tentacles. He thinks of the hillside in his backyard and the vast wilderness beyond. Suddenly his friends are a burden. As always, they'll want to raid the pantry and watch TV. But Gideon longs to get away from it all, to rest beneath leafy canopies and listen to babbling brooks. Out there, free from structure and authority, he could lose himself in the gullies. Out there, there's no time, no rules, and anything he can imagine is as real as the beating of his heart.

Wanda spoils his musings. "What about football practice?"

Gideon feels the tentacles reaching for him. But he won't have it. "I'm through with that."

Dwight examines Gideon's face. "You mean you quit?"

"I never enrolled in the first place."

Wanda, with her usual worry, asks, "But what about the gray lady?"

"I'm not afraid of the gray lady."

·Dwight is still studying Gideon. "You could have fooled me."

Gideon ignores him. "Besides, she's out of town, and what she doesn't know can't hurt her. In fact, I don't believe any of that garbage about expelling me if I don't join the football team. No school administrator has that kind of power. It's unconstitutional."

"Yeah," adds Dwight. "You're entitled to be antisocial, under-motivated, and pathetic. It's your right."

Before Gideon can think of a rejoinder, Wanda surprises them both with a gasp. They follow her gaze back to the school. From behind one of the second story windows, a person is staring back at them.

The gray lady.

"Impossible," Gideon whispers.

Wanda whispers, "She *is* a witch."

Dwight, however, just laughs. "Seriously, guys, the gag's getting old."

As if the gray lady's unholy powers can perceive his every word, Gideon continues to whisper, "I'm telling you, this doesn't make sense. Ms. Primple said she was out of town."

Dwight, with a mean smile, speaks louder than usual. "Obviously Ms. Primple was wrong. Now's your chance for some civil disobedience. Show that old hag who's in control of your life."

Wanda pleads, "Don't do anything you'll regret."

The tentacles have caught up with him, wrapping … squeezing. The only emotion weighing heavier than embarrassment is fear. Without looking at his friends, without saying a word, Gideon begins for the football field.

BRASS KNUCKLES

First there's the familiar shame of being late in front of the entire team. Then there's the agony of running, the taunts of teammates, the pointless slaps, the cruel calisthenics. The autumn air turns cold and sharp, and time slows down as never before.

Finally the warm-ups end, and the armored players line up head-to-head. A whistle blows, and the violence begins. Gideon slips away to the sidelines, but his sweet catharsis doesn't last. Coach McPherson says, "Pay attention to the plays, because soon you'll be tested."

Gideon tries to take mental notes as the quarterback, Doug Rock, shouts strings of seemingly random words. "Blue, forty-two, check, check, set-hut!" What could it mean? He watches the players assume strange, three-legged positions. Then Doug shouts more nonsense — "slant route," "six-eighty-six," "left lover boy" — and the players assume new positions. Gideon tries to memorize the complex geometry of this men's ballet, but it's information overload. What's the difference between the "Quick Ace" and the "Green Eighty"? How is a "Reversed Forward Pass" even possible? It would help if he knew the difference between a linebacker and a nose guard. It all hurts his brain, and he thought football was for dumb brutes!

At one of the end zones, Cynthia McDaniels and her fellow cheer leaders are practicing a tumbling routine. Her hair and skirt bouncing, she runs, jumps, performs a round off, then ends with a triumphant back flip. *Such perfect legs.* She jumps again, and a strong boy seizes her waist, throws her up, and balances her on one hand. Gideon doesn't know who the guy is, but he hates him.

At last, Coach McPherson blows three long whistles. Practice is over. The assistant coach gathers the team for another boring speech. Then there's the druidic circle of team spirit. "Go cowboys!" When the rituals are over, Gideon's mind tells him to run, but for some reason he lingers. This may have something to do with the fact that the cheer leaders are still practicing, and any chance of Cynthia seeing him look like a football player is worth taking.

But then the cheer leaders pack up and go home, and still Gideon lingers. The remaining football players are chatting in tight groups. Gideon finds himself walking among them, pretending he's looking for something. Why? Could he actually be feeling a sense of camaraderie with these guys?

Deep within, he feels a glowing ember of something he's long-suppressed: masculinity. While he, of course, is above the society of jocks, if, out of necessity, he were to lower his standards and find a companion with whom to share his misery, this whole ordeal might be more tolerable. There is that guy, Bula, who seemed friendly enough, but then, Bula probably gives his welcome spiel to every new team member. If Gideon is going to make a *real* friend — or as close to a real friend as one could have with a jock — he'll have to do it the jock way: by proving his manly prowess.

A hard fist slams into Gideon's chest, contracting his ribs, and sending him staggering backward. He impacts against the well-padded back of the towering Koa Kamaka, Hawaiian giant. Koa, with a savage scowl, knocks Gideon in the opposite direction. As Gideon finds himself on his hands and knees, he hears the inane laughter of Kyle Slater, who, no doubt, instituted this senseless violence.

Doug Rock is watching the scene as if it's perfectly normal. "So, Gid, we'll see you at Riverside Park tonight?"

Kyle adds, "Unless you're chickening out."

Climbing to his feet, Gideon has to breathe hard in order to speak. "Um ..." He forgot all about his rash commitment to attend their secret escapade. The way they refer to the mysterious event makes him wonder if they're going to initiate him into some esoteric fraternity … or just murder him. "Tell me when, and I'll be there."

"Midnight," says Doug.

"But it's a school night," Gideon protests. No sooner do the words escape his mouth than he regrets saying them.

Ignoring him, Doug reaches into his duffel bag. "I'm sure this is your first time, so you can borrow some of my gear." He tosses Gideon two metal pieces of something. Brass knuckles. "And in case you get lost …" Doug hands Gideon something else. "Here's my card. You'll find my number on the back."

Gideon examines the card. Printed in elegant cursive are the words:

Douglas W. Rock, Concert Violinist

"What the …" Gideon looks up, but Doug and Kyle are walking away.

As Gideon walks home, the sky has turned golden, the sun beginning to set. Though the air is chilly, he droops his jacket over his shoulder. His stomach growls. The thought of his mother's cooking has never seemed more divine. And he deserves it.

Dwight and Wanda are sitting on his front lawn. Beside them are a messy array of bags, burger wrappers, and soda cups.

"Hey," says Wanda, stuffing a handful of fries into her mouth. She extends an oil-splattered box to Gideon. "We saved you some …" Then she observes the empty contents. "Oh, sorry. I think there's one more burger at the bottom." She shuffles through the crinkly wrappers in one of the paper bags. "Wait, never mind."

Gideon can smell marinara sauce wafting from his house. "Well, I'll catch you guys later."

Wanda frowns. "We're going to *Movies 8*. You wanna come?"

"But it's a school … I mean, I'd like to, but I have too much homework."

Dwight bursts into laughter. "Since when do you do homework? Man, this *gray lady's* got you on a leash!"

"It has nothing to do with her, it's just … if you must know, some of the guys and I were going to meet up for some ... extra practice."

Wanda says, "Wow, you mean you're one of *the guys* now?"

Gideon shrugs. "I guess so."

Dwight says, "I see how it is. You won't be needing us anymore."

"Dwight —"

"Why would you want to hang out with a couple of nerds when you've been accepted into the lofty social circles of Doug Rock and Kyle Slater? Soon you'll have cheerleaders fighting over you and your varsity jacket. Then, my friend, you'll have to choose between those who love you for who you truly are and those who flatter your vain ambition but will forsake you in the end ... the classic conflict."

Gideon applauds. "That was very impressive. Now will you shut up?"

Again Dwight bursts into laughter. "You and I both know you don't have any *friends* on the football team."

"Lay off. It's only my second day."

"So you're really going to stick with it?"

"What do you care?"

"Good point, I don't."

Wanda cuts in. "Boys, be nice. Honestly, Gideon, I think you're brave."

After another whiff of his imminent dinner, Gideon is beyond done with this conversation. He waves goodbye and heads for the front door.

"Gideon ..." says Dwight.

Gideon stops, though he doesn't turn around.

"Remember who you are." Dwight laughs again until slugged by Wanda.

FIGHT

Standing in front of the bathroom mirror, Gideon puts on the brass knuckles and tries to look mean. But there's no looking past those scrawny arms. He gazes out the window, into the black of night. Somewhere a dog is barking. A growling motorcycle rips past his neighborhood. There's something evil and foreboding out there, something more than bloodthirsty jocks, and somehow it has everything to do with the gray lady.

Could this forced association with football players be a plot to get him killed? Maybe the gray lady is a time-traveling agent from the future, sent by a sinister force that knows of his destiny for greatness. Such foreknowledge would explain her knack for being seemingly omniscient.

Gideon splashes his face with cold water. It's time to stop dreaming. She's nothing more than an exceptionally evil school administrator. There's no reason to fear her. At the moment, there are *real* dangers to worry about.

Again slipping his fingers through the cold steel of the brass knuckles, he throws a punch. And another. He grunts. He roars.

Of course, he could take the easy way out and blame his absence on a failed alarm clock, but oh the shame that would follow. Beside taunting, there's something else he fears, a growing ember within him he can only define as conscience. *My conscience is telling me to fight? What's wrong with me?*

Perhaps this is the sort of opportunity he's always dreamed of, a chance to rise up and prove himself against the forces of evil. And what better foes could he hope for than a vicious band of barbarous meat heads? One way or another, Cynthia will hear of tonight's victory. More likely, she'll visit him in the hospital. And wouldn't that be romantic?

It's a foggy night at Riverside Park. The dead leaves, now frozen, crunch beneath Gideon's sneakers. With no moon and no stars, the only light shines from the occasional streetlamp.

He checks his watch. Midnight.

He's standing at the summit of a bowl-shaped park, looking down into the wide, open field. It's empty. His breath, a ghostly vapor, vanishes into the night. Though it's hours after his usual bedtime, he's never felt more awake. And why shouldn't he be? It's beautiful out here. Still. Serene. Almost sacred. Cold ... but refreshing. He can feel the goosebumps beneath his thin jacket. With every chilling breath comes an electric force. Suddenly he's aware of something ... magical.

He studies the misty sky, the mysterious, ominous gray. Whatever it is, he stands at the brink of it, perhaps a seam in space-time or an anomaly in the fabric of the universe. If he could just tear through it, what power, what enlightenment would he find on the other side?

He extends his hands, sculpting the mist.

"The jocks will not come," he orders, a command to the universe.

From this moment on, Gideon Greenwich is in control of his own destiny, and neither the gray lady nor the very laws of physics can interfere.

Enlightenment isn't to be found at the ends of the earth but at the local park. To find it, one need only be awake while the world sleeps. Forget the cold. He's on top of the world, an all-powerful wizard. He alone had the courage to show up tonight. He came, he saw, he conquered.

"I wanted to fight," he says to the night, "but no one showed up. Oh well, their loss."

He passed the test. Like the knights of old, he was ready to lay down his life for honor, and that was enough. The gods have greater things in store for him.

Part of him longs to sit on the nearby bench and just ... be — free from the wheel of time and the confining systems of the world. But an unstoppable yawn works its way into his mouth. That's enough enlightenment for one night.

Then something catches his eye. Down in the field is a silhouette in the fog. No, many silhouettes. At least ten. Spaced evenly apart, the phantom creatures march like an army, like demons from another world.

Jocks.

Suddenly they stop.

"Are you with Westward?" someone shouts.

The shout was directed at *Gideon*. "Umm ..." He can hear his heart beating.

"Cool it," comes a familiar voice ... Kyle Slater's. "It's just mafia boy. Yo, mafs, you gonna join us or what?"

Suddenly the world isn't quite so magical. Feeling a return of the old pit in the stomach, Gideon jogs down the hill. He's admitted into a crowd of familiar faces, guys from the team. Every one of them is wearing a blue and orange varsity jacket, sporting a proud letter E for Eastward High.

As per usual, Doug Rock administers a gratuitous slap to Gideon's back. "Glad you could join us, Gid. You ready for some fun?"

"Umm ..."

Next, Gideon is seized in a hug by Bula. The Hawaiian looks him in the eyes and says, "Welcome, brother. Tonight, we will defend our honor. Don't worry, I will —"

Bula is interrupted as someone shouts, "There they are!"

All heads turn to the opposite side of the park. In the distance are more silhouettes — another army — barely visible in the fog. The silhouettes grow nearer.

"It's Westward," someone shouts, and at this, the battle commences. The Eastward team marches toward the oncoming foe, the mass of bodies forcing Gideon to keep step.

So this is how men kill themselves. What's surprising is how simple it is. No need for justifications. You see your enemy, you fight, you die. And why not? With so much adrenaline, there's no room for rationality. The experience is altogether intoxicating.

Now the armies are charging at each other, the once still night a cacophony of war cries. The silhouettes of the enemy are now fellow teenagers in green jackets sporting the letter W.

With a final surge of sanity, Gideon shouts over the noise, "Why are we doing this?"

But no one answers. Perhaps there *is* no answer. The shouting boys crash and intermix. Punches are thrown, bodies are hit. The air is filled with grunts, wheezes, and the sound of smacking flesh.

Gideon feels his senses heightened amid the omnipresent danger, his only motivation to stay alive. Soon he spots a towering beast, a boy from Westward who's even bigger than Koa Kamaka, some three-hundred pounds of Polynesian muscle and cellulite. The beast smiles, his eyes locked with Gideon's.

Gideon runs. He ducks beneath a stray fist. He narrowly dodges two separate lunges from would-be killers, one an Eastward guy, the next Danny Valesquez, who either forgot that Gideon was on his team or didn't care. Gideon looks back. The smiling beast is getting closer.

Gideon trips over a fallen body, then smears into the cold, hard grass. He lumbers to his feet, but he's too late. A massive hand grips his neck, pulling him up to his tippy toes.

The beast, with his evil smile, buries his fist in Gideon's gut.

VICTORY

For a moment, Gideon is airborne. Then he lands on his back. The wind is completely knocked out of him, and he feels the empty aching of suffocation. At last the air forces its way back in.

Still the beast pursues him to finish the job through the worst means imaginable: stomping.

Gideon rolls, barely avoiding pulverization. The beast is about to go for a second stomp, when a heaven-sent Bula crashes into him, taking him down.

Still on the grass, Gideon can only stare at the epic tackle.

"Get out of here!" Bula orders.

And who is Gideon to questions Bula's authority? Finding a second wind, he climbs to his feet and sprints, never looking back. He runs straight up the hill, and the next thing he knows, his aching body is tumbling down the other side, rolling on the grass.

The hill levels out, and he skids to a stop. He listens to his racing heart and watches his vaporous breath. He looks around for signs of enemies, but the grassy hill is dark and still. The sound of carnage has grown distant.

A shadow is approaching him, a person coming up from the parking lot. Gideon's hands instinctively cover his gut. Whoever it is steps into the light of the nearest street lamp.

Wanda. "Are you okay?" she asks.

In the distance, Dwight is climbing out of a car, his dad's Honda Civic.

Gideon climbs to his feet and looks away. He tries to suppress his heavy breaths.

"You're hurt," Wanda exclaims, placing her warm hand against

Gideon's forehead.

"My temperature's fine," Gideon insists, turning away.

"Hold still. Let me feel your pulse." She forces her prodding fingers against his jugular vein.

"I'm not dead!"

"What happened?"

"I'll tell you later. What are you guys doing here?"

"We were worried about you. We were afraid the jocks would —"

"Kill you," says Dwight, arriving at the scene. "So we waited outside your house and followed you."

Gideon can feel his face flushing in the cold air. "You mean you watched me walk the entire way here?"

"Of course. How else would we have known where you were going?"

"Why didn't you give me a ride?"

"As if that wasn't tedious enough," Dwight continues. "First we had to wait hours for you to leave the house. So come on, what happened?"

"I just got in a little fight."

"Cool. Did you bust anyone in the jaw?"

Gideon shrugs. "I did all right." Fearing that, at any moment, a blood-lusting jock or two would lumber over the hill, he begins for the car. "Now let's get out of here, and I'll tell you all about it."

Wanda says, "What's that sound?"

Gideon stops and listens. He barely makes out the faint sound of a shouting crowd. The jocks. Only something's different from the usual clamor of fighting. Their shouts are growing louder.

Much louder.

Suddenly an army charges over the hill, heading straight toward Gideon, Dwight, and Wanda. It's the Westward football team.

Wanda screams.

Gideon tugs her arm. "Come on." He looks down at the Honda Civic, but it's too far. They would never be able to outrun this charging wall of gladiators. With only moments to spare, he leads the way in hiding behind a nearby tree, and his friends follow.

The Westward jocks whiz past, one after another. To Gideon's surprise, not a single one stops to pummel him or his friends. And then the jocks are gone, scattering and disappearing into the night.

The sudden silence is broken by a cheer from the top of the hill, where a new army stands. Eastward. The jocks are raising their arms in exultation.

Then, following the usual slaps to backs, one of them shouts, "Let's go tell Sportacus!" And the crowd cheers.

Gideon and his friends exchange looks, Dwight whispering, "Who's Sportacus?"

"Wait," says Doug, looking around, "Gid's not initiated."

Gideon ducks lower behind the tree. He hears the voice of Kyle say, "Don't worry, the coward ran off. He won't see anything."

"Hey, Bula, where ya goin'?"

As Bula walks away, he replies, "My mother is waiting for me. You guys have fun. *Aloha ke akua.*"

Gideon peers through the leaves to see the army heading back into the park. A moment later, the only sound is the chirping of crickets.

Dwight says, "Apparently they're going to visit some mysterious guy with an ancient-Greek-sounding name, and Gideon's not supposed to see it."

"It certainly did sound that way," says Gideon.

"So … are we going or what?"

Gideon looks into the mist. Does he really *want* to discover the jocks' secrets? There's something evil in the air, an unseen fuel to this warmongering madness. There's also something exhilarating. How many chances would they have to gaze into the esoteric world of jocks? "I'm game."

Wanda says, "Are you crazy? We're not going after those homicidal maniacs."

Dwight hands her his keys. "Then you can wait in the car."

Wanda's eyes grow wide. She looks down at the parking lot, where the Westward team vanished into the shadows. "You would *leave* me here?"

Dwight says, "Come. We'll keep a safe distance from the jocks."

Gideon adds, "And we'll have each other."

Wanda looks as tight as a ball of yarn. She nods.

SPORTACUS

Gideon, Dwight, and Wanda climb to the top of the grassy hill. Keeping low, they overlook the vast, bowl-shaped park.

The jocks, barely visible in the fog, are approaching the opposite hill.

Gideon takes command; someone has to. "The key is stealth. If we keep our distance and stay quiet, we'll all get home safely." Suddenly he's a quarterback, and in his mind's eye, Cynthia is watching from the front row. "If they spot us, we just act casual. Then we run for the trees. No matter what happens, we must not panic. I'll lead the way. Wanda, you take the rear. Dwight …"

But Dwight is already half-way down the hill, leaving Gideon feeling exposed.

"Dwight!"

"What are you ninnies waiting for?" Dwight hollers back.

To continue the loud discussion is to compromise their safety. Seeing no alternative, Gideon rushes to catch up, and Wanda follows like a clinging duckling. Together they cross the vast, open field, all the while keeping a safe distance from the army of jocks.

We're spies, Gideon muses. *We're willfully pursuing a band of psychopaths.*

The dangerous expedition leads them to the edge of the park and into the wilderness of the adjoining mountainside. They climb over rocks and under whipping branches toward the sight of a glowing fire. The light grows brighter, and the shadows seem darker. They hear shouts and laughter.

Some of the jocks are dragging a large cooler out of the shadows. Others are snapping dead branches and throwing them into the mounting bonfire. Red sparks rise into the dark sky.

Wanda whispers, "This is *not* a legal fire zone. These are very bad boys."

Dwight whispers, "You haven't seen anything yet." He points to the dark, flickering figures of Doug Rock and Kyle Slater. They've opened the cooler and are handing out beer bottles.

"They're under-age!" Wanda exclaims.

Both Gideon and Dwight forcefully cover her mouth.

After ten or twenty minutes of watching the jocks loiter, get plastered, and laugh like idiots, Gideon has had enough. His feet are tired, his body cold, his aching head longing to lie down on a soft pillow. He whispers, "I'm guessing Sportacus is their god of beer."

Dwight nods. "It must be an inside joke. Let's get out of here."

Wanda eagerly leads the way, and Dwight is close behind, but Gideon lingers for a moment longer. Though his body is weary, suddenly he feels unsatisfied. There was something beckoning him in the mist, something he hasn't found yet. There must be more than meets the eye, a deeper reason for this insanity. But upon taking a final look at the reckless scene of debauchery, he knows he's kidding himself. *They're jocks. There doesn't need to be a reason.*

He turns to catch up with the others, when something catches his ear.

Chanting.

The jocks are revolving around the campfire, their bodies moving up and down. It looks like some tribal ceremony.

Is this another inside joke?

Gideon tries to make out the words of the chant, but their voices are too low. He turns to his friends. "Come back!" he whispers.

When Dwight returns, his eyes are also fixated on the strange scene. "Are they saying what I think they're saying?"

Wanda looks just as perplexed. "Oh no," she whispers.

"What?" Gideon asks.

But his friends are too captivated to respond. Gideon tries again to make out the words of the chants. The jocks voices are growing louder … and louder.

Break down the door, big dawg, big dawg.
Break down the door, big dawg!

Have another shot, then tumble to the floor.
Scramble to your feet. You're gonna take more.

Break down the door, big dawg, big dawg.
Break down the door, big dawg!

Wanda asks, "Don't you recognize the most popular rap song of our time?"

Gideon shrugs.

Dwight says, "Don't you remember what happened at the pep rally last year? As soon as they started playing this song, the football jocks fought the basketball jocks, and both Tony Ricci and Carl Manning were put in an ambulance. It got so bad that anyone caught playing the song on school grounds was suspended."

Again Gideon shrugs. "It's just a song."

Wanda shakes her head. "It's evil."

Now the ritual is resembling a Polynesian war dance. With wide eyes, the jocks are sticking out their tongues and shouting with rage.

"Let's get out of here!" says Wanda, rustling the bushes as she distances herself.

Gideon grabs her arm. "Wait." It's too weird to leave now. Whatever it is they came here to see, it's getting closer; he can feel it.

Now the jocks are barking like dogs.

Dwight points to the campfire. "Look!"

The fire is spitting out more sparks; only now they're *green*. As if the jocks threw in an arsenal of fireworks, sparks fly everywhere, and the entire fire turns green. But that's only the beginning. Something is rising *out* of the fire. Some ... *one*.

Wondering if he's hallucinating, Gideon turns to his friends. They look just as confused.

There is a man rising out of the fire.

Now the jocks are chanting a single word:

Sportacus ... Sportacus ... Sportacus!

This isn't just any man; he's a *manly* man: barrel chest, bulging biceps. His tanned skin is perfectly shaved. Over his head is an iron helmet straight from the roman era. His haircut is short and precise, his face handsome, his eyes shining with the green of the fire. From his shoulders hangs a majestic, red cape. Around his waste is a leather ... *skirt*. In one hand he grips a metal spear. Impossibly, he just stands there, unharmed, in the fire.

Gideon can only think of one word to describe this awesome apparition: god. As the supernatural man assumes full stature, the jocks cease their chant and prostrate themselves against the cold, dirty ground.

They're worshiping him. It all seems too much to be real. Again Gideon looks at his friends. Their faces reflect the green light of the fire. They're seeing it too.

Doug Rock rises to his knees. "Almighty Sportacus," he says solemnly, "we have defeated our enemies, and we dedicate our victory unto thee."

The man in the fire — Sportacus — gives a slight nod. "You have done well." His voice is stern, bassy ... *godly*. "I depend on you, my warriors, to defend my kingdom. If there is to be order, it is to be purchased by your blood. The weak must fall. The strong must rise." Barely moving a muscle, he looks down at the prostrated jocks. "When you joined my team, you became men. There's no going back. No seconds thoughts. No ... *infidel*."

At the sound of the frightening word, every jock looks up. Sportacus is pointing a stiff finger at one of the jocks in the back row: Scott Flannigan.

Gideon observes that Scott is the only guy not wearing a varsity jacket.

"How dare you," says Sportacus. The fire seems to burn brighter around him.

With a white face, Scott says, "I ... I couldn't find it."

"Punish him," Sportacus orders.

At once, every other jock leaps to his feet and showers Scott with kicks and punches. For a long time, Sportacus just stands there, watching with approval. At last he raises a gentle hand, and the beatings cease.

Scott is left in the dirt, bruised and limp, while the other jocks resume their prostrations around the campfire. Only Doug Rock dares elevate himself to a kneel.

"Always wear your jackets," Sportacus says. "They are your uniforms, the emblems of your superior class. Wherever you go, you must instill fear of me.

"Tomorrow we will rally our forces, and I will be in your midst. But remember, you must not let anyone know about ..." He trails off, his green eyes scanning the surroundings. "What have we here?" He looks straight at Gideon's hiding place. "Infidels."

Gideon, Dwight, and Wanda need no communication. They run as they've never run before.

PEP RALLY

Gideon stares at the sesame seed buns between his fingers. For the sake of ritual, he opens his mouth and goes in for the bite. But his mind is elsewhere, and the complex operation requires too much coordination. The loose hamburger meat and tomato sauce slop back onto the plate, leaving nothing but empty buns. Gideon spoons the contents back into the buns and starts the ritual over. But once again, gravity prevails.

Dwight isn't even attempting to eat. Staring into space, he says, "What the …" He tilts his head. "I can't even …" He stares at the ceiling. "Huh?"

Gideon puts down his soggy buns. He attempts to drink from his half-pint carton but only succeeds at spilling milk on his shirt. "It appears that the jocks are being controlled by an evil god of war."

"I noticed."

"First the gray lady, now this. Our school's being hijacked by supernatural forces."

Wanda is playing with her peas. "Do you think we just dreamed it?"

Dwight says, "We couldn't have *all* dreamed it. I hate to admit it, but Gideon was right all along. There's something extraordinary going on."

"So what do we do now?"

There's a loud beep as the PA system overrides every conversation in the lunchroom. One of the school administrators says, "Ladies and gentlemen, it's now time to come to the gym for a pep rally. This is mandatory for all students."

The conversations throughout the room resume, more excited

than before. Students discard their trash and file out of the lunch-room.

Gideon perks up. "That's right. Sportacus said they were going to *rally their forces* today."

Dwight adds, "And he said *he* would be there."

With another unspoken agreement, they both turn to Wanda.

"I hate pep rallies," says Wanda. "You know I have no school spirit."

Dwight says, "You'd rather go home than watch the jocks unfold their heinous scheme?"

"Yes."

"Don't you want to learn more about their supernatural leader?"

"Not particularly."

"Don't you think it's our duty to stand up against the forces of evil?"

"No."

Recalling the terrible, green eyes of Sportacus, Gideon secretly agrees with Wanda. The man found them with supernatural sense. Surely he'll find them again. Then what? "Maybe we should sit this one out. I don't really like pep rallies either."

Dwight rolls his eyes. "Don't you remember what happened last time you tried to sluff?"

"I left *two minutes* early. Besides, the halls are filled with students. If we just go now, there's no way the gray lady is going to catch us."

A hand grips Gideon's shoulder, sending a jolt of fear through his body. Fingernails dig into his flesh. He looks up to see Ms. Primple smiling down at him. The air is thick with her flowery perfume.

"Didn't you hear the announcement?" she asks sweetly.

"Welcome to Eastward High's annual pep rally!" shouts Marie Melton, the student body president. For no reason whatsoever, the student body bursts into cheers, their voices reverberating through the packed gymnasium.

Gideon, Dwight, and Wanda, followed by Ms. Primple, are among the last to usher in. Every available seat on the bleachers is taken, forcing them to stand in a crowded corner.

"Tonight our football team will be taking on Westward High," Marie continues, "marking the beginning of our homecoming week celebration."

Again the crowd cheers for no reason.

"So, boys, if you still haven't found a date for Saturday night's dance, you'd better get on it."

This time the crowd laughs, leaving Gideon to wonder what, exactly, was funny.

Before continuing, Marie turns back to Coach McPherson, who sits behind her on the raised stage. The coach nods. "And now, the moment you've all been waiting for. Let's give a big cheer for the one and only … Eastward High football team!"

Gideon is hit from behind with a jolting blast. He turns around to discover that it's his misfortune to be standing right in front of a stack of speakers, shaking his body and blurring his vision. The terrible things nearly blow out his eardrums with booming bass. It's a hellish cacophony of robotic percussion, atonal noise, and an angry rapper going on about who-knows-what.

Meanwhile the football team, dressed in full gear and uniform, jogs into the gym. At the head of the procession is their fearless leader, Douglas Rock.

The crowd goes wild.

Gideon tries to hide himself.

Doug's helmet turns his way.

Doug stops, startling the boys behind him, who collide into each other. He shouts something at Gideon.

"What?" Gideon shouts back, though he can barely hear himself over the noise.

Doug beckons him.

"Umm …" Looking around, Gideon sees hundreds of faces staring back at him. He needs an excuse. Surely an adult will tell him to stay put. He turns to Ms. Primple.

"Go," she shouts.

So, feeling bound by an unseen spotlight, Gideon goes. Soon, without gear or uniform, he's jogging beside the other players, feeling more stupid than ever before. The football team jogs up the steps of the raised stage, where they squeeze together to make room for everyone. As fate would have it, Gideon is standing next to Kyle Slater. Hoping to find a safer spot, Gideon looks around for Bula, but for some reason the guy is missing.

Kyle leans in and whispers, "Deserter."

Pretending he didn't hear, Gideon busies himself with staring into the crowd. On the second bleacher, three seats from the right, sits Cynthia McDaniels. Gideon's heart skips a beat.

Cynthia is staring at *him*.

Gideon straightens up.

At the front of the stage is a podium, where Marie Melton continues her speech. "Now please give another cheer for Eastward High alumni and homecoming guest coach, the celebrated quarterback of the Roxford Invaders, the legendary John Mullins!"

The audience goes wild as a man in a suit jogs into the gym. He's burly and handsome.

A star-struck Cynthia is jumping up and down.

Mister John Mullins takes Marie's place at the podium. "Thank you." His voice reverberates through the suddenly quiet gym. "It's been an honor to work with the Eastward team over the last few weeks."

Gideon doesn't remember seeing this guy at football practice, but then, he's only attended twice. Still, there's something familiar about that voice. Gideon turns to Dwight and Wanda, who, with wide eyes, are nodding back at him.

It's *him*.

"It's rare to find true discipline among today's youth," Mr. Mullins continues, "but I'm proud to say that Eastward High ... has got it." Again the crowd goes wild. "I'd especially like to thank Douglas Rock for being an outstanding team captain, not to mention one of the best quarterbacks I've ever seen."

He leads the way in applauding at an embarrassed Doug. While other girls hoot and holler, Cynthia is quiet.

What's she staring at?

"The team has been working hard," Mr. Mullins continues, "and tonight it's all going to pay off. Tonight we are going to *smash* Westward High."

The crowd cheers louder than ever before.

Realizing it's a game day, last night's shenanigans make a little more sense. It was some opening ceremony, an attempt to intimidate the competition.

"Now that's what I like to hear," Mr. Mullins continues. "Pride. Pride is knowing that your team is the best ... no matter what. It's knowing that your team will *crush* your opponents. In this world, there are winners and losers, and we are *not* losers."

As the crowd follows up with their robotic cheer, Gideon mumbles to himself, "According to who?"

"*Who's number one!?*" Mr. Mullins shouts, initiating the school's famous chant.

"*Eastward! Eastward!*" the crowd responds.

"*Who's gonna win!?*"

"*Eastward! Eastward!*"

"*Who's gonna die!?*"

"*Westward! Westward!*"

Feeling a headache coming on, Gideon rubs his forehead. "Shut up, you morons." Few things try his patience like the school chant.

Something feels wrong. The gym is suddenly silent. Gideon looks up at Mr. Mullins.

The man is staring right back at him. And there they are again: those green, otherworldly eyes.

"What was that?" Mr. Mullins asks.

There's no way he could have heard me. Gideon looks around. Cynthia is frowning. His friends look worried. Nearly everyone in the room is staring back at him, hundreds of silent faces. *This can't be happening.*

Mr. Mullins continues. "I thought I heard you say something ...

unspirited."

Something else catches Gideon's attention: the oblong window above the bleachers. Looking down at him is the gray lady, folding her arms with her usual scowl.

Gideon looks back at Mr. Mullins … *Sportacus*. Surely the man, with his supernatural powers, recognizes him from last night. This must be a setup, a conspiracy, and surely the gray lady is in on it. It's as if they were waiting for an opportunity to single out Gideon and make an example of him.

Still the entire gymnasium is silent. Do they actually expect him to answer?

What has he done? He joined the football team. He befriended Doug Rock. He even attended their extracurricular activity … sort of.

Was that it? Maybe the gray lady — who may have also been watching him last night, even in the middle of a cold night at a public park — didn't foresee the possibility of him escaping from the fight. Maybe she expected him to get plastered with the other jocks and take the appearance of a divine being at face value. Perhaps she hoped that, prostrated on the cold ground, surrendering his mind to the god of sports, Gideon's unruly spirit would have been broken and contained.

And now he's seen too much.

"Well?" asks Mr. Mullins.

Who are these people to control his life? And how is this even legal? Last Gideon heard, freedom of speech was still a thing, and the public humiliation of students could be classified as child abuse.

He looks at the man sitting near the podium: Mr. Bruce, the principal. Even Mr. Bruce is staring at Gideon, a frown on his lined face. Is he too being controlled? Or is he in on the conspiracy?

Gideon clears his throat. "I didn't say anything."

Mr. Mullins smiles. "Good." He turns back to the audience. "Tonight, we're gonna fight. Tonight, we're gonna win. And tonight —"

He's interrupted by Kyle Slater, who shouts, "Actually, coach, I heard Gideon say, *shut up, you morons.*"

Mr. Mullins turns back to Gideon. "Is this true?"

Gideon holds his peace.

Mr. Mullins beckons him. "Come here."

With a pounding heart, Gideon obeys.

Mr. Mullins practically puts his lips against the microphone as he shouts, "*Who's number one!?*"

Gideon has never had a stronger desire to be dead. He says in a small voice, "Eastward."

"*Who's gonna win!?*"

"Eastward."

"*Who's gonna die!?*"

Gideon has no reply.

"*Who's gonna die!?*" Mr. Mullins shouts even louder.

"See, I struggle with that part. Why does Westward have to die? Isn't it enough that Eastward is going to win?"

"You can't have winners without losers."

"That's not always true."

"Are you talking back to me?"

"From my observations, Westward High is no more pathetic than we are, and telling ourselves we're going to win doesn't change reality. I don't care if it's done in the name of loyalty; tooting one's own horn while insulting one's opponents will always be the hallmark of ignorance. Whatever happened to good sportsmanship?"

Mr. Mullins clenches the microphone. "Where's your pride, young man?"

"Pride is one of the seven deadly sins."

"Do you or do you not believe in the pursuit of excellence?"

"What does the pursuit of excellence have to do with being jerks?"

"While ungrateful wimps like you complain about what's nice and not nice, we fight your battles."

Gideon throws up his arms. "What battles? It's just a game."

"In the game of life you can either smash or be smashed."

"That's idiotic."

"You're pressing my button, kid."

"Which one, the stupid button or the jerk button?"

At that, Mr. Mullins walks right up to Gideon. "I'll press *your* button!" He gives him a hard slap to the back.

Gideon falls right off the front of the stage, his hands and feet slamming onto the floor. The audience roars with laughter as Mr. Mullins straightens his suit coat. Thus the jock has put the nerd in his place.

Gideon has been on the receiving end of violence before, and there's no sense in prolonging the misery. He looks up at Dwight and Wanda, calculating the trajectory of his retreat.

An embarrassed Dwight looks away, though Wanda is staring right back at him. She's the one person in the room with an encouraging look on her face.

Gideon is at loss. *You want me to fight back?* What would that accomplish besides further humiliation and broken bones? Besides, it's one thing to pick a fight with a fellow student, but to pick a fight with an adult is grounds for expulsion.

He stands up and begins the long walk across the gymnasium.

"That's right," says Mr. Mullins, "run along home. If you're not with us, you're against us."

Gideon can no longer meet Wanda's gaze. He dares not look at Cynthia. Why can't they understand? This isn't about honor, it's about survival. Until he graduates, he just needs to endure two more years of physical abuse, public humiliation, and delusions of scoring with the opposite sex. In a few decades, these meat heads will be working for *him.* Then who will be laughing?

In the realm of more immediate hope, soon the school day will be over, and he'll be safe in his bedroom playing *Metal Knight V.* By tomorrow morning, he'll have blotted this whole incident from his memory.

He ventures another glance at Wanda. She's never looked more disappointed. He can't bear it. And then there's his conscience. *When are you going to live, Gideon?*

Meanwhile the gray lady looks down with approval. *Yes, Gideon,* she seems to say, *know your limits.* That does it. Something within him snaps. He flips around and charges back to the stage. In an instant, he leaps to the top. An alarmed Mr. Mullins steps back but not fast enough. Gideon administers a hard punch to the guy's chest, who stumbles backward, into the football team.

With wide eyes, Mr. Mullins looks down at his chest, then up at the audience … and explodes.

ESCAPE

Gideon shields his eyes from the firework, a dazzling burst of green sparks. Seconds later, the spectacle is gone, and so is Mr. Mullins.

The formerly silent gymnasium erupts with noise.

Gideon looks again at the empty spot where Mr. Mullins was just standing.

Nothing.

Mr. Bruce stands up, also looking around in wonder.

Doug Rock looks dazed.

Cynthia looks horrified.

Dwight and Wanda look confused.

Kyle Slater looks … angry.

Gideon instinctively steps back.

"Get him!" Kyle shouts. He lunges for Gideon.

But Gideon isn't about to stick around. He weaves through the crowded stage and leaps to the floor. When he looks back, he sees a posse of jocks, led by Kyle, on his tail.

He looks at the nearest exit. It's blocked by Ms. Primple, her arms folded. Behind her stands the school's police officer, Officer Milton, a tall, stern, and frankly frightening man.

His senses sharpened, Gideon feels a rush from his left side. He doesn't need to look to know that a thick fist is flying at him. He ducks out of the way. Another jock lunges from the right, but it's as if the aggressor is moving in slow motion. Gideon dodges the attack with time to spare. Suddenly he's grateful for last night's insanity. It taught him how to think fast and stay alive. It's almost too easy, as if he has some extra-sensory power. Where has this fantastic ability been all his life? Perhaps he just needs to put himself in more life-or-death situations.

He runs straight for the stairs, then up through the bleachers, through crowds of excited students. It seems that everyone is shouting, though whether for or against him, he can't tell.

He reaches the top of the stairs, where's he blocked by the concrete wall. Good thing he's done this before. He just needs to jump, grab onto the railing, and pull himself up and over. Then, safe on the next level of bleachers, he can run for an exit.

He's halfway up when someone — Kyle Slater — grabs his ankle. No matter how hard Gideon tries to pull himself up, he's no match for Kyle's strength. He falls to his feet, and thick hands seize his shoulders. This is where his abilities fail. He braces himself for the pummeling.

But the hands lose their grip. Gideon opens his eyes to see Kyle stumbling down the stairs.

What?

Standing next to Gideon is a tall and burly Hawaiian: Bula. Gideon instinctively braces himself for more violence, but, of course, Bula doesn't attack.

Bula's hands are cupped together, his arms extended. "Go on!" he shouts over the noise.

Gideon understands the meaning, whether or not he understands the motive. With no other option, he grabs onto the bars above, steps onto Bula's hands, and Bula helps lift him up. Gideon pulls himself over and onto the next level. Once safe, he looks down to see Bula single-handedly fending off an onslaught of jocks.

"Why …" Gideon begins, but he can barely hear his own voice over all the noise. He'll have to thank Bula later. He's about to dart for the exit, when it occurs to him how familiar the situation is. He looks across the gymnasium, at the oblong window on the other side.

The gray lady is livid.

Gideon smiles.

WALK

When his parents' phone vibrates with a call from the school, Gideon is quick to turn off the device. When a police car arrives at the Greenwich residence, he's the first to spot it. Letting go of the blinds, he makes sure every TV and speaker in the house is blasting noise.

Officer Milton knocks on the door and waits. He cracks his knuckles. He fiddles with his mustache. He peers into a window. But no one answers. With a frown, he turns and leaves.

Apparently a warrant for Gideon's arrest hasn't been issued yet. That's relieving. Though Gideon won't be able to hide forever. It may only be a matter of time before a swat team shows up.

Moonlight streams through his bedroom window, casting square patterns on the carpet. Everyone else in the house has long since gone to sleep. But for Gideon, that peaceful oblivion that comes through a clear conscience proves unattainable.

I didn't do anything wrong, he tells himself again.

To which another voice in his head has a ready rebuttal: *Murderer.*

How was I supposed to know he'd ... explode?

His life is getting too weird. Just a few days ago, he enjoyed the trouble-free life of an unassuming nerd. He was content to live through comic books and fantasy novels. There was no football practice, scary administrators, or supernatural beings in campfires. Back then no one wanted to hurt him. Back then he was content to live in sweet ignorance of the fact that his school was being controlled by evil beings.

There must be a logical explanation for all this. Maybe Mr.

Mullins was an under-cover Navy SEAL, who was hiding explosives on his body, and maybe Gideon hit him just a little too hard.

That or the guy was, in fact, a god, and it just so happens that gods have conveniently-placed self-destruct buttons on their chests. He did say something about pressing his button …

Surely the world is a reasonable place run by reasonable people. Surely he's only imaging a dark conspiracy. *She's just a school administrator, and he's just a football coach ... who happened to explode.*

Gideon throws off his blanket.

Minutes later, he's strolling alone through the cold night. He looks up at the silver moon, so pristine in contrast to the darkness around it. Yet there's something evil about it.

The neighborhood streets are empty. Only he is awake. Perhaps only he is alive. Hiding within every home are unconscious bodies, tucked away and dreaming of nonsense. It's all so … *weird.*

Let them dream. This, the world of shadows, is his private sanctuary. For these sacred moments, there's only him and the stars. No noise, no pollution, no humans to deal with. Here, reality is subjected to imagination, the way it should be.

And yet, he sees evil lurking in every shadow.

He comes to a stop sign and glares at the forceful thing.

"No."

He continues walking.

There's someone in the distance, a dark, shadowy person. A policeman. It's always a policeman. And he's walking straight for Gideon! Gideon has been harassed before for breaking curfew law. Usually they just send him home, but now, for all he knows, they may have succeeded in obtaining a warrant for his arrest. He is a murderer, after all. Perhaps his face is already plastered around the police station. Should he turn around? No, that would be too obvious. He just needs to stay calm and act casual.

The person is getting closer. Tight, black jeans, pink jacket, long hair … a *girl.*

Dread gives way to fluttering. How often, on these long walks, has he dreamed of meeting a kindred spirit of the fairer sex, a girl who shares his love for quiet streets and all things nerdy? Of course, the wistful fantasy never plays out … unless …

His heart skips a beat. He knows that face. It's Cynthia Mc-Daniels.

Impossible. His life has gotten even weirder … delightfully, wonderfully weirder.

"Gideon?" she says, her brown eyes perking up.

"Cynthia," Gideon whispers. Is he allowed to speak her name?

"Oh, I'm so glad it's you."

She's glad it's me.

"At first I thought you were some weirdo, and I wanted to turn around, but then I thought, *just act casual*. What are you doing out here?"

"I … um … couldn't sleep."

"Me neither! Nice to know I'm not the only one. And I know I really shouldn't be out here alone, what with all the creeps, but I just needed to pace."

"Me too."

"My parents would be so mad if they found out. What about yours?"

"Yeah."

"I swear I'm normally a good girl, but sometimes … I just need to break the rules, you know?"

"Yeah."

"Though I'd feel better if I wasn't alone. You don't mind if I walk with you, do you?"

"Not at all."

"Great. We'll go your way."

They walk together.

Seeing her delicate shadow on the sidewalk, right next to his, smelling her subtle perfume, takin in her bouncing curls, it all seems too good to be real.

Cynthia says, "You were really cool at the assembly today."

"Umm … thanks."

"You don't talk much, do you?"

Gideon shrugs.

"I've been dying to ask you … how did that guy pull off the explosion stunt?"

It takes him a moment to register the question. "That wasn't a stunt. He really exploded." Even while speaking the words, he realizes how stupid they sound.

Cynthia chuckles politely. "Seriously."

If only Gideon knew how to lie. But then, he finds himself longing for a confidant, someone to experience the horrors of this strange, new world with him, someone who is not Dwight or Wanda. "I *was* serious."

After a pause, Cynthia says, "I get it, you can't reveal the tricks of the trade. You know, for a moment I thought the football team really had it in for you, but then I realized it was all part of the show. And then I was like … *whoa.*"

"Actually, they really did have it in for me."

She gives him a soft punch to the shoulder. "You're such a dweeb. And to be honest, you're the last person I expected to find on the football team. I totally didn't even know."

"Well, you know. It's … it's a thing."

"That's cool. I've always had crushes on football players."

"Cool." Gideon's heart rate picks up.

"In fact … do you want to know what's kept me awake?"

"What?"

"There's someone I haven't been able to stop thinking about, and … let's just say it's a major coincidence that I ran into you tonight."

"I see." *This is way too good to be real.*

"This is so embarrassing. I hardly even know you. And yet I totally feel like I can trust you."

"You can." What's he supposed to do now? Put his arm around her? Take her hand? She's practically proposing, and yet he still feels paralyzed. If only she would make the first move, then he could do the rest.

"You won't tell anyone? It will just be our secret?"

A secret love affair certainly isn't as good as openly showing off a trophy girlfriend, but it's better than nothing. "Yeah."

"So as you've probably guessed, there's this guy on the football team — he's in one of my classes — and I've wanted to talk to him for a long time but haven't known how."

Gideon meets both criteria. He feels the heat in his flushing face. "I've wanted to talk to you too."

"Now that we're together, this just makes it so much better."

"So what do we do now?" He honestly doesn't know. Are they supposed to kiss? Or is that only at the doorstep?

"Well, I was hoping you could introduce me to him."

Why the silly games? "I'm sure he would love to be introduced to you as well."

"You know who I'm talking about?"

"Of course."

"And you think he likes me?"

"I know he likes you."

"How do you know?"

This is getting ridiculous. "Well … my pounding heart may have something to do with it."

She stops walking. "What?"

Gideon stops too. How did they go from romantic to awkward? "You … you make my heart pound."

Cynthia looks confused. "Why?"

"Because I …" His defense mechanisms kick in. "Didn't you say …"

"I'm talking about Doug Rock."

First elation, now a stab to the heart. Gideon feels chewed up and spat out. Suddenly he'd rather be anywhere than here with Cynthia. "I know that."

The look on Cynthia's face is somewhere between concern and disgust. "For a moment I thought … never mind." She resumes her pace.

Reluctantly, Gideon follows. He can literally feel his heart sinking, his pulse slowing, his will fading.

"So you really think Doug likes me?" she asks.

"I don't know for sure."

"But you said —"

"I changed my mind."

"You're confusing me."

"I have that effect on people." Somewhere off in the shadows, he just knows the gray lady is watching. Surely this is yet another one of her plots to ruin his life.

"Do you think you could find out for me?"

"Sure."

"You can let him know I like him. Just don't tell him I put you up to this, okay?"

"Okay."

"I'll totally owe you for this. If there's ever anything I can do for you — anything at all — just let me know."

"Okay."

To his surprise, she squeezes his hand, and part of him wonders if there's still hope. "It's been super cool talking to you, Gideon, but I should probably head home now. I'm really glad we became friends."

"Me too."

"See you tomorrow." And with a girlish wave of her fingers, she turns down a side street, leaving him alone in the wide, empty world.

"Tomorrow," Gideon repeats.

Tomorrow. How on earth is he going to show his face at school tomorrow?

PRINCIPAL'S OFFICE

Gideon throws a pebble against the classroom window, but Dwight continues to sit in his desk, oblivious. It takes seven pebbles to finally get his attention.

Minutes later, Dwight meets Gideon at the park adjoining the school. They're encircled by pine trees, where no administrator could possibly see them. (Though Gideon's not sure about supernatural beings.)

Dwight is the first to speak. "Dude, they've already called your name three times over the PA. They want you to go to the main office."

"I don't know what to do," says Gideon.

"I don't blame you. You kind of killed a coach in front of the entire school."

"Is he really dead?"

Dwight shrugs. "At least that's what it looked like. If he's really a god, then maybe he *can't* die. Or maybe he was never alive to begin with. Or maybe … I don't know, Gid. Something weird is going on, and it hurts my head to think about it."

"Do you think I did the wrong thing?"

"I don't know *what* you did."

"Me neither."

"But someone had to stand up to that meat head, and I'm glad it was you."

"What do you think they'll do to me?"

"Maybe you shouldn't go to school. At least not for a few days."

"If I sluff, they'll call my parents."

"Pretend to be sick."

"My mom doesn't fall for that anymore."

"Then … just don't go to the office."

"The gray lady will find me."

Dwight raises his shoulders. "What do you want me to say?"

"Say you'll come with me to the office. Tell them what you saw at the park."

"Let me get this straight. You're going to tell the principal that you *had* to kill Sportacus, because he was an evil god who encouraged violence and under-age drinking?"

"Do you have a better idea?"

"No."

"Then let's go."

Dwight looks at Gideon, at the school, then back at Gideon. "Sorry, man, but you're on your own for this one."

"I thought you were my friend."

"This is too much. I can't deal with it."

"Dwight, I'm begging you. I'm scared."

"I am too." Dwight looks at his feet. "Anyway, I gotta get back to class. Good luck." Never glancing back, Dwight returns to the school.

Gideon sighs. Before long, he finds himself in the main office, where a middle-aged woman stares back at him. She glances up from her computer. "May I help you?"

"I'm Gideon Greenwich," he says simply.

Her eyes widen. "Just a moment." She walks deeper into the office, where, in a hushed voice, she consults with several other middle-aged women. Each turns to Gideon with wide eyes. Then the woman returns. "Mr. Bruce would like to speak with you."

An interview with the principal. Classic. After dealing with the gray lady, this should be easy.

Mr. Bruce is waiting for him, standing in front of his office door. With a pin-striped suit, a thin comb-over, and an eternal frown, the man is the very face of ruin.

"Have a seat," says Mr. Bruce, gesturing to his office.

Gideon complies, entering the dismal room and taking a seat on a hard, wooden chair.

Mr. Bruce doesn't join him. Instead, he walks out of sight.

Gideon can hear the man whispering instructions to someone. He makes out the phrase, "call Officer Milton." Then, at the sound of approaching footsteps, he sits up straight.

Mr. Bruce closes the door as he enters his office. He walks past a wall decorated with diplomas, then takes a seat behind his desk. His stern, tired eyes meet Gideon's. "Well, Mister Greenwich, I'm not one to beat around the bush. As I'm sure you know, your behavior yesterday was unacceptable."

"I know," says Gideon.

"Mr. Mullins was a highly-esteemed coach, and bringing him to Eastward was no small thing. Not only did you insult him in front of the entire school, you … well … it's what happened next that I'd like to talk about."

However inappropriate, Gideon feels the slightest urge to smile. "Go ahead."

Struggling to find the right words, Mr. Bruce rolls his hands. "What … exactly … happened?"

"To be honest, I was hoping you could tell me."

Mr. Bruce's frown sinks even lower. "Don't play games with me."

"I'm telling the truth. I don't know what happened." Is the principal really as clueless as Gideon is? This isn't funny anymore, it's disturbing.

"Let me be more precise. Where is Mr. Mullins?"

"I honestly don't know."

"Mister Greenwich, I'm not sure if you understand the seriousness of the situation. You're being accused of murder."

Gideon feels sudden tears coming on. "It was all so fast and … I swear I didn't mean to kill him."

Mr. Bruce looks down at his desk. "I see." He starts filling out some paperwork. "If you have nothing else to say, I'm going to ask you to step out —" He's interrupted by a knock at the door. "Come in."

The door opens, and Gideon's heart grows even heavier at the sight of the gray lady.

"Good morning, Mr. Bruce," she says, stiff as ever.

Mr. Bruce is in no mood for pleasantries. "And you are?"

Gideon looks between them. How is it possible that they're unacquainted with each other?

"Norma," she says, "from the district office." She doesn't extend a hand. "I'm sorry to interrupt, but I'm aware that Mister Greenwich is being accused of malfeasance, and I felt it my duty to provide some critical information."

Gideon sighs. Now his doom is sealed.

"I'm listening," says Mr. Bruce.

The gray lady opens the door wider as in steps another person: Mr. Mullins.

Gideon feels dizzy. This is beyond weird. It's nonsensical. Impossible.

Mr. Mullins smiles at Gideon. Gideon can only look away.

The gray lady continues. "It was an excellent performance. Even the administrators thought it was real. To you especially, Mister Greenwich, I must say how brilliant your delivery was. Such a strong stage presence. Such witty improvisation. You, young man, should consider a career in the performing arts."

Still frowning, Mr. Bruce says, "You're telling me it was all an act?"

The gray lady snorts with laughter. "Well of course. You didn't think that Mr. Mullins actually ..." She stares incredulously.

Mr. Mullins bursts into laughter. The gray lady laughs with him. Finally, Mr. Bruce's frown lightens up as he too laughs.

"You see, Mr. Bruce," says the gray lady, wiping a tear from her eye, "The student council wanted to take a veer from the usual pep rally, throwing in a little drama and pyrotechnics. Didn't anyone tell you?"

Mr. Bruce is suddenly intent on repositioning the pens on his desk. "Well, someone may have mentioned it. I have so many things to worry about, and ..."

"I fully understand, Mr. Bruce."

"As you can see, I was simply concerned about —"

"I'll only have positive things to say about you to the superintendent."

To quench an awkward moment of silence, it's Mr. Bruce who initiates another round of laughter. The others follow suit. Finally, Mr. Bruce removes his glasses to wipe away a tear. Turning to Gideon, he says, "Well, Mister Greenwich, I guess you're off the hook."

Gideon has given up on making sense of the situation … or his life in general. Though he's not about to question Mr. Bruce's decision. He stands up.

"With one detention," says Mr. Bruce.

Injustice! "What for?"

Mr. Bruce shakes his head as he scribbles his pen over a detention slip. "I don't know. But I know you deserve it."

The gray lady nods with approval.

IDOLS

On Gideon's left is Mr. Mullins. On his right is the gray lady. He dares not ask where they're taking him. At one point Mr. Mullins takes the left hallway while the gray lady turns right. Gideon stands at the crossroads.

"You're coming with me," the gray lady announces.

Gideon regretfully obeys. Even the company of an evil god is better than being alone with the gray lady. Looking back, he sees Mr. Mullins stop in front of a door. The man looks around.

Gideon looks away. When he ventures to glance back, Mr. Mullins is gone, the door swinging behind him. And not just any door.

The girl's bathroom? Who is this guy?

Gideon has half a mind to report this impropriety to the gray lady. Then he wonders if, once again, he's seen more than he was supposed to. However bizarre, perhaps it's best to keep his thoughts to himself … for now.

They pass the picture of the cowboy … one of the *many* pictures of cowboys. But this can't be right; he's certain they've arrived at the door to the teachers' lounge. He was just here a couple days ago. He even recognizes the black smudge and chip in the door's frame.

The gray lady opens the door. Once again, the teacher's lounge is nowhere to been seen. Instead are the familiar stairs leading to an office.

Of course this makes no sense. Why should it make sense?

And then it happens all over again. They're back in her office. The gray lady takes a seat behind her desk, and Gideon dutifully sits across from her.

She breaks the silence. "Mister Greenwich — Gideon — I'll be the first to say it. I'm sorry."

Gideon really didn't see that coming. "For what?" The question is silly, of course, but it seemed like the polite thing to say.

"You must feel so … manipulated."

"Yes, actually."

"Everyone's always telling you where to be, what to do, how to think. Even the best of intentions can go too far, and I'm as guilty as anyone."

Gideon just stares. Is this a trick?

"You don't have to go to football practice anymore, and you don't have to be friends with Douglas Rock. While I hope your time on the team has taught you some life skills, from now on, I just want you to be yourself."

"Okay …"

"You think I'm joking, don't you?"

"Maybe."

"You're wondering what the catch is."

"Yes."

"No catch. You're free to go."

It takes a moment for the words to sink in. Gideon rises to his feet, half expecting her to tell him to sit back down, but she's already turned her attention to her desk. "Um … Norma?"

"Yes?" She doesn't look up from her work.

"No one ever told me about a performance."

Finally she looks up. "What?"

"With Mr. Mullins. I didn't know any of that was going to happen."

"Douglas never told you?"

"No."

She shakes her head. "Boys can be so cruel."

"What do you mean?"

"The student council wrote the whole thing out. A member of the football team was going to pretend to be a student from Westward. He and Mr. Mullins were supposed to have a fight over which school was the best. There was some clever dialog about who had more team spirit, and to prove that we're *bursting at the seams*, they worked in the explosion effect. Compliments of the chemistry club. Quite impressive, really. Though it's a shame the rest didn't go as planned. Apparently the football team thought it would be funny to turn the whole thing into a prank … on you. That would explain why Douglas was eager to find you. Mr. Mullins must have thought you were in on it all along."

Gideon feels a rush of anger. "You're saying Mr. Mullins *wanted* me to punch him in the chest?"

She shrugs. "I didn't read the script either. Luckily, Mr. Mullins was a drama teacher before he was a football coach. He knows how to improvise. You should have seen him at the Shakespeare Festival, never a dull performance. Once he even lit himself on fire. *Green* fire, I seem to recall. He always did have a flare for special effects. But that was before your time."

Suddenly knowledge turns to belief, belief to uncertainty, uncertainty to doubt. "I see."

"Anything else, Mister Greenwich?"

"I could have sworn this was the teachers' lounge."

"The teachers' lounge is in the third hallway after the main office. We took the second hallway."

Gideon fights the temptation to smack himself in the forehead. "You really do work for the district, don't you?"

She takes off her reading glasses. "Who else would I work for?"

"I don't know." With no further ado, Gideon stands up and exits the room.

He finds himself wandering into the commons, though he doesn't recall how he got there. A heavy burden is gone, but in its place is emptiness.

Have I been imagining this whole thing?

He preferred the burden.

The school bell rings, and soon he's standing in the midst of hundreds of hustling students. The goths are the first to announce their presence with their droning music from hell. The football team, coupled with the cheerleaders, announce their presence with barks of laughter.

Gideon steers clear of them. Very clear.

Am I crazy?

Wandering through a hallway, he sees a girl sitting slumped against the lockers. He wants to keep going. He has important things to think about. But at the sight of her pink eyes, his conscience makes him stop. "Are you okay?" he asks.

She looks up. Her hair is a mess, her rosy cheeks stained with tears. "They cast me out."

"Who?"

"The other girls." She points to the end of the hallway, where a group of girls stand chatting. They turn their backs.

"Why?"

She sniffs, struggling to get the words out. "Because I haven't been asked to homecoming."

Gideon has to stifle a laugh. Then he gets another look at her quivering face, and his heart melts. In fact, though he doesn't even know her name, he feels a sudden urge to ask her to homecoming himself. He's never asked a girl to do anything. The thought is paralyzing. In the end, all he can muster is the phrase, "Everything will be okay." The words sound hollow, and he's quick to distance himself from the awkward scene.

Focus, Gideon. He must find his bearings. He must face reality, no matter how horrific.

His thoughts are interrupted by a strange sound. A group of freshman boys are huddled around a locker. Their shoulders are pressed together as if they're hiding something. And they're ... *chanting.*

Gideon can't stop himself from listening in. He hears:

> *Guide us, O Coolar,*
> *Pimp of the universe.*
> *Tear down our enemies*
> *And lift up our egos.*

Their faces solemn, their voices hushed, they repeat the words again and again.

Gideon draws as close as he dares, and then he sees it. Taped to a locker is a poster of a mean-looking rap star. There's something familiar about him. He has jewels in each ear. He's covered with gold and tattoos. Gideon has the unsettling feeling that the guy is staring right at him.

He's shoved to the side. Startled, he sees one of the boys with outstretched hands. Another boy shoves him, also taking him off-guard. It happens a third time. Each boy has turned from the poster to stare at Gideon. In their eyes is that familiar look of death. The resemblance with the rapper is uncanny.

Gideon runs. *Speed walks*. (He's learned from too many experiences how the student body will mock him for running with a backpack on.) When he glances back, his would-be murderers are still staring him down.

He crashes into someone.

"Watch it," snaps a girl. She's tall, blond, and beautiful: Joan Cooper, a senior and one of the cheerleaders in Gideon's Fashion Merchandising class. She's about to say more, but upon getting a better look at Gideon, apparently with no recollection of having seen him before, she turns back to her equally aesthetically-pleasing friends. "And that's the final judgment," she says.

"Yearbook signing?" asks the red-head, Kimberly Fenner.

"No, walking at graduation. The number of signatures you get is important, but true success is measured by the number of cheers … especially by boys."

"What's after that?"

Joan stares into space. "There's nothing after that. Either the student body accepts you or you're a loser."

The brunette, Monica Hawley, points a red claw at Gideon. "Why are you still here?"

Gideon backs up, nearly ramming into another student. Every back is turned. Every face seems wicked. Everything seems wrong. Gideon tries to get away from it all, but the very halls seem to be closing in on him.

GODS

Third period: Ancient World History. Ms. Fitzwater writes a number on the whiteboard:

33,000,000

"Can anyone guess what I'm thinking?" she asks.

Megan Hensley raises her hand. "The total population of India in the fifth century BCE?"

"No."

Ken Garcia raises his hand. "The total death toll from the Persian Wars?"

"No."

James Buchanan raises a hand. "The total cost in sheqels of the Great Ziggurat of Ur?"

"Good guesses, but no." Ms. Fitzwater smiles with satisfaction. "I'm thinking of gods."

Gideon perks up, his mind a haze.

"Historians estimate over thirty-three million gods in the Hindu religion alone. Of course, Hinduism is much more than a single religion. It evolved over thousands of years, a composite of many peoples and cultures. When one tribal people would unite with another, they brought their gods with them. Yes, Joan?"

Joan Cooper is raising her hand. "Wait … do you mean those blue guys with lots of arms?"

"In the Hindu tradition, multiple arms are a symbol of power, much like the many wings of the seraphim as described in the Hebrew bible. Gods are depicted in all shapes, sizes, and colors, though always for a reason and always with a story. Yes, Ken?"

Ken Garcia is raising his hand. "I thought this was a *history* class."

Ms. Fitzwater isn't amused. "Religion played a *major* role in ancient world history, just as it does today. In every culture — without exception — religion determined how people dressed, what they ate, even their laws. From marriage to wars, the laws of men were only reflections of the laws of heaven. When someone got sick, it was a punishment from the gods. When the sun rose in the morning, it was because the gods willed it. Whether you were a king or a slave, it was because a god ordained it. And when your nation lost in battle, it was because *their* god was more powerful than *your* god, so you sure as heck better start worshiping it.

"Death was so common that our ancestors couldn't help but hope for a better world. Hardly anyone questioned whether or not to worship, only *which* god to worship. You see, Mister Garcia, you really can't know a nation in the ancient world without also knowing their gods. Yes, Gideon?"

With his hand raised, Gideon watches Joan Cooper, fearing she'll remember him as the guy who accosted her in the hallway. As far as he can tell, Joan has already disassociated her mind from Gideon's existence.

He says, "This may sound like a dumb question, but … *why* did everyone believe in gods? Was there any evidence?"

Ms. Fitzwater contemplates the question. "We've come a long way in science and technology. We know more about human anatomy, the causes of disease, and how to treat them than ever before. And yet, two-thirds of us are overweight, nearly half of us will suffer heart attacks, and we're addicted to antidepressants, caffeine, and sleeping pills.

"Meanwhile there are parts of the world that have hardly changed in thousands of years, areas with little to no access to modern healthcare, where the cure for the common cold is a visit to your local shaman. Through dances and chants, the medicine men invoke the powers of spirits and gods, and from what I've read, the believers are often healed, sometimes more often than in developed nations. It's a well-documented phenomenon. Yes, Ken?"

"It's called the placebo effect."

"You're right. No one quite knows *how* the placebo effect works, but it *does* work. Amazingly well. So, Gideon, either the gods are real or we hold within our minds the power to change our realities. And that, it seems, would make *us* the gods. Either way it appears that the ancient world might have been on to something."

Fourth Period: Physics. Mr. Periwinkle, his sweater caked with crumbs, holds up his current treat, a chocolate glazed doughnut. It's well known that the fat, middle-aged man loves to torment hungry students with his snacking habits, especially right before lunch.

"There are some who believe that the universe is shaped like a doughnut," he says. "But personally, I subscribe to the *oblate spheroid* model." He swaps the chocolate doughnut for a jelly-filled doughnut. "A more discus shape, just as the planets and galaxies are shaped. Now I know some of you think the earth is spherical, just as everyone did before Galileo. But if there's one constant in astronomy, physics, and especially quantum mechanics, it's that all of our initial assumptions will eventually be proven wrong. The earth is an oblate spheroid."

He takes a sumptuous bite from the jelly doughnut, revealing the red, strawberry glaze inside. With his mouth full, he says, "The classical physicist would say that the exterior universe — the doughnut — existed first, and we — the jelly — developed within it. But Albert Einstein had a different theory. Mister Grady, please pick up on the second paragraph."

Calvin Grady, the scrawny freshman with a stutter, reads aloud, "The space of physics is a function of our conceptual steam."

Mr. Periwinkle sits against his desk, relishing in the blank stares around him. "What do you think that means?"

Calvin shakes his head. "I have no idea."

Mr. Periwinkle licks the jelly out of his beard. "Mister Greenwich?"

Gideon's mind is far away. He looks over the textbook, reading the sentence for himself:

The space of physics is a function of our conceptual steam.

"Umm …"

"Just throw out a wild guess."

"Mr. Einstein seems to be arguing for some connection between our minds and the physical world."

"Interesting interpretation."

Gideon rubs his forehead, trying to sort a sea of fragments. "He must mean that our *conceptions* of the physical world are tied to our minds. Our minds don't actually alter reality."

Mr. Periwinkle's smile widens. "Are you sure?"

Gideon doesn't dare answer.

"Everyone turn to page one-hundred-sixteen. Mister Greenwich, please read aloud."

Gideon does as he's told:

If you drop a rock into a pond, it will fall in a straight line. A rock is a physical thing made of tiny particles. While the water is also made of particles, it won't move in a straight line but expand in waves. The splash will also create waves of air, which your ears and brain will interpret as sound.

Many scientists have tried to determine whether the basic building blocks of our universe, such as photons (light), are made of particles or waves. One famous experiment is to shoot photons against a wall. On their way, the photons must pass through slits. Scientists then observe the resulting patterns on the wall. When there's one slit, the photons act like particles, creating an impression on the wall that mirrors the slit. When there's two slits, the photons act like waves, creating a pattern on the wall like rippling water.

To try to understand this paradoxical behavior, scientists have placed sensors by the slits. The results were even stranger. No matter the number of slits, when the photons were observed, they acted like particles. When the photons were not observed, they acted like waves. The same experiment has been tried with electrons and large molecules, and the results are always the same. It appears that the very act of observation may alter reality.

"So," says Mr. Periwinkle, licking the last bits of jelly from his fingers, "what were you saying about our minds not being able to alter reality?"

Gideon feels a headache coming on. "I don't get it."

Mr. Periwinkle throws up his arms, causing his ill-fitted sweater to reveal his belly. "Welcome to the club. This weird behavior completely contradicted the basic tenets of classical science. It took a whole new branch of science to explain it: quantum mechanics."

Gideon examines his pencil, wondering if it's real or not. "So what do quantum mechanics say?"

"Are you sure I haven't freaked you out enough? Maybe you'd be happier in a universe that makes sense."

Kimberly Fenner blurts out, "That's fine with me. I can't think this close to lunch time." There's murmurs of agreement from the class.

"No," says Gideon, "I need to know."

Again Mr. Periwinkle smiles. "All right." He turns over an apple fritter in his hands, examining the glazed intricacies. "According to some scientists, there *are* no photons. There are no electrons. There are no molecules. Nothing actually exists until we *will* it to exist through observation. While the end result is everything we see around us, before we observe it, it's not there. It appears that our minds don't merely alter reality, they *create* reality."

Kimberly Fenner shoots up her hand. "Are you telling me that if no one's looking at the moon, it disappears?"

"According to the mathematics behind quantum mechanics, yes."

"Then that math is bunk."

"We'd like to think so. But the same math has been used to make successful predictions in chemistry, physics, astronomy, and just about every branch of science. Whether or not we understand it, the numbers *always* add up."

"But … the moon …"

"When tiny particles appear to act in nonsensical ways, it may be because we're incapable of viewing the full story. There's reasons to believe that there are many more dimensions to our universe, but we're trapped in only three. It's like trying to solve a rubix cube while only looking at one side."

Again Kimberly Fenner shoots up her hand. "Can we be done now? This is seriously hurting my head."

Kimberly gets her wish as the bell rings. The class doesn't hesitate to grab their possessions and jump to their feet. Within seconds, only Gideon remains.

Mr. Periwinkle watches him curiously. "Don't you want to get out of here?"

Gideon glances at the door to make sure they're alone. "That's all fascinating theory, but … you don't really believe it, do you?"

"Believe what?"

"All that about the mind changing reality."

"Hmm." Mr. Periwinkle retrieves a book from his desk, then thumbs through it before handing it to Gideon. "Page four-twenty-one, bottom paragraph."

Gideon reads aloud:

> *The very study of the external world led to the conclusion that the content of the consciousness is an ultimate reality" (Eugene Wigner, Nobel Prize winner and leading physicist of the twentieth century).*

Gideon has nothing to say.

"Neuroscientists will tell you that the mind is nothing more than a stream of processes in our brains. But some quantum physicists have another explanation." Mr. Periwinkle stretches out his arms. "What's out there is entangled with what's in here." He taps Gideon's forehead. "Some believe that the mind is one of the fundamental forces of the universe, and everything else is built upon it."

"But —"

"You think *that's* weird? What if I told you that physicists have proven that particles can be tied together over any distance, that what we do here could affect matter on the opposite side of the universe? What if I told you that space and time can be warped, that they're both expanding like a balloon, or that only five percent of the universe is even observable? What if I told you that the vast majority of *everything* is comprised of mysterious substances known as dark energy and dark matter? Or what if I told you that colliding particles in Switzerland have suggested the existence of parallel universes? We've hardly scratched the surface of weird."

"Parallel universes?"

"So it appears."

"You mean with other worlds? And people in them?"

"It's entirely possible. For all we know, there could be multidimensional beings who can see us, though we can't see them."

"Do you mean like … *gods*?"

Mr. Periwinkle laughs. "Something like that. Of course, it's only a theory. We have yet to find any evidence of extraterrestrial life, whether on Mars or a parallel universe."

"It was a dumb question."

"Though I will say this. As far as life in this solar system, it appears we're alone. As far as life on neighboring systems, it's harder to say. As far as life in the galaxy, the universe, the multiverse … we have no idea. Personally I think it's preposterous to conclude that we're the only intelligent beings in all of existence. Even if there's only one other civilization out there, a civilization that has conquered time and space … then of course there are gods. And supposing such beings have a greater dimensional capacity than our own, reaching out to us may be as simple for them as stepping on ants is for us. To the ants, in their flat, little world, the shoe may appear to come out of nowhere, but to us it's perfectly natural."

"Doesn't this stuff ever … freak you out?"

"The first step to enlightenment is admitting that we know nothing. From there, there's endless possibilities, and that is exciting, even empowering." Mr. Periwinkle rubs his greasy beard. "What I'm saying, Mister Greenwich, is much more than the possibility of there being gods out there. What I'm saying is that *you* can be a god. The universe is yours to control if you can only learn how."

"Have you learned how?"

"If I did, do you think I'd be teaching high school?"

LIBRARY

Gideon sits alone in the lunchroom. He's eager to talk to Dwight and Wanda, but they're nowhere to be found. Has he offended them?

As he wolfs down his cheese and pickle sandwich, he catches more than an occasional glance from the student body around him. He can almost hear them thinking, *There's the guy who took on the football coach.*

Yesterday, it seemed, no one would have ever glanced in his direction unless there was something more interesting in the background. Now, from the lowest freshman to the highest senior, it seems everyone's watching him, whispering. Whether they see him as a hero, a villain, or just a performer, no one bothers to say. As he always expected, fame is hollow.

Finally he finds his friends at a table in the library, hunched over a book. Though Dwight doesn't even look up, Wanda runs and embraces him. "You weren't expelled?" she asks, gazing into his eyes.

Gideon pulls away. *Cooties.* "Not yet anyway."

"What happened?"

"Mr. Mullins is alive. It was all an act. And the gray lady was there. She ... saved me."

"She's not a witch?"

"She's just a school administrator, and Mr. Mullins is just a coach who does magic tricks."

Finally Dwight looks up from his book. "Yeah, but ..."

There is no but. Gideon sees in Dwight's face the same existential horror he's been feeling, a realization that they aren't the heroes in some romance, that the forces of evil don't have it in for them, that their reality is random and meaningless.

Gideon leans over the table to see what they're reading. There's an illustration of a man in a toga. Feathered wings protrude from his helmet and shoes. "Who's that?"

"Hermes" says Wanda, "the messenger god."

Gideon rolls his eyes. "Wanda, don't you think it's time we —"

"He's also the god of sports."

Gideon takes a closer look at the illustration. Strong arms, barrel chest … *green* eyes.

"The only question is, if Sportacus was a messenger, who sent him? We know the gray lady is one of them. I think she's the goddess of normality."

"Wanda —"

"But there's got to be more. And do you know who I suspect? Ms. Primple. I think she's the goddess of fashion."

"There's no gods or goddesses."

"That's what they want you to think."

"Wanda —"

"If Ms. Primple is the goddess of fashion, then she's a master of illusion, maybe even a shape shifter. She could have been posing as Mr. Mullins."

"And why would she do that?"

"To cover up the accident. To make everything seem normal. After what you did to Mr. Mullins, they must be scared of you, and their best protection was to fill you with doubts."

"You're looking too far into this."

"Did you notice anything strange about Mr. Mullins?"

"I did see him slip into the girl's bathroom when he thought no one was looking."

"Aha! Because it was really Ms. Primple under a spell of illusion, and she needed a safe place to transform back."

"Interesting theory. But if they really have it in for me, why would they save me from expulsion?"

"Better to snuff out your spark than fight your fire." Suddenly Wanda slams the book shut. Her eyes narrow as she glances between the teachers and librarians in the room. "You know what I think, Gideon? I think we're on the brink of discovering something big, and the dark powers behind it are scared out of their minds. Of course everything appears normal. We're dealing with the goddess of normality, after all, and this is exactly the kind of opposition we should expect. Now, more than ever, we must be strong."

Exasperated, Gideon turns to Dwight.

Dwight can only shrug. Neither of them has ever seen this fiery side of Wanda.

Gideon says, "It's certainly more fun to believe in supernatural beings. And given the depth of the universe, their existence is certainly possible. But is it not more likely that we're just a bunch of nerds with overactive imaginations?"

"But supposing I'm right, *the only thing necessary for the triumph of evil is for good men to do nothing.*"

Dwight says, "All right, Wanda, we'll assume there are evil gods controlling our lives. Now what? You've seen what almost happened to Gideon. We're powerless."

Wanda turns to Gideon. "What do you say?"

Gideon looks at his shoes. "There's a lot at stake, Wanda. I don't know if I'm ready to throw away my life for some crazy idea."

Wanda stands up. She pulls the straps of her bag over her shoulders. "Good day, gentlemen." She walks away.

"Wait," says Gideon.

Wanda stops, though she doesn't look back.

"What do you want me to do?"

"Doug Rock and Kyle Slater are in your next class," says Wanda. "Talk to them and learn everything you can about Sportacus."

"Mr. Mullins."

"Sportacus. Where did he come from? How long have they known him? What are his plans? Can you do that?"

"Those guys want to *kill* me."

"You call yourselves men." Wanda walks off.

INTERROGATIONS

Coach Griffith blows his whistle, beginning another round of hell.

The ball is in Kyle Slater's hands. He dribbles straight down the court, never passing to his teammates.

On the defense, Gideon stands directly in Kyle's trajectory. His hands are extended, his feet spread apart. Though the pose feels presumptuous — as if Gideon has any idea what he's doing — he holds his ground.

With a thrust of his shoulder, Kyle knocks Gideon right over.

Gideon's back smacks against the hard, wood floor, knocking the wind out of him.

There's the sound of Coach Griffith's whistle. *An obvious foul.* But all the coach does is tell the players to come back while another group takes their place.

Struggling to breathe, Gideon climbs to his feet.

Kyle stands over him with the usual murder in his eyes.

"Good game," Gideon wheezes.

Kyle turns a cold shoulder and walks off.

Gideon takes a deep breath. *For Wanda.* Then he rushes to catch up. "So I've been thinking," he says to Kyle, "that assembly yesterday was pretty cool. Did you know all that was going to happen?"

Kyle stops and stares at Gideon. His eyes haven't lost a degree of deadliness. "You'll pay for what you did."

As Kyle walks off, Gideon steps back, his stomach sinking. He doesn't know whether he's more afraid of Kyle or the thought that Wanda might be right.

He turns his attention to the bleachers. Sitting on the top row is none other than Doug Rock. He's been there, alone, for the entire period. And what's that in his hands?

A doctor's note?

A day ago, the thought that Gideon and Doug would switch places would have been inconceivable. How did the great athlete digress into another bench warmer? And did it have anything to do with Mr. Mullins? More importantly, is that a *real* doctor's note?

Only then does Gideon remember his promise from last night. On top of an interrogation for Wanda, now he has to find out whether or not Doug is interested in Cynthia. The things he does for women. Taking another breath of courage, he heads for the bleachers.

Someone grips his shoulders. Fearing a blow from Kyle, Gideon tenses.

"Where do you think you're going?" asks Coach Griffith.

"I … need to talk to Doug."

"Do you have a doctor's note?"

"No."

"Then go sit with the others. There's a seat next to Kyle."

With her legs crossed and on full display, Ms. Primple files her red nails. "Today is your last chance. Mister Farnsworth and Mister Greenwich, you're the only ones left. Are you going to present your reports, or are you going to take failing grades?"

"Failing grade," says Dwight, his eyes glued on Ms. Primple's calves.

Gideon doesn't need any more stress. He also doesn't need an F on his report card. Seeing no alternative, he stands up and walks to the front of the class. The only benefit of standing there is the front-row view of Cynthia McDaniels. She smiles, bringing back the warm, fluttering feelings from last night. Then Gideon remembers how the night ended.

"We're ready when you are," says Ms. Primple.

Gideon clears his throat. "For my report, I chose the … umm … necktie. The necktie was invented in the … fifth century … BC." He steals a guilty glance at Ms. Primple, who looks unimpressed. "It was originally used as a … torture device, similar to the noose. However, as popularized by … Alfonzo the … Great … you know, the king of … Bulgaria … torture for men became fashionable."

Ms. Primple cuts in. "Do you have sources for any of this?"

"Oh, these are all well-documented facts."

Cynthia is no longer smiling. No one is … but Wanda. At least someone appreciates the courage it takes to fight an uphill battle. Thinking of her, Gideon has a sudden idea, an idea that fills him with butterflies. He doesn't like the idea, though he feels bound to go through with it.

"In addition to setting fashion trends, Alfonzo was known for his … powers." He's never dug himself so deep in a hole that he couldn't go lower. "For example, it was rumored that Alfonzo had the ability to shape shift." He steals another guilty glance at Ms. Primple.

Either Ms. Primple has an incredible poker face, or her conscience is clear. Still too early to judge.

"In fact, some people thought he was some sort of deity from a parallel universe, who used his powers to assist the other gods and goddesses in a nefarious scheme to control the minds of unsuspecting teenagers." He steals one more glance at Ms. Primple.

Though her face is cold, there's no sign of guilt. She says, "What does any of this have to do with the necktie?"

Gideon can feel the blood rushing to his face. "Well … it explains how ancient men were able to wear nooses without choking to death."

"And how is that?"

"Supernatural powers."

Following the sound of a slap, Gideon sees that Cynthia has buried her face in her hands.

"I see," says Ms. Primple. "Are you finished?"

"Yes."

DETENTION

Though it's been a long and tiring day, when the last bell finally rings, Gideon has yet another ordeal to face. He makes his way to detention, where there's got to be over a hundred students waiting outside the auditorium. Compared to his first time attending after-school detention as a freshman, attendance has at least tripled. Either the number of teenage delinquents is rising or the school is tightening its grip. As evidenced by the wads of cash being exchanged between students and doorkeepers, Gideon suspects the latter.

This must be the gray lady's fault. He has to check his thoughts. *No, she's a nice woman. This is Mr. Bruce's fault.* Gideon was condemned without reason. Ten dollars to sit in an auditorium for an hour. If this isn't extortion, what is?

Cynthia McDaniels is walking through the hallway. As if Gideon hasn't embarrassed himself enough, now Cynthia will see him as a reprobate. He tries to blend into the crowd.

"Hey, Gideon," she says, "mind if I wait with you?"

"Of course not." His heart is fluttering again. *Stop it. She doesn't like you.* "I ... didn't think I'd find *you* here."

Cynthia shrugs. "Oh, I sluff class now and then."

"Cool."

She plays with her hair for a moment. "That was a very ... interesting report."

"Thanks."

"I had no idea the necktie had so much history."

"Neither did I."

"You made it all up, didn't you?"

" … yes."

"You goof ball."

Is that a term of endearment?

"Anyway," Cynthia continues, "did you talk to Doug?"

"I tried to, but —"

He's interrupted by the woman at the door. "Ten dollars, please."

Frowning, Gideon hands over his crumpled cash. *I'm innocent!*

"No talking beyond this point," the woman says.

Gideon enters the auditorium, where an usher — a girl with a smug air of authority — leads him down a sloping aisle. Though the place is filled with students, the huge room is dead silent. He's directed to take a seat on the front row. Moments later, Cynthia is instructed to sit four seats away.

Gideon smiles at her.

She smiles back.

Perhaps this won't be so bad. Though if they're caught talking, they'll be expelled from the room, then their unresolved detentions will affect their report cards, and precious money would be wasted. *What if adults were treated like this?*

Whether or not his dream girl is sitting nearby, there's nothing to do but open his backpack, pull out a notebook, and draw spaceships. He's etching the flames of a rocket when a wad of crumpled paper rolls in front of his eyes.

He looks at Cynthia.

She winks.

He carefully uncrumples the paper, checking to make sure the usher isn't watching. Then he reads Cynthia's flouncy, girlish handwriting:

> *So do you think Doug likes me?*

Gideon holds in his sigh. Then, forcing a smile, he puts his pen to the paper.

> *As I was trying to tell you, I haven't been able to talk to him*

yet.

He hesitates. Dare he write the next sentence? In his mind, he hears Wanda saying, *You call yourselves men.* He writes:

Though if he's not interested, I know someone who is.

He crumples the paper, checks to make sure the usher's back is turned, then tosses it back to Cynthia. He waits in suspense until, once again, the crumpled paper falls in front of his eyes.

As if I didn't know that. Guys are always asking me out, but I'm only interested in Doug. I'm hoping he'll ask me to home-coming. Do you know if he's asked anyone yet? It's on Satur-day, you know.

Gideon is about to write his response when something catches his eye. At the other side of the auditorium, also on the front row, someone is moving away from his assigned seat. It's Bula, blessed, beautiful Bula. He's crouched on the floor in a runner's stance.

Where's he going to go?

The usher is busy harassing a student.

Bula leaps into action, darting straight for the stage. Beneath the stage are openings to the orchestra pit below. With remarkable stealth, he slips into the pit and falls out of sight, all without making a sound.

The usher is none the wiser.

Gideon knows a hero when he sees one. He turns to Cynthia, who was also watching the great escape. Like Bula was, the two of them are also just feet away from the orchestra pit. They could do this.

Gideon nods at the stage, and Cynthia nods back, smiling. How could he not love such a woman?

His heart rate picking up, he sees that the usher is still harassing the same student, her back turned to them. The timing is as good as it will ever be.

Again he locks eyes with Cynthia. He mouths the words, "On three."

He raises a finger.

He raises a second finger.

He raises a third finger.

Both of them spring forward. Gideon grabs onto the stage, slips his legs into the pit, then falls into the darkness. A second later, his feet impact against a carpeted floor, and he absorbs the momentum with a crouch. Like Bula, he pulls off the stunt without making a sound.

For Cynthia, it's not so easy. She gets stuck halfway through, one leg in, one leg out. Gideon tries to help her down, but she panics and falls without grace. When her shoes hit the floor, it might as well be a bag of bricks.

From the other end of the auditorium comes the shout of the usher. "All right, get out of there!" She tromps toward the stage. "I know you're down there."

Crouched in the darkness, Gideon and Cynthia huddle close to each other. But what's the use? Dragging this out will only make it worse.

You call yourselves men.

Gideon puts a hand on Cynthia's shoulder, then stands up. He's opens his mouth to speak.

"Over here," comes another voice.

In the dim light, Gideon barely makes out the silhouette of Bula climbing out of the pit. "You caught me."

"You're coming with me," says the usher, apparently satisfied with this semi-truthful confession.

There's two sets of footsteps, followed by the creaking of doors, then silence.

Bless you, Bula. Gideon tries to wrap his mind around the greatness of this fellow student, but he can only wonder. Somehow, someday, he'll definitely have to pay the guy back.

Then he has a disturbing thought. Among the hundred or so students in the auditorium, surely there's at least one scrupulous

goody-goody who will betray them when the usher returns. Somehow they need to get out of this place fast.

THE STEAM TUNNELS

Gideon looks around, but there's nothing to see in the dark pit. He can barely make out Cynthia, though he feels her breath on his face. Suddenly there's nowhere he'd rather be than in detention.

His heart doing its pounding thing, he finds the nerve to extend his fingers, and like magic, her own fingers reach back. Together the fingers curl.

She's trembling.

He squeezes her. Then, hand in hand, Gideon and Cynthia feel their way through the darkness. They come to the opposite wall. The wall leads to a metal door. Gideon finds a handle and, cautiously, slowly, creeks the door open. Though he has no idea where they're going, he and Cynthia slip inside and close the door behind them. Feeling indestructible, Gideon leads the way down a dark staircase.

At last they find themselves at the bottom of the stairs. Gideon searches a concrete wall for a light switch.

Success.

They shield their eyes from the overpowering light. Gideon immediately regrets turning it on, because in the same moment, Cynthia lets go of his hand.

It's a large, busy room: racks of costumes, changing curtains, shelves of props, mirrors, and doors.

One door, in-particular, catches his eye. Propped open by a janitor's cart, it reads "Authorized Personnel Only." The magical words practically pull him forward.

"Where are we going?" Cynthia whispers.

"I don't know," Gideon whispers back, "but it might be our way out." He opens the door and peers into the forbidden room, but it's pitch dark inside. He flips another light switch, and a beautiful scene illuminates before them. It's not a room but a labyrinth of tunnels stretching into eternity. Lined with pipes, ducts, tubes, and machinery, the place looks like a scene from a sci-fi movie.

Cynthia whispers, "The steam tunnels. I've heard about this place."

"You have?"

"They say any student caught down here will be automatically expelled."

"Who's they?"

"You know … *they*."

Yesterday the threat of expulsion would have scared Gideon. Now it just feels routine. "Let's go."

"Detention will be over in forty-five minutes. Maybe we should just wait this out."

"We could do that, but it wouldn't be as much fun."

"True."

Cynthia smiles, and this time *she* leads the way.

Soon they're passing through a weird, underground world. Forced to walk single file through the tight tunnels, they take the first left, then the next left. The pipes and ducts look the same everywhere. But when they look up, they notice a familiar sight through one of the vent covers.

"It's the gym," Cynthia whispers. They see the tennis shoes of the basketball team, jumping and scuffling.

The most exciting discovery is when they come to a large, metal cube. It vibrates with the hum of machinery. Protruding from it is a large lever in the "on" position.

Gideon can't help but ask, "What do you think would happen if I turn this off?"

Cynthia pulls him away. "Don't."

"It looks important. Maybe it's the master power switch for the entire school."

"If we get caught, it could be really bad."

Gideon wonders if he would ever really have the nerve to do

something so reckless. It's nice to have Cynthia along, because her lack of inhibition in verbalizing her fears makes him look manly.

They walk on.

"So," Cynthia says, "what's wrong with Doug?"

Though his body tenses at the mention of the hateful name, Gideon keeps his cool. "He's been spending some late nights at a park. Maybe he caught a cold."

"Do you think he would be interested in a girl like me? Honestly?"

"Well …"

"I'm sorry if I sound pushy, but I need to know. I've turned down three guys for homecoming, and if Doug's not going to ask me, then …"

Gideon recognizes that look of hopelessness. He saw it in the girl who was crying by the lockers, and he can't bear to see it in Cynthia.

You call yourselves men.

Whatever the cost, he must defend her. "I'll talk to Doug today."

"Really?

"I promise."

"Oh, Gideon …"

Gideon stops at the sound of footsteps. He looks around, but there's no one else in the tunnels. Then he notices a vent cover. Standing on tippy-toes, he observes one of the school's hallways, where a single person is walking. High heels, gray skirt suit.

"It's her," he whispers.

"Who?"

"The gray lady."

"*Who?*"

"The lady who took me out of class. She's … well, I don't know what she is." Though he almost succeeded in pushing her out of his mind, the sudden temptation to spy on the gray lady is too alluring to ignore. For Wanda's sake, he must do it. "Let's see where she's going."

"Why?"

"Because …" But Gideon has no explanation. "Will you just trust me? We might be on to something."

Now Gideon leads the expedition, glancing through every vent cover along the way. They follow the gray lady, from one hallway to the next. At last, they arrive at a meeting room near the main office, one reserved for teachers and administrators. Thankfully, another vent cover gives Gideon and Cynthia a decent view of this room.

Cynthia tugs his arm, whispering, "I don't feel comfortable with this."

But this is more important than chivalry. Ignoring her, Gideon peers through the vent, studying the faces around the table. It's hard to make them out through the slits, though there's no mistaking the hot-pink wardrobe of Ms. Primple. Who the other two are, he can't say. There's a man in a suit, fat and bald. The other is a woman with a dark, flamboyant perm … a weird clash with her black skirt-suit.

The fat man speaks. "Ah, Norma, we were just talking about you. I assume everything's going according to plan."

The gray lady says, "Test scores are at an all-time high. Disciplinary problems are at an all-time low. Of all the schools in the district, this one holds a special place in my heart."

"And how's your little pet?"

"Mister Greenwich? I really was too hard on him. He's a fine, young man, full of potential."

Gideon smiles. She really is a nice woman. He can hardly wait to tell Wanda about this.

The two voices burst into laughter.

"Okay, seriously," says the fat man, "what's up?"

"You know very well what's up." The mirth in her voice is gone. "We've lost one of our own."

The fat man laughs. "He was never with us to begin with. I say good riddance."

"The football team was our army. Without someone to control it, there's no saying —"

"Will you lighten up? We still control the vast majority of them."

"You underestimate the seriousness of our situation."

"And you worry too much."

The two glare at each other.

"Let me make myself clear," says the gray lady. "Our entire operation is under the risk of exposure. Mister Greenwich and his friends —"

"Oh don't get me started. That kid is harmless."

"Yet you've been entirely unsuccessful at controlling him."

The fat man shrugs. "He's not worth my time."

"None of us can control him, not myself, not Fasha, not Muza, and certainly not Sportacus."

"So somebody's slipped through the cracks, big deal."

"How dense can you be? He suspects who we are."

"But who's going to listen to him? He's at the bottom of the social ladder and digging himself in a hole."

"It's his will that frightens me. Never in all my years have I seen a nerd become a jock."

"Weren't you the one who forced him into it?"

"To crush his spirits. But he wouldn't be crushed. Now he's seen what he shouldn't. We work so hard to create social barriers, and yet he walks through them as if they're nothing. There's no saying what else he can do."

"So get rid of him. Sheesh."

"You know that's against the rules."

"It's only against the rules if it looks unnatural."

"Can't you see this is beyond our power? We must defer to Coolar."

At the mention of the name *Coolar*, audible gasps are heard from around the room.

Ms. Primple says, "No, Norma, you know he hates to be disturbed."

"And you would wait until we have a crisis? Really, Fasha ..."

Fasha?

The fat man leans back in his chair. "Ladies, please. No matter what Norma says, we've got everything under control. There's only two days until homecoming, when, as we all know, our powers will be strengthened. If there are any seeds of dissidence, we'll push them right out of the students' minds."

Ms. Primple says, "But what if Mister Greenwich goes to homecoming?"

The fat man laughs. "He's never gone on a date in his life, and he's not about to start. In fact —"

The gray lady raises a hand. "Someone's listening to us. I can feel it." Her eyes scan the room before turning to the vent. She stares straight at Gideon.

Not again. Gideon backs up, crashing into Cynthia.

"What's going on?" whispers a frightened Cynthia.

"We have to get out of here," Gideon whispers. "Now."

THE ROCKS

Neither Gideon nor Cynthia look back until they're far away from the school. They hide behind a pick-up truck at the edge of a parking lot, where they catch their breaths.

Gideon peers through the windows of the truck at the industrial section of the building, from which they made their escape. The metal door remains shut.

"I don't understand what happened," says Cynthia.

"Isn't it obvious? They're evil beings from another realm who are bent on enslaving us."

Cynthia frowns. "What?"

"I have no idea who that fat guy was, and yet he knows all about me. He's clearly a supernatural entity."

"Or he talks to his coworkers."

"Wanda was right. It's a conspiracy, a supernatural conspiracy."

"I don't know what they were talking about, but I'm pretty sure you're jumping to conclusions. They're just teachers and administrators."

Gideon is pacing back and forth. "They said something about their leader. What was his name?"

"Coolar?"

"We need to figure out who he is. It may be the key to everything."

"Look, Gideon, it was fun hanging out with you during detention, but —"

She's cut off by a distant shout. In the distance are a group of girls: Joan Cooper, Kimberly Fenner, and Monica Hawley, Cynthia's fellow cheerleaders. They wave at her.

"I'll … see you around," says Cynthia.

"Careful," says Gideon, "those are dangerous girls, especially if you don't have a homecoming date."

Cynthia rolls her eyes. "As if you understood any of it." She runs toward her friends. Though halfway there, she stops and turns back. "Don't forget your promise."

"Promise?"

"To talk to Doug."

"Of course." There's that sinking feeling again.

Gideon longs to talk to his friends. He wants to apologize to Wanda for doubting. He wants to tell her that the situation is worse than they ever imagined. But at the moment there's something more pressing than fighting the forces of evil.

With a racing heart, not only from the bike ride behind him, but from what awaits him, Gideon raises his hand to knock on the door. It's a very nice door. Oak, perhaps … maybe cherry. To the side hangs a porcelain plaque with fancy letters:

The Rock Residence

His knuckles almost hit wood before withdrawing.

Will Doug kill him on the spot? Or will he wait for a time when there's no witnesses? What if Doug's dad answers the door? Imagine an even bigger, badder Doug, probably a marine or a professional cage fighter. How could there be any tolerance for nerds in such a family? They'll probably eat Gideon alive.

Gideon steps back. If he's quiet, no one will ever know he was here. He's halfway down the front steps when the door swings open. Standing before him is a tall woman with short, blond hair and a pink, polka-dotted dress.

"Oh, hi," she says.

"Hi," Gideon replies.

"Can I … help you?"

"Umm … Doug?"

"Oh. He's lying down at the moment. Are you a friend of his?"

"Yeah, kind of, in a sort of way. I'm on the football team." *Or at least I* was.

"Oh." The woman looks him up and down as if assessing the truthfulness of his claim. "Well I'm sure he'd love to see you. Come in."

She ushers Gideon inside, closing the door behind him.

No turning back now.

The house is bright and large. The air smells of cinnamon. A crystal chandelier hangs overhead. On the left, a grand piano serves as the centerpiece of an immaculate, well-vacuumed room. On the right is a large painting of Jesus, sitting thoughtfully on a mountaintop. On another wall is a family portrait: a mother, a father, Doug, and … *six* sisters, each in their Sunday best.

"I'll take you to his room," says Mrs. Rock.

She leads him up a spiral staircase, past six doors, until reaching the end of a hallway. The seventh door is partly open, and from within the room comes the sound of a violin. The song is gentle, yet sad. Each note is masterfully bowed.

Mrs. Rock opens the door, revealing Doug. He's sitting upright in his bed. Beneath his chin rests a shiny, red violin. Doug is lost in the trance of his own music, his body swaying with each stroke. He's oblivious to the company.

"Doug," says Mrs. Rock.

Still no response from the maestro.

"Doug!"

Finally Doug looks up.

Gideon instinctively steps back. But there's no disgust, no malice, and certainly no murder in Doug's eyes. The guy continues to play his violin until the end of the song.

Gideon claps, partly out of appreciation, partly out of self-defense.

At last Doug speaks. "Hey, Gid."

"Hi, Doug."

In the silence that follows, Mrs. Rock gets the hint and leaves the room. "I'll just let you boys do … whatever it is you're going to do."

Though it's just the two of them now, Doug no longer looks at Gideon. He stares at nothing at all, just like he was in the gym.

"So," Gideon says, "I hear you're sick."

Doug makes no reply.

"I'm sorry about that. I hope you'll be able to play again soon."

Still no reply.

"You're probably wondering why I'm here. It's … kind of awkward, but … do you know Cynthia McDaniels?"

At that, Doug's interest is finally piqued. "Yeah."

"I have a class with her, and she mentioned that …" This proves to be harder than Gideon imagined. He was too preoccupied with fearing Doug to think about his own feelings. "She really likes you, and she's hoping you'll ask her to homecoming."

Doug's flat lips begin to curve, even if only a little. "I'm afraid I've already been asked."

"As in … a girl asked *you*?"

"Yeah."

"Who?"

"Monica Hawley."

"Cynthia's friend?"

"Yeah."

If Cynthia confided her secret crush to Gideon of all people, surely she also confided in her close friend Monica, which means Monica must have purposely snatched Doug before Cynthia could, a case of back-stabbing betrayal. *Girls are vicious.*

"We're doubling with Kyle and Kimberly Fenner," says Doug.

"I see." What matters is that Cynthia is still available. Gideon's heart kicks back into gear.

Again Doug stares at nothing, as if an unseen weight has taken hold of him.

"Are you okay?" Gideon asks.

Doug shakes his head. "You know that feeling you get when you wake up, and you know you had one too many beers?"

"I'm afraid not."

"You know you were doing something the night before, though you can't remember what. Where you were, who you were with, what you said, it's all a blur. The only thing you know is that you feel sick about the whole thing." Doug rests his head against the wall. "But it's more than that. It's like I've been gone for a long time, like someone else was walking in my shoes, like I've been dreaming. And then I just ... woke up. Whoever that other guy was, suddenly he's gone. And now ... now I don't know what to do with myself."

"Do you remember Sportacus?"

"Who?"

"Mr. Mullins."

"The coach? Yeah, I remember him." The blank stare returns.

"Do you remember the bonfire?"

"You mean after the fight with Westward? Yeah, we always do a bonfire after a victory. But ... I thought you ran away before that."

Gideon laughs awkwardly. "Oh, no, I was there ... at a distance. Anyway, do you remember the man who came *out* of the fire, the man you were worshiping?"

Finally Doug looks Gideon in the eyes. "Is this some kind of joke?"

"You really don't remember?"

"As I told you, it's a blur. I don't know where I've been."

Seeing the great Doug Rock, the hulk, the fear of the boys, the dream of the girls, humbled and vulnerable, Gideon can't help but ... *love* him. "Doug, I know this sounds crazy, but I think I know where you've been."

"And where is that?"

Gideon feels a rush of inspiration. What if his 'friendship' with Doug is for a reason, something deeper than the gray lady could have ever foreseen? "There are dark forces at work, forces that have been trying to control you. I know because they've been trying to control me too. In fact, they may be trying to control everyone." It feels as if he's shared the most tender secrets of his soul.

Doug nods, though it doesn't appear that the words are registering.

This is almost as scary as talking to Cynthia. "And maybe you and I could … you know … work together. With my brains and your brawn — not that you don't have brains — and not that I don't have brawn — well, not that I *do* have brawn … what I'm saying is, together we can fight this evil. Somehow."

Again Doug gives a meaningless nod. "Sure, Gid."

Doug clearly isn't ready for this. Disappointed, Gideon begins to withdraw. "Maybe we should talk another time."

"Yeah."

"I'll let Cynthia know you're already taken." But before he reaches the door, he has another epiphany. "Say, Doug, I wonder if you could do me a small favor."

"I'm listening."

"Since Cynthia will have no one else to go with, maybe *I* could take her to homecoming."

"Sure, Gid."

"There's only one problem. While Cynthia likes me as a friend, I'm not sure she likes me in other ways. So I was thinking that maybe you could help me … *persuade* her."

"How so?"

"It's simple really. We just need to shift her attention from you … to me."

"What are you getting at?"

"I want you to beat me up in front of Cynthia."

Doug smiles, once again free from his trance. "That I can do."

FRIDAY

The gods are real, and they fear him. Doug Rock is his friend. There's hope with Cynthia. For the first time Gideon recalls, he's actually excited to go to school.

As the day advances, math and English classes aren't hard to endure. With so much to dream about, the hours pass by in a blur. Ancient World History is a crime scene investigation, a search for the footprints of his adversaries. Physics is a theoretical glimpse into the nature of their power. Though he can only wonder; if Ms. Primple is one of them, why not Ms. Fitzwater and Mr. Periwinkle? Is the whole staff part of the conspiracy?

At lunch he has everything to tell his friends. It's so exciting that he can't possibly sit down. He paces back and forth, unloading every wondrous detail on his bemused audience, from his romantic excursion with Cynthia, to the secret meetings of the gods.

Dwight, giving an occasional nod, is hard at work on a submarine sandwich.

Wanda doesn't seem to have any appetite. She says to Gideon, "I think you can do better than Cynthia."

But Gideon is hardly listening. "She's one of the most highly sought-after girls in the school. She's gorgeous. And she's the only girl who's shown the slightest bit of interest in me."

"That's not true."

As Gideon puzzles over Wanda's meaning, Dwight finally puts down his sandwich. "Gideon's love life can wait. What matters is that our school is being controlled by evil gods, and we're the only ones who know about it. What are we going to do?"

Exhausted, Gideon finally collapses into his seat. Then, seeing all eyes on him, he throws up his arms. "I don't know."

Wanda asks, "Is Sportacus really gone?"

Gideon says, "They certainly made it sound that way. I think you're right about Ms. Primple being a shapeshifter. How else do you explain Sportacus going into the girls' bathroom?"

"Then they *can* be defeated. We must fight them."

Dwight says, "How?"

Again Dwight and Wanda turn to Gideon, who raises his shoulders. "By … punching them in the chest?"

Still Doug sits alone at the top of the bleachers, while, down on the court, Gideon and Dwight fight for survival. Kyle misses no opportunity to trip, shove, or throw a ball at Gideon, and not once does Coach Griffith call a foul. The man just turns a blind eye to human suffering … as if Gideon somehow *deserves* this.

Despite the pain, there's something invigorating about taking deep breaths and feeling blood rushing through his body. When, for the fifth time, a bruised and scuffed Gideon climbs to his feet, he has a startling realization:

I'm having fun.

When a wide-eyed Dwight passes him the ball, Gideon is glad for the challenge. He can actually dribble. He can actually jump and shoot. Of course, the ball ends up nowhere near the hoop, and, when he lands, there's no avoiding the pummeling crashes of Kyle, but it's exciting nonetheless. Having his wind knocked out on the hard floor is a constant reminder that he's alive.

In Fashion Merchandising, the assignment is to illustrate a new clothing design. As Gideon sketches, he steals more than a few glances at Ms. Primple. The fact that she's attractive has nothing to do with it. He wants to see her glance back, giving some indication that she's watching him, resenting him. But she continues to flip through her terrible magazines.

He's adding the finishing touches to his conceptualization of rocket pants when a folded note lands in front of his eyes. He turns to Wanda on his left, but she's deep in her own sketch. When he looks forward, he sees the chain of girls looking back at him. The note was passed all the way from Cynthia at the front of the classroom. Gideon eagerly unfolds the paper and reads:

What did Doug say?

He knows he must be patient, but it's still hard to avoid feeling the sting. Choosing his words carefully, he replies:

I'm afraid he's already asked someone else. I guess you and I will both be lonely on Saturday.

He folds the note and passes it forward. Cynthia's reply comes much too quickly:

Then ask someone out already. Don't be a wimp!

It would be so easy to write one more reply, to ask Cynthia out on the spot. If she turns him down, he won't even have to see her face. But the possibility of rejection seems so high, he doesn't dare. If nothing else, she'll probably chide him for his unromantic medium of asking.

No, this job calls for a special operation. He must stick to his plan with Doug. After all, there's more at stake here than teenage hormones. By the gods' own admission, they're planning something dubious at the dance. Whatever it is, Gideon must be there to observe it and, perhaps, stop it. *Someone* has to. And if he can only get into the dance with a date, it better be Cynthia.

Without knowing why, his eyes drift to Wanda. She's reading the note on Gideon's desk, and she does not look happy.

ASKING

The bell rings, and another day of school has come and gone. As planned, Gideon jogs to the hallway where Cynthia and her friends congregate after school. He must arrive first.

The crowds begin to usher in from classrooms and other hallways. There's Joan Cooper, strutting her stuff, the admiration of many an eye. Next comes Kimberly Fenner and Monica Hawley. They shake their hands and yap away with the latest gossip. Though every now and then, one of them glances at Gideon, her expression reading, *What's* he *doing here?*

Standing there, exposed, without any social connections, is making Gideon look stupid. In desperation, he turns to the nearest social circle, some guys in sweaters. They're laughing. He laughs too.

The guys glare at him.

He laughs again.

Where are you, Cynthia?

Having already exhausted his welcome with these guys, Gideon meanders over to another social circle, some girls from the lacrosse team. On cue, they too laugh, and he joins in. They're quick to turn cold shoulders.

Gideon never realized how universal the closed-door policy is among high school cliques. There doesn't appear to be a legal way into any of them.

Doug enters the scene with his usual entourage of Kyle Slater and other members of the football team. Though Doug's eyes are distant. Gideon wonders if the guy's lackeys are even aware that their master and commander is only a shell of the man he once was. They just look on with their usual stupidity.

At least Doug has the presence of mind to nod at Gideon.

In response, Gideon delivers the predetermined code, ever so slightly shaking his head.

But Doug only stares back, smacking his fist into his palm.

Gideon shakes his head a little less subtly. *Not yet, Doug. Cynthia hasn't shown up yet.*

Showing no sign of comprehension, Doug raises his fist.

Gideon violently shakes his head.

"Hey," Doug barks with an air of showmanship. He's so loud that he succeeds in turning most of the heads in the hallway. "I thought I told you to stay out of my sight."

Gideon smacks his forehead.

"Now you will be punished," Doug shouts, reciting, verbatim, the words from their rehearsal.

Cynthia's friends are watching. That will have to be good enough. In any case, there's no backing out now. Gideon clears his throat and announces with larger-than-life volume, "It's a free country. I can go where I want to."

"I will beat you up," Doug shouts. His performance isn't exactly believable, but after the pep rally, the student body probably doesn't know what to expect.

"I will not buckle to tyranny," Gideon rejoins.

As Doug approaches Gideon, Kyle shouts, "Let him have it, Doug! He killed our coach." Did Doug initiate Kyle into the scheme? Though Gideon doesn't like the idea, Kyle's touch does add further motivation to the scene. Plus, Kyle is a much better actor than Doug.

All around are excited whispers.

Doug's fist flies, landing a gentle pat on Gideon's cheek.

"Ah!" Gideon shouts, covering his face and falling to his hands and knees. His body clenches in anticipation of the upcoming stage kicks.

From a gentle prod of Doug's shoe, Gideon collapses and rolls to the side. Doug deals another "kick," and Gideon impacts against one of the metal doors, creating a wonderful, painful-sounding clatter.

"Dude, don't hog all the fun," says Kyle.

What? Gideon looks up to see Kyle hovering over him. The next thing he knows, he receives a cold, hard kick to the gut … definitely *not* a stage kick.

Doug pushes Kyle's shoulder. "That's enough."

But Kyle shoves Doug out of his way. He kicks Gideon even harder. One, two, three times, each worse than before. The pain is so awful, Gideon can hardly breathe.

Finally Doug seizes Kyle, shouting, "You don't understand."

The two of them grapple as Gideon attempts to climb to his feet. Before the struggle ends, Kyle breaks free and pounds his elbow into Gideon's ribs, sending him back to the floor.

"What's wrong with you?" Doug demands.

Kyle shrugs. "I was just having a little fun. You started it."

Though the pain is excruciating, Gideon finds comfort in the approach of Cynthia's friends. They look horrified.

Monica Hawley is the first to speak. "Doug, I know he's just a nerd, but … did you have to do it while everyone was watching? I have a reputation to maintain and …" She runs painted nails through well-manicured hair. "I should have said yes to Jim Duckett. Maybe it's not too late." Then she walks off.

This time it's Doug who throws up his arms. "Monica! But … what about homecoming?"

"Forget it," Monica shouts, not looking back.

Next, Kimberly Fenner approaches Kyle. "What she said. You have stained the honor of our tribe. I'm totally going with Robby Haynes." She rushes to catch up with Monica.

Doug and Kyle are speechless.

Meanwhile a sizable crowd has gathered around. Among them are Dwight and Wanda. They help Gideon to his feet, which, for Gideon, is an ordeal of sharp pain in the legs and belly. "Easy," he moans.

A concerned Wanda asks, "What happened?"

"I'll tell you later. Have you guys seen any sign of …"

There she is, standing next to Joan Cooper. Though Cynthia clearly missed the action, a gossiping Joan is quickly bringing her up to speed.

" … and then he started beating up Gideon," Joan says.

"Why?" Cynthia asks.

"Because …" But Joan doesn't have an answer. "Doug, why did you beat up Gideon?"

Doug is a broken man. He turns away.

"I think Gideon must have started it," says Joan.

"What?" Gideon interjects. "That is *not* true. I was just minding my own business when this …" His eyes meet Doug's … those sad, empty eyes. Because of Gideon, the poor guy just lost his girl. Because of Gideon, the poor guy lost his *god*. Once mighty and strong, Doug's body is bent in defeat, as if he has no more pride to defend. The least Gideon can do is swallow his own pride. "All right, the truth is, it *was* my fault."

Satisfied with the confession, Joan continues her story. "Then Kyle joined in, and Monica and Kimberly were absolutely disgusted. I mean, these two big guys against this scrawny, little … Anyway, they dumped Doug and Kyle on the spot."

Cynthia doesn't appear to be listening. Her eyes are locked on Doug's. "You poor thing," she says, almost a whisper. To the bewilderment of everyone present, she approaches Doug and runs a gentle hand along his face. "You have no one to go to homecoming with."

Doug bows his head.

"Neither do I," Cynthia continues. "I know I'm no Monica, but … will you go with *me* instead?"

Doug looks up, a smile gracing his fragile face. "Okay."

Cynthia takes off her backpack, pulls out a pen and a notepad, then scribbles something. "Here's my number." She tears off a piece of paper and hands it to Doug. "Call me." And with that, she walks off, and Joan follows.

Kyle puts out his hands to stop them. "Whoa, whoa, Doug isn't the only guy who got snubbed here. Joan, how about you and me at homecoming?"

Joan gives her answer by whacking Kyle with her backpack.

As she and Cynthia walk off, Kyle clenches his fists. "Now I'm the only guy on the team without a date. Not cool." His face red with anger, he kicks a metal door so hard that it leaves a dent.

Gideon distances himself. He's wiser than reminding Kyle that he's technically on the football team too.

As much as Gideon loathes the guy, he can feel Kyle's pain. Gideon's plan blew up in the worst way imaginable, spoiling his one chance of getting into the dance. In his mind's eye, he can see the taunting glares of the gray lady.

Wait a minute ...

It's not his mind's eye at all. She's literally watching him from the end of the hallway, the goddess of normality surveying this questionable scene.

She is so scary.

Gideon imagines the dance, where the gray lady and her cronies carry out some secret plot against his fellow students — Doug and Cynthia — while Gideon is unable to interfere. His embarrassment turns to rage. Somehow he *must* go to homecoming.

On an impulse, Gideon jogs toward the commons. He can hardly do so without limping. He tries to avoid eye contact with the gray lady as she gets nearer. Finally he catches up with Monica and Kimberly.

"Hey," he says, his determination overriding his anxieties.

The girls frown at him.

"I couldn't help but overhear your situation. I ... I don't have a date either." It's hard to believe how low his shame threshold has dropped. "Would any of you like to ..."

But they're already turning and walking away as if he doesn't exist.

Isn't that considered rude?

In the background, the gray lady folds her arms, a smug smile on her face.

It's not over yet.

Wanda rushes into the scene, panting from the run. "Gideon …
are you okay?"

Wanda. Wanda is a girl. Without a moment's hesitation, Gideon
turns to her. "Will *you* go to homecoming with me?"

Wanda's face flushes. "So I'm your last choice?"

Gideon rolls his eyes. "This isn't about *you*." With the gray lady
so near, he lowers his voice. "I need to find out what the gods are up
to, and I can't go to the dance without a girl. This is strictly business."

"Is that supposed to make me feel better?"

"What do you want me to say?" Gideon flinches at the sight of
an approaching Kyle Slater.

But strangely, Kyle's attention is on Wanda. He looks as embarrassed as Gideon feels. "Hey, uh, what's your name?" he asks.

The anger in Wanda's face vanishes. She makes a double take,
apparently disbelieving that Kyle Slater is actually talking to *her*.
"Um, Wanda."

Kyle nods, staring at the floor. "Wanda. Do you …" He looks
around, then lowers his voice. " … want to go to homecoming with
me?"

Wanda's eyes become wide circles. Her jaw hangs open. At last,
she looks at Gideon, her shock turned to resentment. "I would love
to."

DATELESS

Saturday night, 6:30 PM. The city is alive with newly-washed cars, tuxedos, fancy dresses, pink corsages, boutonnieres, and the smell of hairspray. Myriads of young lovers are enjoying hot garlic bread, lemon-soaked halibut, and strawberry daiquiris on their parents' dollar. And somewhere out there, Douglas Rock, spiffed up and charming as ever, is gazing into the eyes of the vision of all visions, Cynthia McDaniels.

Curse you, Doug. Our friendship is over.

What more, Wanda's out there too, subject to the whims of the worst human being in the world, Kyle Slater.

Dwight is shuffling a deck of cards. "Will you stop gazing out the window and come play already?"

Gideon lets go of the blinds. "I just don't get it. How did my plan fail so miserably?"

"How else? *You* saw her standing there."

"You really think the gray lady was behind it?"

"She's clearly an evil genius, playing us like pawns. She must have known that Doug would betray you and crush your hopes."

"Do you think she's omniscient?"

"She's probably listening in to this very conversation."

Gideon knocks over a pile of books. "Curse you, gray lady!"

"Dude, what's gotten into you? Up until now you've been perfectly content to stay home from every dance."

"It's different now. I actually like a girl. And … you know … Wanda."

"You like Wanda?"

"No, of course not. I like Cynthia. I'm *worried* about Wanda."

"What was she thinking, saying yes to that creep?"

"Maybe we should check up on her."

"Check up on a homecoming date? You do that. As for me, I'm going to sit here and enjoy some spicy cheese puffs."

You call yourselves men.

Gideon parts the blinds and resumes his stare.

"What are you looking for?" Dwight asks.

"Do you ever feel that there's a bright, exciting world out there, and you're missing it?"

"All the time. That's why I play video games. The virtual world is so much more manageable than the actual world."

"The virtual world is lame."

"You are *killing* the spirit of the loser party."

"Maybe I don't want to be a loser anymore."

"Then go hang out with your jock friends. Oh wait … they kind of sabotaged you and tried to kill you and stole your girl, didn't they?"

"Maybe I don't want to be a jock *or* a nerd."

"To set the record straight, there was never a remote possibility of you becoming a jock. You are a nerd. You were born a nerd, and you will die a nerd."

"That's what the gray lady *wants* us to think."

"Then why did she try to turn you into a jock?"

"As you said, she wanted to crush my hopes … and it worked." Gideon collapses on a couch. "Maybe you're right about me. I was never meant to hang out with cheerleaders. I never had a chance with Cynthia. I'm a loser."

"Admittance is the first step to recovery. Now eat some cheese puffs."

Dwight leans back on the couch and drops the deck of cards. In a softer voice, he says, "Hey, Gid, I'm sorry how things turned out. I really am. But don't you think it's time to face reality?"

"Reality?"

"You know … to let go of the whole gray lady thing."

"What do you mean?"

"Don't you think it's a little convenient that whenever something goes wrong in your life, you can just blame it on the gods?"

"Dwight, I know what I saw and heard. Cynthia was there too."

"I don't doubt there was some private meeting of school administrators. Maybe they even talked about you. But that's not exactly proof of anything."

"I thought you were on *my* side."

"I am on your side. I've been with you from the beginning. It's been a fun game."

"This is not a game. You saw Sportacus."

"He's a magician."

"The teacher's lounge …"

"You were confused."

"What happened yesterday."

"Social ineptitude. Come on, man."

"You think I made this whole thing up?"

"It's called wishful thinking, romanticizing, confirmation bias. If you want to see gods, you'll see them. But don't take it personally. Everyone does it. It's a mass delusion the world has bought into since the beginning of time. Only … now we should know better."

Gideon sighs. He's never felt more empty. "Maybe you're right."

THE PRIESTS OF ISHTAR

Gideon taps a button with his thumb, and the knight jumps. He twiddles the joystick, and the knight runs. Slashing monsters right and left, the knight explores a fantastic, colorful forest where the laws of physics are only suggestions. Such strength, such speed. He's tireless, boundless … without feeling.

Dwight looks up from his book. "Listen to this. *Ishtar was the goddess of fertility, love, and war.* How could she be the goddess of both love *and* war?"

His eyes never leaving the screen, Gideon asks, "What are you reading?"

"It's the book Wanda checked out, *The Gods and Goddesses of the Ancient World.*"

"I thought you don't believe in that stuff."

"I don't, which is what makes it all the more interesting."

"How do you figure?"

"Well, once you give up your delusions, you can examine things from all sorts of interesting angles that you couldn't before. It's hard to imagine how people *ever* believed this stuff. Get this … *because only females were allowed in Ishtar's temple, where her sacred shrine was housed, the priests of Ishtar would dress up as women.*"

"Can we change the subject?"

"No need to get touchy. I'm just saying it's interesting."

Arriving at the banks of a swamp, the knight confronts the final boss of the level, the dreaded hydra. With myriads of heads and snapping jaws, the serpentine monster proves to be a formidable foe. The knight slashes left and right. But in the end, his health points run dry. He falls and dies.

A second later, he's resurrected and back at the beginning of the forest. It will take a good five minutes to retrace his journey. The world is cruel.

"I know it's just my imagination," says Dwight, "but don't you think this statue kind of looks like … Ms. Primple?"

Gideon pauses the game. He follows Dwight's finger to a photograph in the book. Ishtar. She's beautiful, and the resemblance to Ms. Primple is stronger than Gideon cares to admit.

He resumes the game. The knight continues his gallant quest, sloshing through water, cutting through grass, vanquishing creatures of the deep. He comes to the old willow, whose branch points to the direction of the hydra. Only the knight takes another path. Trudging into deeper water, he loses his bearing. Health points drop.

Dwight looks up, "Dude, what are you doing? That's not the right way."

The knight treks deeper into the swamp. Health points drop faster.

"You can't swim with all that armor on."

The knight dies. A suicide.

"That was your final life."

Game Over.

Gideon tosses the controller. "Let's go."

"Go where?"

"To the dance."

"What?"

"I have to know for certain."

"Know what?"

"If the gods are real."

"We can't just … it's a *date* dance."

"Will you be my date?"

"Heck no."

"If you put on enough makeup, no one will even recognize you."

"I'm not going to dress up like a girl!"

"Come on, be a man."

"Out of the question."

"All right, *I'll* be the girl."

"You can't seriously —"

"They said their powers would be strengthened at the dance. I have to know what that means."

"And what if it means nothing at all?"

"Then we'll know you're right, and I'll never mention the gray lady again."

Dwight thinks for a moment. "And if I'm wrong?"

"Then our friends are in trouble, and if we do nothing about it, we're sorry excuses for men. Aren't you the least bit curious?"

Dwight sighs. "I don't want anyone thinking I'm gay."

"No one will even recognize me."

Moments later, they're struggling to haul the Greenwich family's costume box out of the garage.

"I can't believe we're actually considering this," says Dwight.

"We're not considering it, we're *doing* it," says Gideon.

At last they drop the heavy box on the carpet. Gideon falls to his knees and digs through the fabric and accessories. He throws out a red dress ... a curly wig ... a sequined purse.

"Gideon, this has got to be the worst idea you've ever had, and that's saying something."

Gideon goes to the bathroom mirror and tries on the wig. "Works for me." He tries on the dress. It's a tight squeeze, but it fits. Next come clip-on earrings, and a big smear of rouge. Feeling slightly insane, he grins at the fake woman staring back at him. "You know, it's hard to feel depressed when you're about to throw yourself into the fire. Anxious ... maybe even terrified ... but not depressed."

Could such a courageous act go unnoticed by the benevolent eye of the universe? No matter how outrageous, somehow this just feels right. Somehow it *has* to work.

Dwight gives Gideon a good look. "If the lights are just dim enough and the observer is standing at least ten feet away — and is partially blind — the illusion just might work."

GIDWINA

The night is still young. Arm in arm, Dwight and *Gidwina* approach the front doors of the school.

"Slow down," Gideon whispers, stumbling to balance on his high heels. Every breath of cold air is exhilarating. Every exhalation leaves him feeling empty, exposed, and — frankly — doomed. To his dread, there's only a little more parking lot between them and the front doors, where students wait in line to buy tickets.

They take their place in the back of the line. Gideon whispers, "We're not going to fool anyone. My jaw is too masculine."

"Don't flatter yourself," Dwight whispers back. "You look lovely."

The line of couples moves painfully slow. Though after a good five minutes, not one couple has taken a second glance at Gideon's flamboyant curls or bright, red lips. Either they're too enraptured with their dates or the illusion is actually working.

When they reach the front of the line, Gideon's sickly foreboding elevates to a pounding heart.

"Two tickets, please," says Dwight, handing over Gideon's cash.

As if the exorbitant detention fee wasn't enough, the tickets leave Gideon broke. *The things I do for the greater good.*

Trying not to think about how many cheeseburgers this could have purchased, and, more importantly, trying not to call any attention to himself, he looks up at the evening stars. But in the silence that follows, he can almost feel the ticket lady's gaze upon his jagged face. He steals a glance.

She's staring right back at him, her eyes narrowing.

Gideon's heart rate picks up. He knows she's about to call him out. In a panic, he turns to Dwight.

Dwight has never looked more nervous. He turns to Gideon.

Look at her, *not me!*

Dwight clears his throat. "You know, Gidwina, no matter what anyone else thinks, you've always been beautiful to me."

Both of them turn to the ticket lady. She looks down at her table. She appears to be somewhere between confusion and shame. At last, without making eye contact, she hands over two tickets. "Next!"

Arm in arm, Gideon and Dwight step into the school. It might as well be another world. Their ear drums are pounded with a deafening beat, shaking their internal organs. The lights are a spectacle of insanity: red, blue, green, swirling, beaming, and flashing through a chaotic sea of bodies. And yet it's not chaotic. The bodies sway back and forth like a school of fish.

"What is this?" Gideon shouts over the noise. He can barely hear his own voice.

"I don't know," Dwight shouts back. "Why anyone would pay money for this is beyond me."

"Maybe we're in the wrong place. I thought homecoming was supposed to be ... elegant." But upon getting a better look at the swaying bodies, Gideon sees familiar faces, dresses and tuxedos.

"Maybe it's been hijacked by the gods."

"I thought you don't believe in the gods."

Dwight shrugs. "Nothing short of the supernatural could explain this magnitude of awfulness."

"By the way, you were brilliant back there."

"I know."

The darkness and blinding strobe lights will further mask Gideon's identity. Surely it's all downhill from here. Only one question remains: what in the world is he going to do? Getting through the front doors was so consuming, he never thought of what to do next.

Dwight asks, "So what do we do next?"

Gideon's heart resumes its pounding. It's not the administration he's afraid of or even the gods. It's Cynthia. If she recognizes him, will she be impressed or scandalized? Will she laugh or scream? "Umm … we keep our distance and … watch."

"Watch for what?"

"Supernatural activity."

Dwight looks as uneasy as Gideon feels. "Works for me."

They go for a sparsely-populated corner of the commons, where, as fortune has it, the refreshments table awaits them. *Perfect.* While Dwight stuffs his face with eclairs, Gideon fills a cup full of red punch, with which he covers his face. Feeling a little safer, he scans the premise. Though it's hard to make out anyone, his senses are heightened by the will to survive. He spots Cynthia.

She and Doug are dancing a slow song … if swaying back and forth counts as dancing. Though Doug's hands are wrapped around her shoulders, his arms are straight, their bodies far apart. Doug is staring at the ceiling. Cynthia looks bored.

Gideon can't help but smile. If even the great Doug Rock suffers from social awkwardness, maybe there's still hope for Gideon.

The long song drags on, and still Doug stares at the ceiling. The guy looks lost. Is he still suffering from *god separation anxiety*? Gideon's smiles fades. He hates to admit it, but to some small degree, his heart goes out to the guy.

At last the song ends. Doug goes one way, perhaps to a restroom; Cynthia goes another. She's headed straight for the refreshments table.

Gideon turns to Dwight. "This was a bad idea. Let's get out of here."

"We didn't get this far only to chicken out. Now's your chance to win back your girl."

"That's *not* why we're here."

"It is too, and you know it. Tell her you just *had* to see her."

"She'll never understand."

"Fine, *I'll* tell her."

There's no time to argue. Gideon starts to walk off, but Dwight grabs his arm, saying, "Oh no you don't."

"Let go of me!" Gideon struggles, but it's too late. Cynthia is staring right at him. Just as with the ticket lady, he can see her studying his features, trying to work out what that thing with curly hair *is*.

Thankfully, Cynthia's friends come out of nowhere, diverting her attention. Chatting and laughing, the group of girls walk off and are swallowed up in the crowd.

Gideon sighs. *That was close.*

"Hi Gideon," says an unexpected voice.

Gideon nearly jumps out of his high heels. Standing beside him is Wanda. Gone are the Pokémon t-shirt and pink sweatpants. She's wearing a sparkling, lavender dress. Her hair is crimped and curled. Her freckles are gone. She smells like roses, and she's wearing … *makeup*. She has eyes and lips.

Gideon has to fight the temptation to reach out and touch her. "You look beautiful." The words roll off his tongue before he can assess their propriety.

"And you look horrible," Wanda replies.

Gideon looks down at himself. The contrast between him and Wanda is like night and day.

"If you came here to make a fool of yourself, you're well on your way."

"It's the *gods*," says Gideon. "As I told you, they're going to do something evil tonight. I had to come in disguise so they wouldn't recognize me."

"And I'm sure the fact that you couldn't get a date had nothing to do with it."

"Well …"

"And I'm sure it has absolutely nothing to do with being near Cynthia."

Gideon busies himself with straightening his wig. "Come on, Wanda, why would she want to see me like this?"

"You're not exactly known for your rationality."

Dwight interjects, "Wanda, aren't you supposed to be with Kyle?"

Wanda looks at her high heels. "We're just … taking a break

from each other."

"Off to a smooth start, I see."

"Perhaps you should mind your own business."

Gideon says, "We're concerned about your choice of friends."

Wanda looks incredulous. She throws up her arms and walks away. But after only a few steps, she stops and turns to a passing girl.

"Hey, Stephanie," she says loud enough for Gideon and Dwight to hear, "see that *thing* over there?" She points to Gideon. "That's Gideon Greenwich dressed in drag."

As Wanda walks off, Stephanie's eyes open wide.

Gideon and Dwight turn to each other. With no need for words, they run off as fast as Gideon's high heels will allow.

CONSPIRACY

They fly up the nearest set of stairs. On the next level, serving as a railing, is a short, brick wall. They duck behind it. For a while they lay low. Gideon's gaze is glued to the bottom of the stairs. He half expects the news Wanda gave Stephanie to spread like a wildfire and for a mob of curious spectators to materialize. But when nothing happens, he climbs to his knees and peers over the wall.

He has a great view of the dance below. Up here, with a little distance, the pounding beat is less threatening, the flashing lights less blinding. The crowd no longer constitutes *everyone* but merely a congested group of teenagers. What before was overwhelming is now contained and comprehensible. Now he can actually hear himself think.

"Who's that?" asks Dwight.

Gideon follows his finger to … the fat man. Sitting on a chair atop a raised stage, the fat man overlooks the dancing crowd. He's dressed in a tuxedo, holding a wireless microphone.

"That's him," Gideon says, "the guy from the meeting with the gray lady."

"He's just sitting there in plain sight," Dwight observes. "Where's the conspiracy?"

"To answer that, we'll first need to find the conspirators." Gideon scans the massive room and soon discovers another attendee of the secret meeting: the dark woman with curly hair. Wearing large headphones, she's sitting near the speaker stacks, moving her hands over a disk jockey console.

Gideon points her out. "Muza," he recalls.

"Who?"

"The gray lady mentioned three names: Sportacus, whom we know, Fasha, whom I think is Ms. Primple, and *Muza*. This must be Muza, goddess of … music, I guess."

Dwight cringes. "You call this music?"

"Well, so-called music, anyway."

"Nice to know who's putting us through this hell. So if Ms. Primple was in on the conspiracy, she should be here too, right?"

Together they scan the commons … so many faces. Soon Gideon points to the opposite corner. "There!" Looking as ravishing as ever, Ms. Primple, the lady in red, is watching the dance.

"She sure looks giddy," Dwight observes.

"Of course she is," says Gideon. "She's surrounded by a decadent display of sequins and polyesters. It's one of the few times when fashion matters most."

"So what?"

"So … it must make her more powerful or something."

Dwight rolls his eyes. "I don't see the gray lady anywhere."

"Oh, she'll show up eventually. She always does."

Gideon's gaze gravitates back to the fat guy. "But who is *this* guy?" He can see how the goddesses of music and fashion have a place here, but this guy? Looking closer, he notices something strange. The man's free hand is slightly raised, moving gently back and forth. It looks as if he's petting an animal.

Hand signals? Gideon studies the curly-haired lady, then Ms. Primple, but neither of them are paying the fat man any attention.

There's a rhythm to that swaying hand. *Where have I seen that before?* Gideon wonders.

Oh.

It's everywhere, the motion of hundreds of teenagers moving to the music. The fat man's hand is mirroring them in perfect synchronization.

"Look," Gideon exclaims, "he's *conducting* them."

Dwight follows Gideon's finger. "He's just moving to the beat."

"He moves them like puppets. He's the leader of the crowd, the god of … popularity. Yes." It's all starting to fit together. "Sports …

music … fashion … popularity … these are the things that control the minds of our peers."

"But not ours, of course."

"As you said, we're nerds; we have no concept of any of those things, and therefore the gods can't control us. That's why the gray lady has tried to beat the nerdiness out of me."

"I have to admit, I kind of like this new religion of yours."

"The glitzy appearances, the peer pressure, the worship of rap stars, it's all one big offering to the gods of … *cool.*"

"Beautiful. Keep going."

"With every concession to the latest trends, individuality is suppressed, rank and file submission is reinforced, and the gods and goddesses of this world gain more control."

"Don't stop."

But Gideon is done monologuing. His eyes gravitating back to the fat man, suddenly he knows what he must do. "I'm going to press his button."

"What?"

"I'm going to press the god of popularity's button."

"What are you talking about?"

"Do you think it's a coincidence that when I punched Sportacus in the chest, he just happened to explode? Surely we discovered the gods' weak spot."

"Just because it happened to one of them doesn't mean it will happen to all of them."

"It's our best shot."

"Don't you think this is getting a little … ridiculous?"

"The idea that gods walk around with self-destruct buttons on their chests? Yes, that does seem ridiculous. Had I not observed it firsthand, I wouldn't believe it. Is it possible that reality is, in fact, ridiculous?"

"Supposing you're right, *how* are you going to get close to him? According to you, the commons are surrounded by omniscient beings."

"They're not omniscient."

"How do you know?"

"Just look at them. They're oblivious to us, and we've been saying all sorts of heretical things."

"Regardless, they outnumber you, and there's no saying what they'll do. Besides, half the dance probably knows you're here by now. Discretion is no longer an option."

The conversation is interrupted as their attention is drawn to the fat man, who has risen to his feet. Raising a microphone, he looks at Muza, who nods, and suddenly the booming music cuts out, leaving only ringing in the ears.

"And now the moment you've all been waiting for," his voice blasts through the speakers, "the selecting of this year's homecoming royalty."

The audience voices their excitement.

"We'll start with the queen. Are there any nominations for the queen?"

Hands shoot up, names are called.

"I hear a nomination for Joan Cooper. Will anyone second it? … We have a second. Joan Cooper, come on up here. Who else? Kimberly Fenner. Do we have a second?"

As the girls walk up to the stage, Gideon's stomach sinks. Again he knows what he must do. He turns to Dwight. "I need you to nominate me."

HOMECOMING QUEEN

"You know, Gideon, sometimes it's hard to tell whether you're joking or not."

"I'm dead serious."

"Then you're insane."

"Do you think I *want* to do this? It's for the good of the school."

"How in the world is this for the good of the school?"

"It's the only way I can get close to this guy."

"No one is going to elect *you* as homecoming queen."

"I don't need to be elected, I just need to be nominated, so I can stand on the stage."

"You are absolutely nuts."

"I get it. Now will you please nominate me?"

With his booming, bass voice, the fat man asks, "Any final nominations?"

Gideon says, "Nominate me!"

"You'll regret this," says Dwight.

"Okay, just do it."

The fat man says, "Going once … going twice …"

Dwight shouts, "Up here!"

All heads turn up to the second level, where Dwight waves and points to Gideon. "Right here."

For a moment the entire room falls silent as every last person, no doubt, tries to make sense of Gideon's face. Thankfully, Gideon has distance and darkness on his side. At last the fat man asks, "And this is … ?"

"Gidwi —"

Gideon slugs him.

"Umm … Ros … a … linda … Rollins … worth."

"Does anyone second Rosalinda Rollinsworth?"

Still the room is silent. Though one brave soul raises her hand: Stephanie Snyder, the girl who knows Gideon's secret. She has a big grin on her face.

"All right, Miss Rollinsworth, come on down."

With a slap to the back from Dwight, which either means good luck or good riddance, Gideon makes the long journey down the stairs and through parting students. He makes no eye contact. If the pounding in his chest keeps up like this, he's going to have a heart attack. At last he jogs up the few steps to the stage, where he takes his place behind the other nominees.

"And now," continues the fat man, "it's time to nominate the king."

Again hands shoot up, and names are called. Boys start coming up to the stage.

You made it, Gideon thinks. *Run up to the man and pound his chest.*

But he doesn't.

What are you waiting for? When he glances at the second level, Dwight is staring back at him, the same question on his face. Daring another glance, Gideon sees a couple of girls staring right at him. One is whispering to the other. The recipient of the secret then whispers to another girl.

You must act now!

"Why do you look so familiar?" someone asks. Gideon knows the voice.

Cynthia. She's standing right next to him.

"Umm …" Gideon begins in his normal range, then slides up to falsetto, " … I don't know."

"Are you in any of my classes?"

"I don't think so."

"I know I've seen you before."

"Interesting."

"You know who you remind me of?" But before she can continue, someone walks between them.

Doug.

"Oh," says Cynthia, happy to divert her attention, "you were nominated too?"

Doug shrugs. "I tried to talk them out of it." He also stares at Gideon, who promptly busies himself in adjusting his pantyhose.

Fortunately, Doug and Cynthia get lost in their own conversation. Unfortunately, they're blocking his path to the fat man, who's saying, "Now that we've settled our nominations, let's start the voting." The fat man points to the nearest boy. "Let's hear some love for James Rogers."

The friends of James applaud, shout, whistle, and scream.

"Not bad. How about for Dustin Holmes?"

The response is even louder.

When did amplitude become a viable form of democracy?

"Moving on, how about Douglas Rock?"

A plethora of female fans hold nothing back in expressing their approval. There's so many of them, thus far Doug is clearly the winner.

"And one more. Kyle Slater."

Gideon's body tenses at the mere mention of the name. He peers through the crowded stage to locate his enemy ... a safe distance away.

Meanwhile the shouts from the audience are deafening. It helps that nearly the entire football team is hooting, hollering, and jumping up and down. There's no competing with the sheer force of their lung power.

Why didn't they vote for Doug?

"And we have a winner," the fat man announces, "Kyle Slater!"

Following the cheers, Kyle raises his arms and joins in with the barking chant of his teammates:

> *Break down the door, big dawg, big dawg.*
> *Break down the door, big dawg!*

"And now for the queen," the fat man continues.

Every boy but Kyle leaves the stage, exposing the girls.

Gideon glances at Wanda, who now stands alone. With her eyes on Kyle, she's putting on a smile, but Gideon knows her too well to be deceived. *Gosh, she's beautiful.* Suddenly he wishes he'd had the presence of mind to nominate her for queen, because no one else would. Though if anyone deserves it, she does.

Wanda's eyes meet his, and Gideon looks away. When he ventures to glance back, Wanda is whispering to the girl beside her.

No, Wanda!

"Do I hear any votes for Joan Cooper?" asks the fat man.

The crowd cheers.

"How about Kimberly Fenner?"

It appears that Joan is more popular than Kimberly, who slumps in disappointment. Even so, Kimberly has it easy. No mob is going to erupt and call *her* a fake. No evil gods will punish *her*.

To buy himself a little more time, Gideon steps around Cynthia, putting himself last in line. Meanwhile it appears that just about everyone, boy and girl, is whispering into the ear of their neighbor. Each is staring at Gideon.

You're running out of time!

Feeling something like guilt, Gideon habitually looks for the gray lady.

She's standing near the front doors, her arms folded. Of course, she's staring right at him.

"Not again!" he cries, stepping back. Though he's thankful that the cheering audience masks his outburst, it's only too plain that his operation is doomed. *Maybe the gods* are *omniscient.*

Now the crowd is cheering for Cynthia, who's more popular than both Kimberly and Joan.

"Last but certainly not least …" continues the fat man, "Rosalinda Rollinsworth."

With the boys gone, there's only a few girls between Gideon and the fat man. If he runs now, he can strike before the gray lady can intervene. But with hundreds of eyes watching him, he couldn't feel more trapped in a straight jacket.

"It's a fake!" a male voice cries from the back of the auditorium.

Another guy shouts, "That's not a —" But before he can even finish the sentence, he's drowned out by an explosion of opinionated voices.

Gideon feels the wave of shouts beat against him. He takes in the sea of excited faces. Some are outraged, some are laughing, some look … *sadistic*. Whatever the reaction, there's not a teenager in the commons who doesn't have something to say about Gideon, and as far as amplitude goes, there's no contest.

"The crowd has spoken," shouts the fat guy. "The new homecoming queen is Rosalinda Rollinsworth!"

SLOW DANCE

The crowd goes wild.

Gideon is dumbfounded.

Dwight looks like a deer in the headlights.

Weird doesn't begin to describe Gideon's reality. Even ridiculous falls short. For a moment he feels light-headed, wondering if the voices and faces are products of his imagination. Were it not for his deep breaths, this would be indistinguishable from a dream.

The girls begin to exit the stage.

Gideon follows.

"Oh no you don't," says Cynthia, pushing him back. "You're not finished."

Only three people remain on the stage: Gideon, the fat guy ... and Kyle Slater.

Kyle looks how Gideon feels: absolutely horrified.

But what does he *have to be afraid of?*

The fat guy has a big grin on his face.

Does he know what's going on? Is this a trap?

The fat guy says into his microphone, "How about a slow dance, Maxine?"

Muza — apparently also known as Maxine — nods, her curls bouncing and a wicked smile stretching across her red lips. She fiddles with her disk jockey console.

"I don't know about you," continues the fat guy, "but I'm dying to see the new homecoming royalty dance together."

The audience simultaneously voices their approval, disgust, and laughter.

The music begins, a soft classic from the 1980's ... an androgynous, crooning voice, a cheesy, electric piano, snares with too much reverb. Ordinarily this would be torture enough. Coupled with Kyle Slater, the devil incarnate … Gideon has no words. He can't move.

Thankfully, Kyle isn't budging either. He just stares at Gideon, his face pink from shouting. Does he know Gideon's secret, or was he too absorbed in his own victory to put two and two together? But then, if Kyle realized he was staring at Gideon Greenwich, he would have murder in his eyes, not fear. The meat head must simply take Gideon for an exceptionally ugly girl. No doubt he's wondering how the system could be so broken as to pair a work of art like himself with something so hideous.

"Do we have to push you two together?" laughs the fat guy.

I won't budge if you won't budge. So far so good. They've already managed to wait out an entire verse of the terrible song.

But the audience won't have it. "Dance, dance, dance!" they chant, including voices from the football team, to Cynthia, to Wanda. Even Dwight is joining in.

"I resent that," Gideon mouths at his friends.

As the chant grows louder and louder, Gideon feels a pulling sensation. It's as if the floor is moving beneath his feet. He looks down.

It is!

When he looks up, he sees Kyle moving closer. Kyle looks just as confused as an unseen power pulls them together. They fight against the force in vain.

Gideon turns to the fat guy, who has one hand raised, a subtle smile on his lips.

"I know you're one of them," Gideon says, not even bothering to hide his masculine timbre.

The man's smile fades.

Shouldn't have said that.

The next thing Gideon knows, his body collides with Kyle's, and to keep themselves from hugging, the two have no choice but to grab each other's arms.

And so they dance. Gideon, of course, has no idea *how* to dance, though apparently Kyle doesn't either. With locked arms and as much distance between them as possible, they sway back and forth, slowly circling around the stage.

Meanwhile the audience taunts them with hoots and cat calls.

Kyle, staring at the ceiling, is the first to speak. "So … are you new to this school?"

"Actually," Gideon squeaks, a less than elegant transition to his falsetto, "I go to another …" If he says he's from another school, Kyle could challenge his right to be homecoming queen, making a bad situation worse. If he can just survive the dance long enough to get close to the fat guy, he can hit and run. "I mean, yes. Yes I am."

"Cool."

"Yeah."

Gideon tries to direct their dance toward the fat guy, but the unseen force is locking them in place. There's nothing to do but endure. Though it occurs to him what a rare opportunity this is. He asks, "Is it true that your friend Doug is the captain of the football team?"

Kyle's face reddens a bit. "He *was* the captain. Now I am."

"Oh, really? What happened?"

"We used to be friends, but … now I hardly know the guy. He stopped coming to practice. He brings doctors' notes to P.E. He never wants to hang out with the guys anymore. You know who he reminds me of?"

"No."

"That nerd, Gideon Greenwich. But you probably don't know who that is."

Gideon forces an awkward laugh.

For a moment Kyle is silent. It's clear that Gideon has flipped a switch in the guy's head. Kyle's face a little redder, he blurts out, "And do you know what really gets to me? One day Doug's my right-hand man. The next day, he betrays the entire order."

"Order?"

"Forget it. You wouldn't understand."

"You mean the cult of Sportacus?"

For the first time, Kyle stares right at him. "How did you know that?"

"I too am a … a believer in the gods."

"Really?" Kyle's voice softens a bit. "I misjudged you."

Another awkward laugh. "But isn't Sportacus … you know … *dead*?"

Kyle laughs. "You can't kill a god. He *will* return. Besides, as you already know, Sportacus is just one of many gods. The time is close at hand when they will redeem this school."

"What are they going to do?"

"As if you didn't know."

"Um … should I?"

"I thought you're a believer."

"I'm … new to the faith."

"As soon as the link between our world and theirs is completed, they'll take full control."

"And how, again, will that link be completed?"

"How else? With a tower."

"A tower?"

Kyle's face is a mix of wonder and disgust. He's staring at something just above Gideon's head.

Gideon looks up. His wig is falling off. He's about to straighten it, but Kyle beats him to it, pulling the wig right off his head.

Kyle's face grows even redder. "You."

The audience goes wild with gasps, laughs, and screams.

At last, Gideon breaks free from the unseen force. He backs up, unsure of what to do. Though when Kyle's fist comes flying at his face, he knows exactly what to do. As at the pep rally, his senses are sharpened, and time seems to slow down. Dodging the blow is easy. Running is even easier. That is, until he trips on his high heels. Still on the stage, he falls on his hands and knees, but this only sets him back a moment. He looks up, his eyes locked on the fat guy.

The fat guy backs up.

Gideon kicks off his high heels and charges. His dignity is gone. His expulsion is guaranteed. *Might as well go down with glory.* A second later, he gives the fat guy a hard punch to the chest.

The chest jiggles, absorbing the impact, though the man looks unfazed. In fact, he's smiling. "Looking for something?" he asks.

Gideon slaps him again and again. He slaps high and slaps low. He finds a lot of jiggles but no button.

The man has had enough. He waves a hand, and though no contact is made, Gideon feels himself flying through the air, over the stage, and into the startled crowd. He topples several students, who cushion his fall.

Whoa. Whatever keen senses Gideon has, they're no match for this guy.

Students look at each other, each as if to say, *Did that really just happen?*

Gideon gets to his feet and runs. Mission failure. Backup mission: stay alive.

The startled crowd parts before him, creating a pathway to the front doors. Everything is confusion and shouts.

Someone is standing in his way.

The gray lady.

"Gideon Greenwich!" she shrieks. He's seen her angry before but never like this.

Gideon keeps running.

"Stop!" she commands.

Gideon runs faster. In the final moment, he wins the game of chicken.

AFTERMATH

Sitting on his wig, Gideon lays low in the passenger seat of Dwight's car. His finger presses against the automatic lock switch. Now and then he hears voices, and he slumps even lower. He removes the clip-on earrings and wipes his lipstick onto the sleeve of his dress. If only he brought a change of clothes.

He jumps as someone knocks on the driver side window. But it's only Dwight. Soon the two of them are sitting in silence. The keys are in the ignition, unturned.

"Can we go?" asks Gideon.

Dwight leans his seat back, staring up at the bright moon. "You really outdid yourself this time."

"You win some, you lose some."

"Yeah, well … you definitely lost this one."

"No human could have thrown me that far."

"He's a big guy. You're a little guy."

"Yeah, well he didn't even touch me."

"Didn't touch you? You were assaulting the poor man, and he pushed you away in self-defense."

"It may have looked like that from where you were sitting, but I assure you, it was supernatural."

"They're going to arrest you for this."

"The fat guy, Ms. Primple, the DJ … they were controlling minds. You saw the students, swaying back and forth like zombies."

"It's a *dance*. Of course they were swaying back and forth."

"Kyle even admitted that he worshiped the gods. He said they're planning something big, and it's gonna happen as soon as they finish building a tower. What do you think he meant?"

Dwight pounds the steering wheel, honking the horn. "Gideon, there was no button."

"What?"

"I played along. I even tried to believe. But I couldn't, because it's not real."

"Dwight, the fat guy was controlling me like a puppet. I felt his power."

"Once again you're the only witness."

"He was controlling Kyle too."

"Kyle's the last person I'd believe."

"Whether or not you understand, I did what I had to do."

"When I signed up for this, you didn't tell me that you were going to act like a psychopath in front of everyone. Now they're gonna think I'm crazy too."

"You're worried about your reputation? No wonder you can't see it. The gods are controlling you as well."

"There are no gods!"

Gideon sighs. "I'm sorry. I didn't mean —"

More voices are approaching. Gideon and Dwight slump down, hiding themselves from view.

"I knew it was him the whole time," comes the muffled voice of Kyle Slater. He's just outside their car. "I was just playing along, you know?"

"Not really," replies a female voice.

Dwight peers through the passenger window and whispers, "That scum bag. He ditched Wanda for another girl."

Gideon's own curiosity gets the best of him. He rises just enough to spy Kyle walking with his arm around Joan Cooper. *Of course.* As the homecoming king, Kyle must think he's entitled to the best. And with Cynthia, the first runner up for queen, off limits, that leaves Joan as the next trophy to claim. Not that Joan was without a date … but whoever the poor guy was, Kyle clearly didn't fear him as he must have feared Doug.

"Well, the joke was on him, eh?" Kyle laughs.

"What joke?" asks Joan.

"Just get in the car."

Kyle jangles his keys, then opens the driver-side door of a red Lamborghini. Joan is left to walk around and open her own door. As she climbs in, she says, "So you're not going to get back at Gideon?"

"Oh, I'll get back at him. Next time I see him, I'll kill him."

"Literally or figuratively?"

"Literally."

"Meaning figuratively?"

"Yeah."

The doors slam, and the car backs up and drives off.

A moment later, Dwight starts his own car and, without another word, takes Gideon home.

As Gideon climbs out, grabbing the wig and earrings, he looks at his somber friend. "I'll … see you on Monday."

Dwight shakes his head. "If you're not arrested by then, they'll expel you."

Gideon nods. Such is his burden. "Well … thanks for being a friend."

Dwight has no reply.

"We're still friends, right?"

"Good night, Gideon."

"Good night, Dwight."

Gideon slams the car door, and Dwight drives off, leaving Gideon alone in the dark neighborhood.

There was no button.

Gideon has lost friends, made enemies, and dug himself into the pit of all pits. Neither *weird* nor *ridiculous* come close. *Disaster* seems about right. *My life is falling part.* And for what? Perhaps there are some fights that can't be won. Perhaps it would be better to forget what he knows, swallow his pride, and go with the flow. Maybe then people would like him. Maybe then he'd be kissing a girl instead of standing alone on a dark street.

Sunday afternoon. Gideon pedals his bicycle through the autumn air, the wind beating against him. He can't go fast enough. Passing Eastward High, he wants to get as far away as possible. But there's no escape. Behind every corner, peering through every window, the gods are always there, watching him.

But then, if they knew what Gideon was up to last night, why didn't they stop him sooner? Only one answer makes sense, what he suspected all along: they *didn't* know. They're *not* omniscient. They may not even be very intelligent. And perhaps god is the wrong word.

He turns onto Eastward Drive, where he and Cynthia spent a magical night. At least it started out magical. If there was ever any hope for the two of them, surely he blew it last night. How could she possibly fall for a freak like him?

He pedals faster, driving his fury into the wheels. The pain in his legs is sweet.

Another face enters his mind, those red lips and blue eyes … such lovely eyes.

No. He can't think about Wanda like that. Some things are just wrong. But she won't leave his thoughts.

He takes a sudden left and pedals up a hill. Though his legs burn, he doesn't let up until arriving at an old, pink house. He throws the bicycle onto a lawn that's months overdue for a mow. Then, gasping, his scorched body covered with sweat, he lumbers to the front door. Hanging from the roof are a hundred potted plants, growing every which way. Above the door is a pink plaque shaped like a pig. In faded letters are the words *"The Biggles Residence."* Gideon bangs the brass knocker, which is also shaped like a pig.

Wanda answers the door, but no sooner does she see Gideon than she tries to shut it.

"No, please," says Gideon, shoving his hand between the door and the frame.

"I'm surprised you haven't been arrested."

"Why does everyone keep saying that? All I did was slap a guy's chest."

"His name is Mr. Phillips. He teaches drama."

"Are you sure? I never saw him before Thursday."

"Maybe you should do more research before you jump to conclusions … or attack people."

"Wanda, he was one of them. He had power."

"I'm not in the mood."

Not in the mood? Is this a game to her too?

Gideon takes a deep breath. "I just wanted to say I'm sorry."

"Then get on with it."

" … I'm sorry."

"There, you said it. Now remove your hand."

"Can I ask a stupid question?"

"You will regardless of my answer."

"I know I should be sorry for something, but … what exactly is it?"

"You asked me to homecoming as your fourth choice."

"Oh, right. Won't happen again."

"Girls don't like feeling used."

"You mean like how Kyle totally dumped you for Joan? That was —"

Wanda slams the door on Gideon's fingers. Gideon recoils in pain. The door is then shut and padlocked.

For a moment, Gideon just breathes. Then it's back to the bicycle.

Fighting gods is manageable. Dealing with the opposite sex is a challenge he may never surmount.

Well after sunset, he's lying awake on his bed, staring at the ceiling, when his phone vibrates. He looks at the glowing screen.

1 new email from Douglas Rock.

"How did he get my contact info?" He opens the message.

Gid, meet me at the football field at midnight.

Gideon's stomach sinks. As if his life wasn't ruined enough, he now has to fight Doug Rock.

MIDNIGHT

How did I offend him? By attacking another one of his gods? By standing too close to his girl. *Cynthia was supposed to be* my *girl.* Gideon slaps his fist. "You're not the only one with skin in this game, Doug."

If he takes the guy out, no one will stand between him and Cynthia. Of course, that's a big *if.*

To set the record straight, there was never a remote possibility of you becoming a jock. You are a nerd. You were born a nerd, and you will die a nerd.

Gideon kicks his mattress, shoving it right off the frame. "I'll show you, Dwight."

Not fighting is not an option. Whether or not he's about to be expelled, there are some things he can't hide from. Sacred honor is at stake.

He looks in the mirror, at those determined, bloodshot eyes. "Who are you?" Certainly not the pathetic recluse he was a week ago. Once again he puts on Doug's brass knuckles.

Crickets chirp. A cool breeze blows through the grass. There, in midst of the unlit football field, one can actually see the stars. Were it not for the knowledge of his impending doom, it would be a beautiful night.

The manly silhouette of Doug stands on the fifty yard line, lit by the moon.

Trying to keep his heart rate low, Gideon takes deep breaths. He walks, the grass crunching beneath him.

Doug holds his ground. Doug is in power.

What a shame it is to end like this. There was something revolutionary, almost beautiful about the short-lived friendship of a jock and a nerd. And *why* is it ending like this? Can't they talk out their differences? Is it at least fair to ask for a reason before being pummeled? But then, do jocks really need a reason to pummel? Maybe Doug repented of his transgression from jock orthodoxy. Maybe beating up Gideon is an act of penance.

Gideon stops at the forty yard line, where the face-off begins. Doug is stoic, unreadable.

Gideon spreads his legs, straightens his back, clenches the brass knuckles.

Doug is the first to make a move. He turns away. "Follow me."

Oh no. Is Doug taking Gideon to meet the rest of the team? Regardless, Gideon follows. They walk to the corner of the field and around a chain link fence, then suddenly stop.

"Look," Doug orders, pointing up at something.

Gideon looks up. The moon? The stars? "I … don't see anything."

"The tower!"

Only then does Gideon notice the cell phone tower right in front of them. Made of gray, industrial steel, it's easy to tune out with the fences and power lines. "Umm … okay."

"Look closely."

Craning his head, Gideon observes the panels, the wires, the triangular bars. It's one ugly piece of machinery, though nothing unusual. "It's just a cell phone tower."

"It's evil."

"What?"

"Don't you see that green glow?"

"No."

"And it's missing a panel on the west side. I've been watching the construction workers. They'll probably finish it on Monday."

As soon as the link between our world and theirs is completed, they'll take full control.

"Come to think of it," says Gideon, "Kyle said something about a tower. You wouldn't know anything about that, would you?"

Doug shrugs. "My memory's failing me, man. I don't even know where I've been for the last year."

"Why were you watching the construction workers?"

"I haven't been feeling up to football practice, but I didn't want to go home, so I've been hanging out by myself. Sometimes I just like to watch, you know? And man, the things I never noticed before … the girls in this school … the way they talk and act … they're morons. And the guys are even dumber. And that's when I started noticing a green glow in some of their eyes."

"Do I have it?"

"Nah, you're good, man. But a lot of people do. And when I noticed the same light coming from the tower … I knew something was wrong. I know it sounds crazy."

Recalling the green eyes of Sportacus, a man standing in a green bonfire, Gideon says, "It doesn't sound crazy at all."

"I had to tell someone, though I didn't think anyone would believe me … except you. I wanted to tell you last night, but … you know … things were a little crazy."

"So you don't want to beat me up?"

"Why would I want to beat you up? You're my friend."

"Really?"

"Of course."

"Thanks for telling me about the tower."

"Do you know what it means?"

"I have a theory. I tried to tell you about it at your house, but I don't know if you were all there. I think our school is being controlled by supernatural beings."

"Makes sense to me."

"Really?"

"The way teenagers act … I've never been able to put my finger on it, but I've always known it wasn't natural."

"Your wisdom is beyond your years."

"My mom says I have an old soul."

"Anyway, I don't like the idea of others controlling my life, so

I've been fighting them. That's why I took on the fat ... uh ... *Mr. Phillips* at the dance, and that's why I took on Sport ... I mean, Mr. Mullins. They take the form of ordinary people."

"How do you know who they are?"

"To be honest, I don't know anything. I could be dreaming this whole thing up."

"Then I'm dreaming it with you. Sometimes I have this feeling that Mr. Mullins is still there, watching me."

Gideon can't help but smile. "You can't know how much I relate. I'm glad we became friends."

Doug smiles back. "I'll help you fight them."

"You will?"

"What do I have to lose? My reputation? I don't care about that stuff anymore. I just wanna do something ..." He searches for the word, shaking his fists. " ... good. You know?"

"Yeah. I do."

"Only ... *how* do we fight them?"

"I wish I knew. If this tower is the source of their power, maybe there's a way to ... stop the transmission. I don't know."

"We'll figure it out, you and I."

"Yeah."

There's a moment of thoughtful silence.

Doug plays with the loose gravel beneath his shoe. "I don't know how to say this, but could you ..."

"Yes?"

The great Doug Rock actually looks embarrassed. "Could you teach me how to become a nerd?"

It takes a moment for the words to sink in. "Teach you ..."

"You know, with the comic books and computer stuff. I want to be smart. And cool. Like you."

Gideon feels dizzy. "I don't know how you got this impression, but I'm not —"

"You were incredible last night, disguised, on a secret mission, fighting the system. Jocks don't do that. We just get drunk and hit each other. But you ... every time I see you, I can tell you know stuff. Cool stuff. And I want to know it too. I want to be like you."

"And I want to be like *you*. Doug, you're the coolest guy in school. Guys admire you. Girls adore you. You don't want to be a nerd."

"I don't care about any of that stuff. Not anymore. I'm empty, Gid, and I need something different. Please, I'm begging you."

"All right, I'll … teach you what I know. Though I'll probably be expelled tomorrow for what I did at the dance."

"Not if I can help it."

"You can't help it."

"Don't underestimate my power."

Gideon laughs. "All right, whatever."

Doug smiles, opening up his arms. "C'mere."

Gideon has to fight the instinct to run.

"C'mere," Doug repeats, a little firmer.

When Gideon doesn't come, Doug walks to him instead, seizing him in a tight hug … a painful hug. His voice quivers a bit as he says, "You're the best, Gid."

EXPELLED

Barely has Gideon entered the building before he hears his name over the PA system. "Gideon Greenwich, please come to the main office."

Finally. He's more than ready to meet his fate. He wouldn't have even bothered to come to school were it not for his desire for closure. The wait was killing him. Now the only troubling thing is the question of how he's going to explain this to his parents.

On the way to the main office, he's not surprised when the gray lady steps into the hallway.

"Well, Mister Greenwich," she says, straightening her clothes, "it appears that your time is up."

Gideon stops. "You're not going to rescue me again?"

"I helped you once, but you've proven less than grateful."

"You didn't want me expelled, because you feared what I'd do outside of your control. You thought that if you could convince me that you were my friend, that everything was normal, then I'd forget all about your little operation. But as you've seen, it's not so easy to shut me up. Whether at school or not, I will continue to fight you."

The gray lady frowns, her eyes narrowing. "I have no idea what you're talking about."

"Now you just want to get rid of me, don't you?"

"This is where our paths part."

"You'd like to think so."

"You, young man, belong in a correctional facility. I've seen to that."

"Do what you want with me. I know your secrets."

"You know nothing."

"What was that, goddess of normality?"

"For your information, Officer Milton is waiting for you in the office. He's a large, strong man, and he loves to put delinquents in their places. As soon as you're finished with Mr. Bruce, Officer Milton will take you to the youth detention center. Last week he left empty-handed. We will not disappoint him again."

"Don't you get it? The more you try to *correct* me, the more I'll rebel."

"You can rebel all you like in your prison cell."

A staring contest ensues. The gray lady wins.

Unable to bear her smile, Gideon turns away. He enters the main office, walking right past the front desk and past Officer Milton.

"Oh," says the secretary, looking up from her computer, "Mr. Bruce —"

But Gideon is already approaching Mr. Bruce's office. Not even bothering to knock, he opens the door.

A startled Mr. Bruce looks up from his desk. "I uh … please shut the door and have a seat."

Leaving the door wide open, Gideon steps into the office. He doesn't sit. "I'd like to get this over with as soon as possible."

With his usual frown, Mr. Bruce takes off his reading glasses. "The reason I asked you to come here is —"

"I know. I assaulted a faculty member. Again. My conduct was unacceptable. I'm expelled."

"Do you care to give your side of the story?"

"No."

Mr. Bruce's face grows a shade darker. "What is wrong with you, Mister Greenwich?"

"I'm a hopeless delinquent, sir."

Mr. Bruce pounds his desk. "What were you thinking?"

"I wasn't thinking. I'm dumb."

"Don't get smart with me."

"I'll try to be dumber."

Mr. Bruce glares at Gideon, his expression a mix of confusion and defeat. "Don't you care?"

"It's out of my power, so why worry about it? I've spent too much of my life worrying."

"You're right, it's out of your power. You will be expelled, and that's a fact. Technically, I'm supposed to tell you about the appeals process, but we both know —"

"We both know I'm at the mercy of Norma."

"Who?"

Gideon is taken aback. "The woman from the district."

"What does she have to do with this?"

Does he really not know he's being controlled, or is this part of the act? "Last time I was here, she tried to buy my loyalty. Now that she knows I'm not for sale, she'll want me as far away as possible."

Mr. Bruce throws up his arms. "What are you talking about?" The confusing thing is, he looks genuinely ignorant. He may have no idea that he's being played by a dark conspiracy, as clueless as the student body. *Who else are the gods controlling?* Perhaps the better question is, who are the gods *not* controlling?

"Forget it," says Gideon.

With a frown, Mr. Bruce grabs a pen and starts filling out some paperwork. "Let's just get this over with, shall we?" He's about to sign his name, when he's interrupted by a vibrating phone on his desk. His red face turns to concern as sees who the caller is. He answers. "Coach McPherson. How are you?"

Finally Gideon takes a seat, throwing his head against the wall. How long must they delay the inevitable? He overhears Coach McPherson's shouting voice. Though he can't make out any words, the anger is unmistakable.

" ... No, I wasn't aware ..." Now Mr. Bruce sounds nervous. " ... I ... I had no idea."

Gideon sits up.

" ... Well, the decision isn't final ... I'll see what I can do." Mr. Bruce puts away the phone. He removes his glasses and rubs the top of his nose. "Why don't you just go to class."

Gideon has a double take. "Me?"

"Who else?"

Gideon doesn't budge. "What's going on?"

"Apparently you're on the football team now."

"And?"

"Coach McPherson isn't happy."

"What did I do?"

"He's mad at Douglas Rock, not you."

"Why?"

"As you know, Doug is our star quarterback. He's helped our school win state for two years in a row. And now he's threatening to quit … unless a certain running back stays on the team."

"I don't follow."

"He says this teammate is the best athlete he's ever worked with."

"Who?"

"You."

"What?"

"You certainly are full of surprises, Mister Greenwich. I had no idea you were so good at football."

"Umm …"

"As you know, sports are very important to our school. They're a huge source of funding. When you're out there in uniform, you represent the students, the staff, and the community. It's not something to take lightly."

"Okay …"

"All I ask is that you take out your aggression on your opponents … not on the faculty."

"Okay …"

"You can go to class now."

" … I'm not expelled?"

Mr. Bruce rolls his eyes. "If we expelled you, you wouldn't be able to play football, would you?"

Gideon steps out of the main office. So does Officer Milton. The tall man gives Gideon a good stare before turning a cold shoulder and walking away.

Maybe next time.

Gideon is about to go to class when he hears his name. He turns to see Doug coming out from his hiding place behind a trophy cabinet.

"Did it work?" Doug asks.

Gideon laughs. "You're something else, Doug."

"You better come to practice today. Coach McPherson will be expecting great things from you."

"Do you have any idea how bad I am at sports? I have no coordination whatsoever."

Doug smiles. "I noticed."

"I'm just not cut out to be an athlete."

"And maybe I'm not cut out to be a nerd, but people can change. Together, you and I will bring balance to the force."

Gideon laughs again. "So you're feeling up to playing football and basketball again?"

"I'm ready to conquer the world. But before I can do that, I have to pass Biology. I'll catch you later." Doug administers a back slap — as painful as ever — then walks away … actually, it's more of a strut than a walk.

"Hey, Doug …"

"Yeah?"

"Thanks."

"This nerd training better be good. I'll see you at lunch."

Gideon feels relieved from a great burden … and weighed down by another. How in the world is he going to be a running back? What does a running back even do? As he heads to his math class, he stops at the intersection where he encountered the gray lady. Though the hallways are empty, he can almost feel her presence. And maybe it's his imagination, but for a moment he thinks he sees her reflection in a classroom window.

"Looks like your plan backfired," he says to the doors and lockers. "You hoped Doug would make me normal. Instead I made him weird. Weirdness will prevail."

Surely it's his imagination, but for a moment he thinks he can feel her anger, fierce and burning.

"Though you were right about one thing. I was meant to be a football star. Go cowboys!"

NERD TRAINING

Wanda sits alone in the lunchroom. She's there, but she's not there.

Holding a steaming tray, Gideon makes for her table. But in the same moment, Wanda picks up her food and leaves.

Gideon searches the cafeteria for Dwight. The guy is playing cards with another group of friends.

Not those guys. Notwithstanding his prejudices, if Gideon could befriend Doug Rock, he could befriend a rival tribe of nerds. He steps forward.

Dwight immediately meets his gaze, and the message is clear: *Back off.*

Finally Gideon sits at an empty table. So this is the cost of war, so much higher than he ever imagined. Somehow he thought standing for principle would earn him *respect.*

From all around, he catches peers staring and whispering, but as always, no one comes to talk. Apparently he's a thing to be discussed, a topic of controversy, not a living, breathing person.

But at last, someone *does* approach him. Doug. And who's this trailing behind?

"Hey, buddy," says Doug, his fingers interlocked with Cynthia McDaniels'. Cynthia's attention is on the opposite corner of the cafeteria, where her friends are sitting and laughing.

Gideon puts down his milk carton and wipes his mouth. "Hi."

Finally Cynthia turns to him, not even trying to mask her disgust. "So … that was totally weird at the dance."

"Yeah, well …" Gideon rotates his peas with his spoon, "it got a little out of hand." It takes concentration to avoid staring at Doug and Cynthia's interlocked fingers. For a moment, he and Doug lock eyes, then Doug looks at the floor. Apparently this is painful for Doug too, which forces Gideon to love him all the more … which is annoying, because right now Gideon really wants to hate him.

"Why did you do it?" asks Cynthia.

Gideon has no answer, so Doug answers for him. "I told you, babe. He was on a mission to expose the gods."

Babe?

Cynthia shifts her weight. "Doug, you know I like you, but … normal people don't talk about … gods."

She was there in the tunnels. She saw the gods! Is it more illogical to believe in the supernatural or to doubt one's own experiences? Gideon is surprised at how much Cynthia's betrayal hurts.

"Anyway," says Doug, "let's get on with the training." He takes a seat across from Gideon. "Where do we start?"

Cynthia folds her arms, looking away. This would be much easier if she wasn't here.

"Well," says Gideon, putting down his spoon, "if you want to be a nerd, you've got to …" — he searches for the words — " … exude a certain … lack of confidence."

"Lack of confidence," Doug repeats. "Should I be taking notes?"

"That would be a nerdy thing to do."

"Excellent." Doug unzips his backpack and pulls out a notebook and pen. "Go on."

"Never look people in the eyes. Mumble when you talk. Slouch when you walk."

Cynthia buries her face in her hands. "I can't believe I'm hearing this."

Gideon can't help but smile. "Wherever you go, you need to give a clear message that says, *I hate myself.*"

"I hate myself," Doug repeats.

"Say it and mean it."

"I hate myself!" Doug shouts.

"Good. Next, your hygiene will have to go."

"Hygiene?" Doug's eyes widen.

"Absolutely. You're not allowed to bathe more than once a week, though once a month is better. You'll need to stop wearing expensive designer clothes and limit your wardrobe to one pair of slacks and three or four t-shirts."

Doug looks up from his notes. "What kind of t-shirts?"

"Preferably ones exhibiting sci-fi characters from previous decades. A true nerd is never up with the times."

Doug nods as he writes. "It's a lot to take in, but I can do this."

As Gideon puts on smelly gym clothes, it occurs to him that he's actually … *excited*. Perhaps, after preparing to fight Doug Rock, there's still some adrenaline in his body. Perhaps, with the gods always watching him, he feels a need to prove himself. Whatever the reason, though deliverance is only a forged doctor's note away, he finds himself voluntarily walking into the arena and grabbing a basketball.

Dwight is beside him. Without saying a word, the two of them dribble, throw, and miss.

Coach Griffith blows his whistle and announces the torture for the day: full-on team basketball. *How creative.* To no one's surprise, Kyle Slater is appointed as a team captain. To everyone's surprise, Gideon is appointed as the other captain. This is, no doubt, another payback for all the periods of skipped class.

Gideon can feel the hateful stare of Kyle burning into his cheek. While the guy couldn't exactly murder him in a public school, it wasn't hard to imagine Kyle *accidentally* committing a foul that resulted in Gideon's broken bones.

Kyle starts off by choosing Chris Stanley, the tallest and most aggressive boy in the class.

Gideon looks around. As if his gaze is contagious, the other boys seem to step back. Someone is going to be mad no matter who he calls. At least he knows who's *already* mad at him. "Dwight."

With a groan, Dwight steps up beside him.

Of course, Kyle chooses the second-tallest boy in the class.

Gideon studies his options. Not one boy will look at him. "Umm

..."

From the back of the gym, someone shouts, "Choose me!"

It's Doug, hopping as he puts on a shoe. "Sorry I'm late, coach," he says. "I had to meet with a counselor."

Coach Griffith asks, "No doctor's note today?"

"No way." With his shoe in place, Doug jogs straight to Gideon and Dwight. "I'm ready to get back into action. That is, if it's okay with the team captain."

Without hesitation, Gideon says, "I choose Doug." Beside him, he can feel Dwight's frowning disapproval. Even more obvious are the murmurings from the other boys, as if a sacred line has just been breached. Notwithstanding, when it's Gideon's turn to choose another player, the remaining boys seem less terrified.

Though the ball starts in Gideon's hands, he's quick to dispense the cursed thing to Dwight.

Dwight, at the appearance of an oncoming stampede, is quick to pass the ball to someone else.

Soon the ball finds its way to Doug, the master and commander, who dribbles the ball between his legs, charges down the court, and plows right through the defense. He jumps at the three-point line and scores without hitting the rim.

Coach Griffith shouts, "Nice team work!"

Gideon has never been on a winning team before. It's kind of addicting.

There's something different about Ms. Primple. No leopard spots, no frills or lace, just a gray, flannel skirt suit.

Where have I seen that before?

Once everyone has taken their seats, she announces a pop quiz and hands out paper.

Gideon reads the first question:

> *What color was Katie Taylor's dress at the Oscar awards, last Spring?*

"What kind of question is that?" Gideon finds himself vocalizing.

"No talking," Ms. Primple snaps.

Gideon reads the next question:

List the five best providers of ladies undergarments.

Again, Gideon can't help himself. "How am I supposed to know that?"

"If you talk one more time, you will fail the quiz, which, by the way, will count toward half of this term's letter grade."

Feeling blood rising to his face, Gideon reads the third question:

True or false, Scott Martin, featured in the September edition of Vainglory Magazine, looked better in his leather pants than in his blue jeans.

Gideon shoots up a hand.

Ms. Primple sighs. "Yes, Mister Greenwich?"

"These questions are subjective."

"That's the nature of the fashion industry."

"Yeah, but —"

"If you can't handle it, maybe you shouldn't have signed up for this class. But then, as our resident cross-dresser, I thought you, of all people, would know a great deal about fashion." The room fills with snickers. "After your so-called report on the necktie, I decided it was time to raise the bar. For those who belong here, there's nothing to fear. For those who don't ..." She glances at Dwight and Wanda. " ... they can thank *you*, Mister Greenwich."

As usual, Gideon can feel the frowns of his friends. He stares at Ms. Primple, wondering what she's trying to accomplish. To make his life a living hell? He almost wishes he *was* expelled. His one comforting thought is that the school day will be over in forty-five minutes.

Then he remembers football practice. *How am I going to get through this?*

Ms. Primple says, "Oh, and there will also be practical exams, as it doesn't do any good to study fashion if we don't practice it. Starting tomorrow, every student who enters my classroom who is not wearing a color-coordinated wardrobe will be docked ten points. Sweat pants and Pokémon t-shirts will result in a half-letter-grade drop."

Dwight raises a hand.

"Yes, Mister Farnsworth?"

"*Star Wars* t-shirts?"

"One letter grade."

"Isn't this a violation of our rights?"

"You're minors. You have no rights."

"Actually, I just turned eighteen."

"In my class, you will do as I say, or you will fail. Any further questions, Mister Farnsworth?"

Gideon fumes. Being forced to play football is one thing, but being forced to dress fashionably? *This means war.*

FASHION CLUB

Football practice is a constant nightmare of hits, clobbers, and dog piles ... always with Gideon on bottom ... and Kyle Slater on top. Then there's the confused glares of Coach McPherson, who's probably thinking, *You call that a running back?* Though a few days ago, Gideon couldn't have cared less, now he longs to prove himself, at least so he doesn't let down Doug. From the way he outran his pursuers at the pep rally ... at the fight ... at the dance ... he knows he can do this.

More than once, Gideon recovers from a fumble or a dog pile to see an embarrassed Doug avoiding the glances of his teammates. No doubt, they're all wondering the same thing: *why in the world would you give the ball to Gideon?*

The next morning, Gideon's calves, thighs, and back are still aching. He tries to make his way to first period math, but every step is painful. *How long can I keep this up?*

There's a voice coming over the P.A. system. "Attention, students, because the administration and faculty are concerned about an increase in delinquent behavior ..." It's Ms. Primple! " ... we'd like to make you aware of some new school policies." *No.* "Beginning today, all students must be affiliated with an official school club ... and only *one* club. Each club must be sponsored by a teacher. All clubs will be required to hold mandatory meetings. Failure to attend or comply with club rules will result in detention. Enrollments will take place in the commons in lieu of first period. Please proceed to the commons immediately."

Soon Gideon finds himself following a bewildered crowd. The commons are filled with teachers, tables, and lines of students. The fact that Ms. Primple is behind this makes him suspicious, but then, how can he complain about something that gets him out of Pre-Calculus? While school-sponsored clubs have never been his thing, he wouldn't mind joining the Chess Club, the Astronomy Club, or the Live Action Role-playing Club.

Mr. Snodgrass, a bald man with thick glasses and a bristly mustache, is sitting behind one of the tables. On top of the table is a sign that reads *Science Fiction Club.*

Ooh. Gideon gets in line. When it's his turn, Mr. Snodgrass asks, "Name?"

"Gideon Greenwich."

Mr. Snodgrass raises an eyebrow and gets a good look at Gideon before scanning a roster. Apparently Gideon's name is just as infamous among the faculty. "I'm afraid you're in the wrong line. This booth is for students with last names between A and E. You're at the next table over."

"I don't understand. I want to join *your* club."

"I'm afraid that's not how it works. You're assigned a club."

"Assigned?"

"Don't blame me. I just do as I'm told. Next!"

Gideon approaches the next line over. To his horror, Ms. Primple is sitting behind the table, a grin on her unnaturally red lips.

"Yes, Mister Greenwich," she says, "you'll be joining the Fashion Club."

As fate would have it — or as the gods would have it — none of Gideon's friends have been assigned to the Fashion Club, which must be the smallest club in the school. It's just him and the three girls he has nothing in common with: Joan Cooper, Kimberly Fenner, and Monica Hawley. Together they follow Ms. Primple to another part of the school, where she stops them in a hallway.

"This will do," she says. "We will begin with inspections." She looks over Joan. "Designer boots ... beige leggings ... a well-ironed burgundy skirt — a direct compliment to the beige — and a matching wool blouse. But the brand? Let me see the tag. Ah. *Beau Fromage.* Very nice. Moving on ... a pearl necklace, silver earrings, and a seamless hair piece. You pass." Next Ms. Primple examines Kimberly and Monica, who also pass with flying colors.

Then she examines Gideon. "Worn-out tennis shoes, complete with holes and grass stains. Wrinkly slacks with a mustard stain. Aren't these the same slacks you wore yesterday? A tacky green t-shirt that in no way compliments your lower half. And as for your hair … never mind, we won't go there. You fail." She places a slip of paper into Gideon's hand.

"What's this?" he asks.

"Your detention notice. I filled it out in advance."

"But I didn't do anything."

"You're violating the Fashion Club's dress code. As I said over the P.A., failure to comply with club rules will result in detention."

"But you never *told* us the rules."

"Yesterday I warned you there would be penalties for unfashionable wardrobes. Did you think I was joking?"

Gideon crumples the paper and stuffs it into his pocket. As tempting as it is to lash out, he knows the gods must be looking for another excuse to expel him. *I must stay calm.*

Ms. Primple approaches a random girl in the hallway.

"Stop," Ms. Primple orders.

The girl stops, alarmed. She looks young and shy. She's probably a freshman, not a day over fourteen.

"You'll be our first subject." Ms. Primple turns to the club. "Now we're going to critique other students' fashion. I've shown you how it's done. Joan, you'll go first."

With some timidity, Joan approaches the girl, looking up and down. "Okay … her pants are purple and her shirt is red, which totally clash."

The poor girl looks horrified.

"Are those brown socks? Ew. And I don't mean to be rude, but your hair is a nightmare. Get a straightener, hun. Then there's your face. Looks more like a pizza, if you ask me."

Ms. Primple and the other girls laugh. Meanwhile, the freshmen girl, her eyes welling up with tears, walks off as fast as she can.

"Well done, Joan," says Ms. Primple. "I couldn't have said it better myself." She wastes no time in stopping another passing girl. This girl is overweight, wearing too much makeup, and even Gideon can tell that her clothes are unfashionable.

Ms. Primple says, "Your turn, Mister Greenwich."

Gideon doesn't budge. He just stares at the frightened eyes of their next would-be victim.

"I said it's your turn."

Gideon shakes his head. "No."

"No?"

"I won't do it."

"How would you like another detention?"

"Do what you will, but I'm not going to harass this poor girl."

The way Ms. Primple looks at Gideon reminds him very much of the gray lady. "Club meeting is over. Mister Greenwich and I need to have a private meeting."

Gideon follows Ms. Primple through the school and into her classroom. He knows the situation is dire when she not only closes but locks the door. Though when she begins lowering the blinds, he feels something else altogether. However much Gideon disdains Ms. Primple, she is, nonetheless, a vision of feminine perfection, and he's a teenage boy with raging hormones.

"What's this about?" he asks, tortured by the conflict within him.

"Oh, Gideon," she says sweetly, almost seductively, "why do you fight me?"

"I …" He tries to divert his attention from her curves.

She comes closer. "I know you think fashion is vanity, but you're wrong. In this world, where seeing is believing, appearances matter. If you can't make it look good, then it's no good, because no one will buy it. Gideon, you poor, stupid soul, clothes make the woman. Do you have any idea what I look like without clothes on?"

"Um …"

"Would you like to see?"

"Um …"

Ms. Primple begins to unbutton her blouse, and a tormented Gideon instinctively looks away.

Ms. Primple laughs. "Such a gentleman. Though it's not what you think. Look again."

With a tinge of guilt, Gideon obeys, and his pounding heart skips a beat. Ms. Primple isn't there at all. In her place is a monster.

Gideon stumbles backward, crashing into a desk and falling to the floor.

The towering monster, brown and hairy, resembles a wild boar, though it stands like a human. It's covered with horns, tusks, and claws, and it has way too many arms. Beneath its hideous, wet snout are a set of yellow, sharp teeth. Its green eyes are dead-set on Gideon.

"You see?" the beast speaks with the voice of Ms. Primple.

Gideon glances at the door. If he runs now, he might escape.

But the beast is on to him. "Really, Gideon, do you think I would hurt you? I'm only trying to help you understand. This is how the ancient Sumerians saw me. They were a stubborn lot, only worshiping out of fear. So I gave them something to fear."

Suddenly the classroom appears to be warping around the giant beast, contracting from all sides. The walls are rippling like water. The next moment, the beast is gone, and in its place is a beautiful woman. Ms. Primple. Wearing a flowing, red gown, she sits on a golden throne that's carved to resemble male lions. She wears a towering crown, a style from centuries long gone, and she has … *wings*. Where has Gideon seen this image before?

"The Assyrians and Babylonians had better sense," says Ms. Primple. "They wanted a goddess of love and beauty, so I became their Ishtar."

Of course! It's the goddess from Wanda's book.

"It's far more useful to be beautiful. Empty-headed men would do anything to please me. Wars were fought on my behalf, and all from the power of appearance. As times have changed, we deities had to change. But one thing never changes: man's compulsion to worship; a golden calf, a queen, a pop star … Whatever you mortals desire, we're at the front of it, controlling it, controlling *you*. Are you beginning to understand?"

Gideon shakes his head. "I don't know what you want from me."

She closes her eyes, revealing blue eyeshadow. Once again the classroom appears to warp around her, and the next moment, *Sportacus* is standing in her place, that herculean horror in the white toga. Just as alive and real as that unforgettable night at the park, the man thrusts a spear at Gideon's chest, the sharp tip stopping only inches away.

"Perhaps you'd prefer a more classical threat," Sportacus says, though the voice is Ms. Primple's.

Gideon fumbles backward until trapped against the wall. "*You're* Sportacus?"

The classroom warps for a third time, and suddenly Ms. Primple is back to her usual self. "Of course not. You took out that meat head, for which I thank you. The pantheon is better off without him. The imbecile would never leave me alone. Not that I can blame him."

"Then that was *you* at the principal's office."

"Norma and I had to clean up your mess."

"So Sportacus really *is* dead."

Ms. Primple laughs. "He's just … let's say … sent away. You cannot kill a *god*. We're immortal. We're all-powerful and all-knowing. Which brings me back to my point, Gideon dear. While you have a certain charm, you little rebel, it's time you learn your boundaries. The first rule is that you do not disobey a god or a goddess. That is sin. You do not challenge a god or a goddess. That is blasphemy. We are the powers that keep this world in order. Serve us, and you will be blessed. Anger us, and you will suffer. We've tolerated a lot from you, but no more. We could kill you with the snap of our fingers."

"Then why haven't you?"

Ms. Primple laughs, betraying the slightest bit of nervousness. "It is not your privilege to know our secrets. But believe me, if you fight against us any more, we *will* do away with you one way or another. We could start by throwing you into the juvenile detention center. Or, if you're so eager to feel the full force of our power, I could have you sacrificed. We goddesses do love sacrifices. Stabbed on an alter perhaps? Burned at a stake? Thrown into the fiery furnace of Molech? I'm sure we could come up with a creative punishment for a heretic." Then she adds in her gentle, breathy voice, "On the other hand, please us, and we will please you. Understand?"

Gideon can only manage a nod.

"You probably wonder why we've tolerated so much from you. It's because you have so much potential. You can see beyond what the others can … those sheep. You could be our mouthpiece, our prophet. All you need is a little re-education. Work for us, worship us, and we can give you anything you want. Or any*one*. A certain girl in our class, perhaps?"

Gideon has no words.

"I'll give you some time to think it over. You can go now."

At first Gideon wonders if this is a trick, but then, any chance to get out of this room is worth taking. He darts for the door.

"Oh, and Gideon …"

She's waving her fingers flirtatiously. "This conversation will be our little secret. Got it?"

"Got it."

HIT

As punishment for being a terrible running back, Coach McPherson, always distant and looking on through his unreadable sunglasses, drafts Gideon to the defensive line. There, more than ever, Gideon finds himself the target of the aggression that Kyle and his cronies couldn't get away with in the gym. Bruised and battered, he's thrown to the cold, hard grass, again and again, clobbered, and beaten.

So ... much ... pain.

When, at last, a whistle blows, and his tormentors withdraw, Gideon rises to wobbly legs and straightens a sore back. Though he wants to keel over and die, for Doug's sake, he chooses the path of insanity. He turns to Kyle and shouts loud enough for everyone to hear, "Is that the best you can do? Bring it on, girly man."

Kyle is not amused.

The only plus side to the position of lineman is that it doesn't require any actual understanding of the game of football. Without any strain to the brain (except for the occasional hits to the head), Gideon's job is to serve as a human crash dummy. There's plenty of time to stare at the clouds and ponder his place in the universe. He thinks of the gods and whether to fight or surrender. He thinks of Cynthia and Ms. Primple's tempting offer. Then there's sudden flashes of violence and pain. During these rude awakenings, spiritual meditation must give way to a consuming awareness of his mortality. All in all, he finds being a lineman enlightening.

That is, until Kyle hits him for the fifth time. Then, lying on the ground, seeing spots in the gray sky, something snaps within Gideon. Again he stands up and brushes off the grass. But when comes the sixth charge from the offensive line, he hits back, and he hits hard.

There's something deeply satisfying about watching a wide-eyed Kyle fall to the ground. Even more satisfying are the looks of confidence in Doug and Coach McPherson. As if that weren't enough, when Gideon happens to glance at the end zone, he sees Cynthia and the other cheerleaders watching him. It's hard to tell from the distance, and maybe it's just wishful thinking, but it certainly looks like Cynthia's smiling.

When practice is over, Gideon has never been in more pain, and he's never felt better. The sky is golden. The clouds are pink. To sweat is to live! If only Dwight and Wanda knew what they're missing. Holding a scuffed helmet, limping with every step, he's halfway home when a car pulls over on the other side of the street.

Oh no. His heart sinks at the thought of a vengeful Kyle. Who else could it be?

Then comes a feminine voice. "Gideon!" He turns to see none other than Cynthia McDaniels stepping out of the car.

In a panic, Gideon looks himself over. He's wearing his pads, covered in sweat and grass stains. His hair must be a disheveled mess. He must look … *manly.* A smile gracing his lips, he hollers back, "Hey!"

Cynthia runs across the street. Still in her cheer leading uniform, her hair permed, her makeup immaculate, she looks more beautiful than ever. "I'm so glad I found you. I really wanted to see you."

"Oh," is the most intelligent response Gideon can muster.

"Doug's been acting really weird, lately."

Of course this is about Doug. Gideon can't help but sigh. "I tried to talk him out of the whole nerd thing, but he wouldn't listen."

"You've been a true friend to him, and I really appreciate that."

"Well … you know." Ever so slightly, Gideon sucks in his belly and lifts his chest.

"The thing is, I need a break from Doug."

And so you come to me?

She plays with her hair, meeting his eyes. "As in forever." She smiles. Her brown eyes are too much. There's a hint of green he hadn't noticed before.

Gideon's heart rate picks up, but he's been burned too many times. This can't be what he thinks it is.

"You know what I really want, Gideon?" She steps closer, her warm hand taking his. "You." Then, without warning, she leans forward and kisses him on the lips.

The feeling, soft and intimate, makes Gideon feel lighter than air.

There's a honk from the car across the street.

Cynthia withdraws and turns away, but not before revealing her blushing face. "I better not keep my friends waiting. See you tomorrow?"

"Yeah."

They part, and Gideon continues the walk home, though this time there's no pain. In fact, it doesn't feel like a walk at all but a drift through clouds.

That night, lying in bed, his mind is a confused mess of darkness and light. On one hand there's the gods and all their horror. On the other hand, Cynthia loves him, which makes no sense whatsoever. But who cares? He's so wound up, sleep isn't a possibility. He needs to talk to someone, someone like Doug.

No, not Doug. I just stole his girl! ... Wanda? No, that might be worse.

That leaves only Dwight, who isn't a good option at all. But why not? Just a few days ago, they were best friends. Must bad feelings fester, or is someone allowed to be the bigger person?

Gideon calls Dwight but gets a voice mail greeting. He calls again. Voice mail again. He tries a third time, and finally Dwight answers.

"Dude," says an irritated Dwight, "I'm trying to sleep."

"It's only ten-thirty-five, and *Star Trek* doesn't end until eleven."

"All right, you called my bluff. What's up?"

"So much has happened, and I ... just need someone to talk to."

"Gideon, I can't handle any more craziness in my life. I've got enough to worry about with Calculus and AP Chemistry, so if this is about the gods —"

"Cynthia McDaniels kissed me."

"What?"

"She *kissed* me … on the lips."

"Was she possessed?"

"Very funny."

"The only way a girl like that would kiss a guy like *you* is if (A) she's insane, or (B) she's possessed."

"Seriously, man, she just showed up on my way home. She said that she and Doug were through and that she wanted *me*. What should I do?"

"I find this harder to believe than the existence of gods. Unless … it was the gods that possessed her. That would explain every-thing. Maybe they *are* real."

"I'm looking for some guy-to-guy advice here."

"Then you're talking to the wrong guy. You know I've never *touched* a girl."

"Does this mean she's my girlfriend now?"

"Sure, why not? She was almost certainly possessed, but in the rare chance that I'm wrong, I'm happy for you."

"Thanks."

"Anything else?"

"Umm … Ms. Primple turned into a pig."

"I don't want to hear it."

"All right, you don't have to believe me. It just gets a little lonely when your friends think you're delusional."

"I thought you were above the company of nerds."

"Doug is as weird and awkward as we are. He's lost his friends too and he needed someone to confide in … like I need you."

"Go cry on your jock's shoulder. Seems you two were meant for each other."

"Have I ever lied to you?"

"I can think of a few times."

"When it really mattered?"

Dwight is silent.

"This *really* matters, Dwight. You *know* I'm not crazy. I know it's hard to believe that one guy could have it right while everyone else is wrong, but … isn't that how it's always been? Truth is never popular, and when people stumble on it, they look the other way. I didn't want any of this, but I *know* what I've seen. I know there's something dark going on, and I know *you* know it too."

"Gideon … it's just not … logical."

"Forget logic. The universe is wonderfully complex, and we're kidding ourselves if we think we've got it all figured out. Sometimes we just have to do what *feels* right, even if we can't explain why, because if we do nothing —"

"Yeah, yeah, evil triumphs."

"I need your help, Dwight."

Dwight sighs. "I'll … I'll try to keep an open mind."

Gideon relaxes on his bed. "It's good to talk again."

"Yeah."

After the phone call, Gideon still finds sleep hard to come by. "*Possessed*," he murmurs. "He's just jealous." But in Dwight's defense, the voice of Ms. Primple replays in his mind:

> *"I can give you anything you want. Or anyone. A certain girl in our class, perhaps?"*

Dang it.

Could the gods really make Cynthia his? That might explain the green he saw in her eyes. Though disturbing, the idea is beyond alluring … leading to another question: Why, again, is he fighting them?

Sleep is nowhere to be found. It's two AM when Gideon tiptoes out of the house, welcoming the cold air on his skin. Tying the belt of his bathrobe, he walks to the side of the house and leans against the bricks. From here he has a great view of the city below. And there, in the twinkling lights, he imagines it all over again: young lovers, tuxedos, dresses, interlocked fingers, gazing eyes … could he really be a part of all that?

Cynthia actually kissed him. Who cares *why*? What matters is that she wants him, and he must do everything in his power to hold on to this wonderful reality. What would be so terrible about a little compromise? He could choose his battles. Sports, fashion, music ... even popularity; these are good things. Maybe the gods are good. Surely it wouldn't hurt for Gideon Greenwich to be a little more normal.

There's something strange at the school, a light that wasn't there before. Though hazy, the green glow appears to be coming from the ... *cell phone tower.* The more he looks, the more light he sees, weird and unearthly. Like a rising spotlight, it connects the tower to the clouds above.

Doug was right.

With a sudden curiosity, Gideon looks across the city until identifying the bright mass of Westward High, a few miles away. He just makes out their football stadium and, after some searching, what might be another cell phone tower. He looks closer, and what at first was invisible becomes undeniable: another green glow, a pillar of light between heaven and earth.

He turns to the north end of the valley. It's a good ten miles away, but somewhere out there in the busy lights is Mountain Ridge High. He doesn't know where, exactly, though his newly-trained eyes soon find what they're looking for: another pillar of green light.

Chills spread over his skin. "They're everywhere."

It's four o'clock when he gives up on sleep altogether. He flips on the light and grabs Wanda's library book, *The Gods and Goddesses of Ancient Mesopotamia.* He stares at the illustration of Ishtar and the rows of priests in women's clothing. He turns to another page to see a statue of a human-boar, multi-armed and covered with horns ... the very monster he saw yesterday.

Prostrated before the monster are hundreds of worshipers. There was a time when he would have disdained such small-minded submission. Now he can hardly blame them. It's their way of life, the only life they've ever known. Everyone's doing it.

He reads about the stone masons who carved an idol, then coated it with gold, and adorned it with jewels.

"We *make* them," he whispers to the silent bedroom. "We give them their power, and we can take it away."

He turns back to the image of Ishtar, wondering what would happen if the kneeling priests were to just stand up and leave? What would happen to a goddess of beauty if no one worshiped her and no one cared?

He reads about Molech, a giant, stony furnace carved like a face. Cruel priests would throw unwilling victims into its fiery mouth. It's hard not to imagine the demonic eyes, the black smoke, and the cries of suffering. What could lead human beings to do something so terrible?

The answer comes with further reading. The priests made good money.

Wealth. Power. Prestige.

And what of Gideon Greenwich? Will he sell out for a girl?

SUBMISSION

Gideon shows up to the Fashion Club with clean slacks and a collared shirt, brown shoes and a coordinated belt. His hair is gelled, his stubble shaved.

"By the power of Ra," says a smiling Ms. Primple, "it appears that there's hope for everyone."

Gideon catches Joan, Kimberly, and Monica stealing glances at him. It's a good feeling.

When it's his turn to criticize a random passerby's wardrobe, he doesn't shy away. "Clearly," he says, looking over the girl's red, curly hair and colorful outfit, "the striped tights are at odds with the plaid skirt, an insult to the eyes. And that green, collared blouse? Are you *trying* to make us puke?"

The red-headed girl turns up her head and walks away. Meanwhile Gideon is met with applause.

"Well, Gideon," says Ms. Primple, twirling a lock of her golden hair, "you are full of surprises."

In Ancient World History, Ms. Fitzwater reads aloud the following:

> *In 1095, as tensions mounted with the violent situation in Jerusalem, Pope Urban II urged the Frankish knights to stop killing each other and to kill Muslims instead, for which they would be justified by God. Reversing centuries of Christian doctrine, he declared, "Set out on this journey and you will obtain the remission of your sins and be sure of the incorruptible glory of the kingdom of heaven."*

Ms. Fitzwater looks up from her book. "What do you think of the pope's decision? Was it justified?"

Ken Garcia answers, "Of course not. The crusades were one of the darkest chapters of history."

Ms. Fitzwater nods, stifling a yawn. "Anyone else?"

Gideon raises a hand. "Hindsight is twenty-twenty. If you read the whole speech, the pope describes the horrible things the Muslims were doing to the Christians. Everyone there agreed that the mandate came from God."

Ken rolls his eyes. "That doesn't make it right."

"How can *you* claim to know what's right? Were you there?"

Ms. Fitzwater cuts in. "There's no need to get defensive, Gideon."

"I'm just saying, what choice did they have? To these people at this time in this place, God told them to go war, and that's all there was to it."

Joan Cooper says, "Are you all right, Gideon? You don't seem your ... *normal* ... self."

Gideon smiles. "I've never felt better."

After taking a sumptuous bite from a Danish pastry, Mr. Periwinkle says, "For extra credit, who can name the four fundamental forces?"

Gideon shoots a hand up. With so much on his mind, his grades have been suffering, and he needs all the help he can get. "Gravity, electromagnetism, the weak force, and the strong force."

"Very good."

Seeing that half the class is zoning out or asleep, Gideon continues. "But do those four, simple forces really control the *whole* universe?"

"As far as we've been able to observe, everything is held together by those four irreducible interactions."

"But what about the crazy stuff? You know, like quantum leaps ... entanglement ... electrons with minds of their own ..."

"Hmm. I seem to recall it was Richard Feynman who said, *We do not know what the rules of the game are; all we are allowed to do is to watch the playing.* There may very well be additional forces out there. As far as more complex interactions, we're always discovering new laws."

"And is it not possible that those laws could be broken?"

"It is not possible. That's why we call them laws."

"But suppose we were to observe *supernatural* phenomena."

"Supernatural phenomena?"

"You know, like the tugging of an unseen force, or … a weird, green light … things that don't make sense. Wouldn't that suggest that there's something higher than the laws of physics?"

"No, it would suggest that there's a new law or force to learn about. Everything in the universe, no matter how strange or complex, is bound by the laws of physics."

"Even God?"

"If there is a God, then yes. He, like us, would have to play by the rules. Without laws, there could be no universe. Nothing could exist."

"But supposing there's an exception —"

"There are no exceptions. The laws *must* be obeyed."

"Then supposing we could master the laws of physics —"

"We would be gods."

For whatever reason, Doug doesn't show up at lunch for his nerd training. Gideon can only wonder what's transpired between Doug and Cynthia and what Doug must think of him. He hates the thought of losing Doug's friendship.

Gideon spies Cynthia sitting with her friends. Occasionally their eyes meet, and smiles are exchanged. Surely the gods couldn't force something so beautiful. Surely it's a *real* smile.

When Dwight appears, carrying a tray, he looks between Gideon's table and that *other* table of nerds. With some apprehension, he chooses Gideon's table. "What are you wearing?" he asks.

Gideon looks down at his collared shirt and ironed slacks. "I … uh … was drafted into the fashion club, and … you know, Ms.

Primple said she'd dock our grades if —"

"I get it, you're a sell-out."

"You were right, Dwight. Some battles aren't worth fighting."

They talk, they laugh, and Gideon realizes that as nice as new friends are, there's nothing like an old one. If only he could win Wanda back.

In the P.E. locker room, Gideon is tying his basketball shoes when Dwight taps him on the shoulder. Trying to look nonchalant, Dwight nods to the other end of the locker room, where Kyle Slater and his friends are talking in a huddle, their voices hushed. On occasion, one of them glances at Gideon.

Dwight whispers, "I overheard part of their conversation. Today's the day. Kyle's hiding some brass knuckles in his pocket. As soon as you get the ball, two guys are gonna grab your arms while Kyle takes it out on you. They're gonna make it fast and dirty so it looks like an accident."

Gideon looks around. "Where's Doug?" His guardian angel is nowhere to be seen.

"I heard someone say he's sick today. You'd better be sick too. Write a doctor's note."

The thought is tempting. It might just save his life. But there's more at stake than the life of Gideon Greenwich. No matter how difficult, he must *stick* to his plan. "No, I've got this."

"Are you crazy?"

"I need you to trust me."

Gideon and Dwight are the last to enter the gym, where they feel the eyes of the conspirators upon them.

Meanwhile an oblivious Coach Griffith appoints Kyle and Gideon as team captains again (apparently it's a running gag). Of course, Kyle calls the tallest and scariest guy in the school, Koa Kamaka, as his first pick.

Dwight whispers, "Koa is one of the conspirators. The other guy is Matt Wilson. Choose Matt to spoil their plan."

Gideon nods, then announces, "I choose Dwight."

Dwight smacks his forehead.

Kyle, however, looks amused. "I choose Matt Wilson." Matt is the second tallest guy.

As Dwight glares at him, Gideon says, "I choose Pablo Gonzales," and the gym fills with laughter. Pablo is, by far, the *shortest* guy in the class.

Next, Kyle chooses Joe Munson — big, tough, Joe Munson — and Gideon chooses Elvin Banks, perhaps the most quintessential nerd in the school.

At that, Kyle blurts out, "What's wrong with you, man? Are you *trying* to lose?"

Keeping his cool, Gideon responds, "I just think it would be better to respect the natural distinctions between our social groupings."

Kyle can only stare.

"What I mean is," Gideon continues, "why should we, the physically underdeveloped, bring down the scores of genuine athletes like yourselves? If we're ever going to overcome our nerdish tendencies and achieve physical excellence, it won't be through an unnatural association with our betters but through hard work and discipline. In the meantime, we fully expect you to put us in our proper place."

Kyle's only rebuttal is, " … you're going down, poindexter."

"Yes, I most certainly am."

"We're gonna cream you."

"I look forward to being creamed. Failure is an excellent teacher."

Confused, Kyle looks to his friends for backup, but they've got nothing. Finally he turns away and grabs a basketball.

The whistle is blown, and the game begins. Gideon starts with the ball. He immediately throws it to Dwight.

Dwight wants nothing to do with it. He throws it to Pablo Gonzales.

Pablo is mulled over by Joe Munson, who picks up the ball.

Joe throws to Kyle, who's standing at the three-point line. Kyle jumps, shoots, and scores.

Gideon claps his hands. "Good job, Kyle! And way to go, Pablo. Everyone's a winner."

The ball is thrown back to Gideon for the next play, which has a similar theme, only this time it's Elvin Banks who's knocked to the floor.

As Kyle scores another three points, Gideon helps Elvin to his feet. "Good effort. Way to go, team."

Kyle rolls his eyes.

For the third play, Gideon holds on to the ball, dribbling straight toward the other hoop. He only makes it about six feet before running into Matt Wilson. Though Matt makes no attempt to steal the ball.

Coming in on Gideon's left is Koa Kamaka.

Gideon glances at the bleachers. Coach Griffith is chuckling to himself as he watches a video on his phone.

Matt grabs one of Gideon's arms. Koa grabs the other.

As the ball bounces away, Gideon forces a smile. "Please, my friends, show me how it's done."

All three of them turn to an approaching Kyle.

Kyle looks disgusted. He shakes his head. "This isn't even fun anymore." He picks up the ball and dribbles to the other end of the court.

Meanwhile Gideon's captors look at each other, shrug, and release their grip.

"Come on, guys," says Gideon, "I thought you were going to teach me a valuable lesson."

And so the game continues. When the score is sixty-nine to zero, a yawning Coach Griffith puts an end to the misery.

With a clear line between jocks and nerds, it's back to old times. Only one thing is different: Gideon. *Am I the only one having a good time?* he wonders.

Glancing up at the oblong window, he sees the gray lady. Of course he sees her. But unlike usual, she's smiling.

Gideon can't help but smile himself.

TEACHER'S ASSISTANT

Before entering Fashion Merchandising, Gideon stops in the boy's bathroom to ensure that his hair is perfect, his shirt tucked in, his belt properly aligned. Even then, he's the first to arrive in the classroom. He walks straight up to Ms. Primple, who's reading at her desk.

She looks up, her eyes bright. "Why, hello."

"I … enjoyed our club today."

She studies him. "What's gotten into you?"

Gideon checks over his shoulder to make sure that no one else is listening. "I thought about your offer, and I accept."

"You accept?"

"I want to be your prophet."

She narrows her eyes. "Why?"

"For purely selfish reasons. You give me what I want, I return the favor."

"So my little bribe paid off."

Gideon's heart sinks, though he knows he shouldn't be surprised. "You could say that."

"I still have my doubts about you, but Norma has been saying good things."

"Has she?"

"She said you've been shaping up in your classes, especially P.E."

"I've tried."

Ms. Primple gives him a good stare. "I could use an assistant in this class. That will be your first assignment."

"What do I do?"

"Whatever I tell you to."

The conversation abruptly ends when other students enter the classroom. Gideon joins them, walking to the back of the classroom.

"No," says Ms. Primple, "you'll be sitting by me."

Gideon nods, taking the nearest desk.

Apparently Ms. Primple has run out of actual curriculum, for when the bell rings, she gives the class the familiar assignment of critiquing each other's fashion. Then she adds, "And I'd like to ask my new assistant, Mister Greenwich, to lead the discussion." She then leans back in her chair and resumes her place in her magazine.

As puzzled girls whisper, Gideon walks to the front of the class. He hears the familiar sounds of awe and wonder at his gelled hair and color-coordinated wardrobe. Though the position is perfect, he tries not to stare at Cynthia ... not an easy thing to do. "Thank you, Ms. Primple."

He surveys the class. So many pretty girls and perfect wardrobes. Then there's the back of the room. Over purple sweat pants, Dwight is wearing a *Battlestar Galactica* t-shirt. The words are faded, and the shirt has been washed so many times that it's shrunken well above his belly button.

Dwight shakes his head, the message clear: *Don't you dare say my name.*

Then there's Wanda. On top of her *pink* sweat pants is a white t-shirt featuring an ironed-on cat and sparkling sequins. She wore this same shirt in fifth grade. Of course, her hair is a mess, her face without makeup, and her eyes ...

Yep, she's still mad at me. "To start off," Gideon says, "let's talk about ..." Getting desperate, he takes another look at the frightened faces before him, wondering who scares him the least. "Janelle Sprankle."

Janelle looks beyond nervous. Sitting in a corner, she's always kept to herself.

"The orange skirt and white blouse go well together. Good job, Janelle."

Janelle makes an audible sigh of relief.

Following some light applause, Gideon glances back at Ms. Primple. She's buried in her magazine. "However ..."

Janelle's eyes widen.

" ... while the colors are well balanced, the overall effect lacks a certain ... chutzpah."

"A what?" asks Janelle.

"Orange is a very bold color, and no offense, Janelle, but you're just not a very bold person. If I were you, I'd play it safe and wear brown."

As a blushing Janelle buries her face in her arm, Gideon glances back at Ms. Primple, who gives an apathetic nod.

"Next up," he continues, " ... Monica Hawley."

Now Monica looks terrified.

"Well, Monica, I have to say you've done it again. The frills, the braided belt, those tight shorts. Dynamite."

Monica smiles.

"Only ..."

Monica stops breathing.

"I hate to say it, but ... those shorts kind of make your butt look big."

Again Gideon glances back at Ms. Primple, who's looking up from her magazine, her interest piqued. He continues, "You know I mean it as a friend, right?"

Monica nods. "Of course." But she can't keep his gaze.

"I could be wrong. What do you think, Dwight?"

Dwight nearly falls out of his chair. He and Gideon exchanges looks.

Gideon mouths the words, "Trust me."

After a long pause, Dwight stands up. He takes a good look at Monica. "I'm sorry, Monica, but Gideon's right. Big butt."

Sitting next to Dwight, an embarrassed Wanda is the next to bury her face.

Gideon surveys the class. Not one girl dares look back. "Kimberly Fenner," he announces, and this time there are sighs of relief from the girls who are lucky enough to not be Kimberly. "I like the stripes. I really do. But horizontal? Sorry, babe …"

"Babe?" Kimberly says with disgust.

"Babe," Gideon repeats, holding his ground. In the end, he wins the staring contest. "Do you really want people to see you as a hot dog? Think twice next time and go hamburger. Am I right, Dwight?"

"You are so right," says Dwight, his fear giving way to a smile.

Like clockwork, down goes Kimberly's head.

"Next," Gideon continues, "Joan Cooper."

As Gideon approaches her, Joan is quick to say, "You can just skip me."

"Joan," Gideon repeats. "Joan, Joan, Joan. I love the flower patterns. But you, my friend, are not a flower. You're a dragon."

Joan scowls. "I am *not* a dragon."

"Oh, but you are. Strong and fierce. What you need isn't flowers but spikes and chains."

Ms. Primple stands up in her chair. "That's enough, Gideon."

Every last girl is hiding her face. Gideon has never felt more powerful. "I'm sorry, Ms. Primple, but they've gotta hear it as it is."

Monica looks up, her eyes pink. "He's right. These shorts *do* make my butt look big. I knew they did. I just knew it."

Ms. Primple says, "Those shorts are fine. There's nothing wrong with horizontal stripes, and Joan is not a dragon. You may sit down, Gideon."

But Gideon doesn't budge. "Who are you going to believe," he asks the class, "two guys" — he gestures between himself and Dwight — "who totally notice these types of things … or another girl?"

Kimberly is sobbing.

Ms. Primple says, her voice growing cold, "You have overstepped your bounds, Mister Greenwich. Sit down."

Still Gideon ignores her. "You know what guys really want?"

Every last girl looks up.

" … ponchos."

"*Ponchos?*" the room seems to echo.

"Girls look totally hot in ponchos."

A few girls start taking notes.

Meanwhile a glaring Ms. Primple steps right up to Gideon. "That is not true. Girls do not look hot in ponchos."

But no one seems to be listening to her. Kimberly asks, "What else do guys like?"

Gideon smiles, glancing at Wanda. "Of course, every guy is different, but if there's one thing that's universally attractive on girls … it's sweatpants and t-shirts featuring cats. Write that down."

The room is filled with the noise of girls unzipping backpacks and pulling out notebooks.

"This is heresy!" Ms. Primple shouts.

"Is it?" Gideon turns to her. "Or are *you* heresy? You're supposed to be the goddess of fashion, and here you are wearing a beige cardigan over a charcoal shirt."

Ms. Primple gasps, then takes a step back. "There's nothing wrong with that."

"Maybe not last month. But have you even read the latest addition of *Vainglory Magazine*? Beige on charcoal is an unforgivable sin!"

"I read every edition of *Vainglory*. Show me where it says that."

"I don't have to show you anything. You know why? Because now I'm the fashion authority around here."

"Says who?"

"Says the class. They actually *care* about what I have to say. And I say ponchos are in, cardigans are out, and horizontal stripes make you look fat."

"You know nothing about fashion."

"Fashion isn't about knowledge, it's about looks. You've either got it or you don't, and *you* don't."

Looking as horrified as the girls, Ms. Primple turns to the class. "Tell him there's nothing wrong with beige on charcoal."

But no one backs her up. Instead, Joan asks, "Where do they sell ponchos?"

Furious, Ms. Primple pushes over an empty desk. "Are you even listening to me?"

Now Dwight is walking forward, his eyes on Ms. Primple. "Face it, you're a walking contradiction. You, of all people, are out … of … style."

Ms. Primple backs up, waving her hands, her eyes wide. She crashes into the wall …

… and explodes.

FUGITIVES

The class covers their eyes as a shower of sparks sprays over them. When they look again, Ms. Primple is no more. The room fills with chatter as the class tries to make sense of what just happened.

There's a change in the air. Gideon can feel it. Everything seems *lighter*. Everyone looks relieved. Yet there's confusion.

Cynthia turns to Gideon, her smiling face gone. In fact, she looks sick. (He's seen that look before, in Doug.) "I can't believe I kissed you."

The door bursts open, revealing the teacher from the next room down, Mr. Purkey. "We heard a bang. Is everything all right?"

Joan has a different look in her eyes, a look Gideon has also seen before. Reminding him of Kyle Slater at the pep rally, Joan points to Gideon and Dwight. "They … they *killed* Ms. Primple."

Gideon turns to Dwight. "Run."

Within seconds, the school has become a mass of confusion. As crowds of students and teachers gather around, Gideon and Dwight bolt for the front doors of the school.

Soon they're running down the sidewalk of Eastward Drive, the school well behind them. Gideon is alright, but Dwight is a big guy. Between gasps, he says, "I can't run any farther."

Gideon looks around. "We'll take a back road."

Taking turn after turn, they lose themselves in a neighborhood. Their only goal is to get lost.

Dwight says, "My house isn't far from here."

"The police might find us at your house."

"We can't run forever. What are we gonna do?"

"I don't know."

And so they keep running.

Dwight, regaining his breath, asks, "How did you know that would happen?"

"What?"

"The explosion!"

"I finally realized what happened with Sportacus. He didn't have a button on his chest. He exploded because I made him look stupid in front of the entire school, which is an unforgivable sin for a god of cool."

"Why do you call them that?"

"It just fits."

"And with Ms. Primple?"

"Same thing. She was only a goddess because we *gave* her power. That's how it was in ancient times, and that's how it is today. But we can take that power back, and when we did, it destroyed her … literally."

"*How* do we take the power back? By fighting them?"

"By outthinking them. All we had to do was back her into a logical corner. The gods hate logic."

"Are they really gods?"

"They certainly want us to think they are."

"You're something else, Gideon. I'm sorry I doubted you."

"I'm sorry I had to drag you into this, though I'm glad to have you."

A siren blares a sudden warning as a police car turns a corner. Officer Milton is inside, a look of triumph in his eyes. *Got you at last*, his smiling face seems to say.

Gideon contemplates running, but he knows that Dwight won't be able to make it. With a sigh, he puts his hands in the air.

Doing likewise, Dwight whispers, "How did he find us so fast?"

"How else?" Gideon replies. "Supernatural assistance."

After a long, silent ride, the car stops at the youth detention center, a compound of brick and steel. There's a chain link fence, barbed wire, and … a cell phone tower.

Interesting.

Officer Milton opens the door, and Gideon and Dwight lumber onto the pavement. Their hands are cuffed behind their backs, the hard metal digging into their wrists.

Once inside the building, Gideon actually has to shield his eyes from the florescent lights overhead. Aside from the electric buzzing, the place is quiet. Young inmates, wearing bright, orange uniforms, walk in single file, trailed by security guards, their steps in perfect harmony. No one talks. No one smiles.

Officer Milton removes the handcuffs, and a security guard confiscates their keys, wallets, and phones.

Gideon and Dwight are led through metal detectors and through one locked door after another. Their first destination is in front of a blue screen, where a woman photographs them. Next their thumbprints are scanned. Finally, Officer Milton locks them in a small room with a telephone and a thick window.

"You each have five minutes to call home," he announces before leaving the room and locking the door.

Gideon whispers, "Should we tell them you're eighteen?"

"Are you crazy?" Dwight whispers back. "Then they'll put me in a *real* jail."

"They're gonna find out eventually."

"Not if we get out of here first."

"How can we possibly get out of here?"

"If you can defeat two gods, I'm sure you can find a way."

"Dwight, we've been arrested. They're going to accuse us of murder. This is everything you feared."

But Dwight is smiling. "I don't care anymore. I've been asleep for too long. Now I'm ready to fight."

"I thought *you* were the logical one."

"Dude, this is freaking awesome. We're taking on the forces of evil. We're freeing our minds, and I've never felt more alive."

"You should probably keep it down. There's no saying who's listening."

"Sorry," Dwight says in a quieter voice, "it's just been so long since I felt that my life had a purpose."

"Well, I guess we better call our parents now."

"They'll find out soon enough. Right now there's more important things to do. We should call … Doug. Yeah, he'll understand."

"Doug?"

"Maybe he could help us find a way out of here."

"I thought you didn't like Doug."

"I changed my mind."

Gideon shrugs. "I guess it's worth a try. But I don't know his …" Having a vague recollection, he reaches into his back pocket. Sure enough, he retrieves a crumpled business card that reads:

Douglas W. Rock, Concert Violinist

"I'm so glad I never change my pants," says Gideon.

"Eat that, Ms. Primple," says Dwight.

Gideon calls Doug. The dial tone rings and rings, and Gideon is about to hang up when, finally, there's an answer. Far from the silence of Doug's bedroom, there's the noise of a crowd and heavy breaths.

"Doug?" Gideon asks.

"Gid." Doug's voice is strained, exhausted.

"Are you all right?"

"I slept through the first half of school. I was gonna stay home, but something told me I needed to be here. I was right. It's crazy, here, man. I'm doing what I can, but … we need you."

"What's going on?"

"It's the gods. They're … taking over." Someone screams in the background.

"What?"

"I …"

Then there's the voice of a woman, not far from Doug. "Douglas Rock. Hand over the phone." There's no mistaking the gray lady.

It's hard to make out what happens next. There's grunts and struggles, a loud crack, and then … nothing. The call is over.

"What's happening?" Dwight demands, trying in vain to listen in.

"I don't know," says Gideon, hanging up the receiver, "but somehow we gotta get back to the school."

Now Dwight picks up the receiver. "I'll call Wanda. She's the only other person who would understand."

"Wanda? But —"

Dwight leans forward, pressing the receiver against his ear. "Shh … Wanda? Wanda, can you hear me? It's Dwight." As he listens to someone talk, his face pales.

Gideon leans in close. He hears someone say, " … and we're taking her somewhere safe" — the voice of a woman. "That is, unless you and your friend decide to interfere. Then she won't be safe at all."

Gideon whispers, "What's happening?"

"Someone's kidnapping Wanda," Dwight whispers back.

The woman continues. "Though I'm glad you called, because I didn't know how else we were going to send you the message. Stay away from the school, and no one gets hurt. Come back, and your girlfriend dies."

The call ends suddenly, and Dwight hangs up the receiver.

"Who was that?" Gideon asks.

Dwight shrugs. "Poor Wanda. We have to do something."

"Like what, report the incident to the police? Given the circumstances, I don't think that's going to jive."

"Do you think it was one of the gods?"

Gideon shrugs. "She did sound familiar. Maybe it's the goddess of music. Muza."

"Why would they drag Wanda into this? We're already locked up!"

"They must be scared out of their minds. We killed two of them." Counting on his fingers, Gideon thinks of the gray lady, the fat guy, and Muza. "That leaves only three."

Dwight has an epiphany. "Or maybe they know something we don't."

"Like what?"

"The way out of here!"

"Come on, man, you know there's no way out."

"Maybe we just need to think like the gods."

"We can think all we want, but that's not going to change our reality."

"Unless it does."

"What?"

"You say the gray lady is everywhere you go, right?"

"Yeah, so?"

"So she must have a way of getting around," — Dwight places a hand against the bricks — "ways that aren't constrained by walls."

"What does that have to do with thinking?"

"Maybe that which we call reality is nothing more than a state of mind."

"Dwight, the laws of physics can't be broken."

"Including the *Law of Observation*."

"What's that?"

"You're taking Physics this year with Mr. Periwinkle, right? Haven't you heard of the double slit experiments?"

"Well … yeah, but —"

"Maybe we only *think* we're trapped in this room, because every time we look that way, we see a wall. But so long as we're not *observing* the wall, the atoms aren't actually there."

"Dwight, Wanda's in trouble. We need a *real* solution."

"Do you have a better idea?"

"No."

"Then we're gonna close our eyes and walk through that wall."

Dwight leads the way, and with nothing to lose, Gideon eventually follows. Dwight smacks into the wall. So does Gideon.

"It didn't work," says Dwight.

"No, it didn't," says Gideon.

"What do we lack?"

"Common sense?"

"No, I mean … there must be another law we're overlooking.

What's the opposite of observation?"

"Ignorance?"

"Yes, the *Law of Ignorance!* It didn't work, because we still *think* the wall is there. We must first achieve a state of utter ignorance. We must lose all grasps of reality."

Gideon throws up his arms. "We don't have time for this! Where do you think they took her?"

Taken aback, the excitement drain's from Dwight's face. "Well … come to think of it, I did hear a train in the background."

"That could be anywhere. Do you remember anything else?"

Dwight closes his eyes. He's silent for a moment. "No, the train was nearby. I distinctly remember hearing it moving on the tracks."

"That could still be anywhere."

"I also heard bells."

"Bells?"

"You know, the warning bells at an intersection."

"Hmm …"

"And unless I'm mistaken, I can only think of one place in town where the train tracks cross the street."

Gideon looks up. "Fifth West?"

"By the old farmer's market."

"That's a bad side of town."

"Yeah."

"What do you think they're doing to her?"

The door is unlocked as Officer Milton steps in. "Time's up." Standing next to him is a security guard with a fat neck. Judging by the girth of his tattooed arms, the man could probably kill them each with one hand if he wanted to. "Clyde will take you from here."

Clyde grins.

Their final destination is on the other side of an automatic, steel door: a small room with brick walls, two bunk beds, and a camera in the corner of the ceiling.

"Get cozy, gentlemen," says Clyde. He steps out of the cell and closes the automatic door, sealing them to their confinement.

Dwight collapses onto the nearest bed, rusty springs creaking beneath him. "So, any bright ideas yet?"

Gideon collapses on the other bed, grateful for a chance to rest. It's been so long since he slept. "What do you want from me?"

"If you can outthink gods, you can get us out of here."

"I'm nothing special, Dwight. All I did was stand up to them, just like you did. The war isn't over, but we've lost the battle. Now all we can do is wait."

"When Wanda needs us?"

"The only reason the gods endured my antics as long as they did was because they hoped I would defect to their side. Now that they've realized I won't, we're going to feel the full brunt of their power. They're supernatural beings. We're mortals. We have to pick our battles."

"Is that what we're destined to do? Nothing?"

"Nothing's destined. The universe is random."

"No way. If there's bad gods, there must be good gods. Something or someone helped us defeat those imposters, and that someone is going to help us escape."

Starting at his scalp and moving down his spine, Gideon feels chills come over his body. It never occurred to him that he hadn't been fighting his battles alone. "I don't know, man."

They're startled by the sound of creaking springs as a third voice says, "Will you guys keep it down?"

BULA

Gideon climbs off the bottom bunk to get a better look at the top bunk. What they had mistaken for a pile of blankets is actually a body ... a big body. He knows the face. "Bula."

Half asleep, Bula opens one eye. Though groggy, he manages a weak smile. "*Aloha ke akua*," he says with his Hawaiian accent.

Gideon is at a loss. He turns to Dwight. "It's Bula, from the football team." Then to Bula, "What ... what are you doing here?"

The Hawaiian rolls over, facing the wall. "I stole a library book."

Dwight says incredulously, "They put you in here for a *library* book?"

"You could say I'm a repeat offender."

"Why didn't you just check it out?"

"That would defeat the purpose."

"What purpose?"

"The ways of Bula are mysterious before men. Now will you keep it down? I'm trying to sleep."

"In the middle of the day?"

"You're obviously new here. Once they put you to work, you'll sleep every chance you can get."

Gideon says, "We'll keep it down. But first I just want to say thanks. You saved me at the pep rally. You saved Cynthia and I at detention."

"It was nothing."

"Why did you do it?"

"Because you are my brother."

"You hardly know me."

"As soon as you joined the team, I could tell you were a fighter."

"You've got the wrong guy."

"No. Any big guy can push people around. But when a little guy joins the team, that's something else. And when you stood up to that coach, I realized you were the best kind of fighter: you fight the system."

"What system?"

Bula sighs and throws off his blanket. He rolls over to face his prison mates. "You know, the system of the mind."

An excited Dwight slaps Gideon's shoulder. "He's one of us."

Still smiling, Gideon says to Bula, "You're not like the other jocks. You know something, don't you?"

Bula shrugs. "I need a Slurpee."

"What?"

"From Seven-eleven. Do you know how long it's been since I've had a Slurpee?"

"No …"

"As soon as I get out of here, I'm gonna buy a Slurpee."

Bula covers himself with the blanket and rolls over again.

Dwight whispers to Gideon, "He helped you escape twice, and now we just happen to run into him? This is what I'm talking about; it's fate, man. You gotta get him to talk."

Gideon nods. "Umm … Bula … about the system of the mind …"

"I don't wanna talk about it."

"We don't mean to bother you, but … a friend of ours is in trouble."

Bula rolls over, his hard face softening. "The fat girl?"

Biting his lip, Gideon nods.

"What's wrong?" Bula asks.

"She was kidnapped?"

"By who?"

"This might sound a little crazy, but we call them the gods. They pose as teachers, but they're not. They're powerful, and they try to control our minds."

Bula sits up, his face dead serious. "They didn't send you here?"

"What?"

"Ever since I arrived, every counselor and case worker has tried to convince me that I'm crazy. They want to tell me how to think and to doubt what I know. They're all being controlled. And when you started asking questions, I feared you were also part of the system."

Gideon shakes his head. "We're on your side."

Bula thinks for a moment, looking them over. "I'm an outsider. I never belonged in a clique. I'm not a jock, I'm not a nerd, I'm just Bula. And that gave me a perspective. I could see things others couldn't. I could see the system and how everyone was a prisoner. I thought I was the only one who knew, and I tried to fight it."

"How?"

"They want you to look straight ahead. They don't like it when you look around. So I looked around."

"What did you see?"

"Layers."

"Layers?"

"Lots of them."

Gideon turns to Dwight. Dwight shrugs.

"They only tell you about the one in front of us," Bula continues. "That's why we're prisoners. But if we could just step to the side, there's no walls."

Dwight jabs Gideon with his elbow, nodding.

Gideon asks, "Do you mean like … parallel universes?"

"Something like that," says Bula. "Do you want to know why I'm really here? I didn't care about the library book. I wanted to see if I could pass between layers. If I could just get past the detectors without tripping the alarm, I would know it's possible. It didn't work the first time or the second time. On the fifth time, a police officer was waiting for me."

"But … *how* could you pass between layers?"

"The Hawaiians call it lüng. The Hindus call it prana. The Chinese call it chi."

"Which is?"

Dwight says, "Come on, Gid. You've never heard of the power of the kung fu master, the unseen energy that flows around everything?"

"Well," says Gideon, "I did learn that almost seventy percent of the universe is made of a mysterious something called dark energy. Could that be the same thing?"

Bula nods. "Maybe. All I know is that it's real, but most people don't notice it, because they're only aware of the physical layer. To feel it, you have to be in touch with your spiritual side."

"And then what?" asks Gideon, his eyes glued on Bula.

"Then you're in control, because the chi has power over everything. It can move the physical layer. It can move *you*. It responds to your mind."

Dwight slugs Gideon again.

Finally Gideon slugs him back. "Cut that out." He turns back to Bula. "So why didn't it work?"

Bula rolls onto his back, staring up at the ceiling just inches above him. "I don't know."

Dwight says, "*I* know. It's the Law of Observation. You were so focused on the detectors that it forced the molecules to stay in place. If you would have just closed your eyes, they wouldn't have been there."

Gideon slaps his forehead. "No, Dwight, that's not how it works."

Bula says, "I think he's on to something. Maybe I wanted it so much that I trapped myself in the physical layer. Maybe I just needed to let go."

Having another epiphany, Dwight asks, "Do you think these layers ever intersect?"

"Maybe," says Bula.

Gideon says, "I know this sounds wrong coming from *me*, but don't you think this is getting a little crazy?"

Dwight, who isn't listening, stands up and starts feeling along the walls.

"What are you doing?" Gideon asks.

"I'm looking for an intersection between layers," says Dwight, "a rip in space-time. There's gotta be a way out of here."

"Oh my gosh. This isn't going to get us anywhere."

Meanwhile Bula hops down from the top bunk. He joins Dwight in feeling the walls.

Dwight says, "Come on, Gideon, you're supposed to be our leader. Help us."

But Gideon has had enough. He sits down on the bed and just watches, bemused. Though staring at the walls of the tiny room reminds him of something. He recalls being alone with Ms. Primple, who transformed before his eyes. But the transformation affected more than just her. The very walls seemed to warp around her.

But what *caused* that warp? Gravitation? Electromagnetism? She had no tools, she said no magic words, all she did was *think*. Could it be as Mr. Periwinkle mentioned, the theory that mind itself is a fundamental force, the fifth irreducible interaction?

Even if that were true, surely there's differences between the mind of a god and the mind of a mortal like him. But as he ponders on what those differences could be, he can only think of one: the gods are less intelligent. Though the thought is crazy, ridiculous, insane, he can't help but entertain Dwight's idea. If the gods can do it, then why not him?

During his previous adventures with jocks, when his life was in danger, he felt a clarity of mind that empowered him to think and move faster. When, on the night of the fight with Westward, he was alone at the park, for a brief moment, he felt as if he could control the elements. What if the very power of the gods was already within him, and all he needed to do was figure out how to unlock it?

Could it really be possible that he could beat them at their own game, the game of the mind? Whether it is or not, what does he have to lose? Wanda needs him.

Having an epiphany of his own, Gideon says, "Guys, I think there may be a way out of here."

LAYERS

Gideon joins them at one of the walls, feeling, searching, until …

"There." He bends down, pointing to a small vent cover.

Dwight looks less than impressed. "Somehow I don't think we're going to fit through that."

"The gods have the power to warp physical space," says Gideon. "I've seen it with my own eyes. And they do it with their *minds*. If we can just learn to think like them, maybe we could expand this vent."

"Now you're talking." Satisfied to have Gideon take over, Dwight resumes his seat on the bed. "Ready … go."

"I didn't say I know *how* to think like them."

"It's like Bula said. Connect to your spiritual side, find the chi, and push it against the wall. Oh yeah, and don't think about it. *Law of Ignorance*, remember?"

Bula places a hand on Gideon's shoulder. "I believe in you." Then he also climbs up and gets comfortable on his bed. He and Dwight watch and wait.

Gideon rolls his eyes and turns back to the little vent on the wall. He takes a seat. He stares at the metal slits.

"Are you thinking?" Dwight asks.

"Yes," says Gideon.

"Well stop it."

Gideon closes his eyes. He tries not to think.

"You're still thinking, aren't you?"

"How could I respond to your questions if I wasn't thinking?"

"Point taken. My lips are sealed."

Keeping his eyes shut, Gideon imagines the vent cover. He imagines the chi between him and it. He breathes the stuff in. The power flows through him. In his mind's eye, he's wearing a white karate gee, his bare chest exposed and well-oiled. As a tai chi master, he gathers the energy with his hands. He rolls it into a glowing ball. He pushes the ball against the vent. The mystical power infuses with the atoms, providing a direct line to his mind.

Grow, he orders. The command ripples through the stream of chi, pushing against the metal. *Grow!* Now the atoms are rippling, the molecules expanding. The iron cover, the aluminum duct, and the bricks all warp outward.

It's a nice image, but when he opens his eyes, nothing has changed. Perhaps he was thinking too hard. He tries again, and this time he tries not to think about anything. If the cloud of his consciousness happens to collide with the spirit atoms of the vent, so be it. But he doesn't will it. He doesn't will anything. He is an empty room, a blank canvas. He is not thinking.

It turns out that trying not to think is identical to thinking.

When the door of the cell opens, and Clyde the security guard ushers them out, Gideon has lost track of time. He may have been sitting there for hours.

"Come on," orders Clyde, leading the way through another bright hallway lit by florescent lights. He leads them in a single file line, with Bula at the rear. Bula walks with his head hanging low, off in his own world.

Dwight makes sure Clyde isn't listening in, then whispers, "Did it work?"

Gideon shakes his head. "No matter how hard we think or don't think," he whispers back, "the fact is, we're not gods."

"Psalms eighty-two six."

"Huh?"

"*I have said, Ye are gods, and all of you are children of the most high.*"

"Since when do you recite Bible verses?"

"I can't tune out everything in Sunday school."

Clyde glares at them.

Awhile later, Dwight whispers even more quietly, "You can do this."

While Bula is taken somewhere else, Gideon and Dwight are escorted into a small auditorium. The seats are nice and comfortable. Clyde stands by while they watch a video with a friendly-looking man in a suit. The man says:

> *Welcome to the Bright Horizons Juvenile Correctional Facility. This will be a pivotal time in your lives for discovering your true potential and developing the habits that will help you become productive members of society.*

There's inspiring music while smiling teenagers sweep floors, wash windows, and pick up trash along the highway. The same teenagers, who have great teeth and are remarkably diverse in ethnicity, explain how cool it is to follow the rules. There are many rules: no running, no touching, no unapproved talking or singing.

Gideon wonders how much money these actors made. Getting paid to have nice teeth would certainly be better than working in call centers or fast food. He'll have to look into the opportunities when he gets out of here. Ms. Primple seems like the type of person who would know people with nice teeth. Maybe she could set him up with the right contacts.

Oh wait, I blew her up ...

Yet in his mind's eye, she's still there, watching him on her throne.

How did she do it?

One moment she was a beautiful temptress. Then the walls warped around her, and she was Sportacus. The change was instantaneous. There was no sleight of hand, no costume change. As far as Gideon could tell, she didn't *do* anything.

He can't get the image out of his head. Her throne was golden, her gown red, her eyeshadow blue.

Eyeshadow? How did he observe eyeshadow unless ... *That's right*. She was closing her eyes just prior to the transformation. Far from *observing*, she tuned out her surroundings, entering a state of concentration.

But I tried that.

He whispers to Dwight, "I don't care what the Bible says, we're just not gods."

"Mark five thirty-six," Dwight whispers back.

"What's that?"

"*Be not afraid, only believe.*"

"This isn't about fear, it's about physical impossibilities."

From the back of the room, Clyde shouts, "Watch the movie!"

On the screen, a teary-eyed girl is bearing her testimony about how the Bright Horizons Juvenile Correctional Facility changed her life.

Supposing it's possible for Gideon to do what the gods do, what is he missing?

He ponders this throughout his meeting with the case worker. He nods his head and says what he's supposed to say, but his mind isn't there. It's somewhere high above, wondering, searching.

Are you there? Can you hear me?

When a mop is placed in his hands, he wets down the floor, but his mind isn't there. It's somewhere between Eastward High, ancient Babylon, and the ethereal heaven above.

Will you help me?

There's no response from above, so he looks down at the floor. There's something there, hidden beneath the grime. He mops and mops until the glistening tiles reveal the reflection of his weary, blood-shot eyes.

Hello.

Could *observing* really affect the physical world? He closes his eyes. He opens them. The reflection is still there. Only it's not *really* there, not like *he's* there. It's an illusion. Maybe the entire physical world is an illusion, a facade to something deeper.

Maybe it's not observing as in *seeing* that's the problem but observing as in *obeying*. After all, seeing is believing ... believing is *accepting* ... and accepting is ... *submitting*?

Gideon rubs his forehead. Either he's thinking too hard, and he's on the brink of insanity, or he's onto something brilliant. Regardless, he finds himself sinking further down the rabbit hole.

What if for the majority of his life, because he accepted his reality, he's been subjected to the whims of the gods? Has he, like the atoms around him, been manipulated? If so, then Dwight's theory was dead wrong. Ignorance wouldn't be the solution, it would be the *problem*. The true opposite of observation, or submission, wouldn't be ignorance but *control*.

We either submit ... or we control.

Could it really be that simple? It's as if there's only two categories in the universe: things that act and things that are acted upon. But what makes the difference? *Magic, power, force ...*

Intelligence. The gods control the weak-minded by telling them how to think and act. But when people start thinking for themselves, the gods have *no* power. It's simply a matter of intelligence.

But that can't be right. Judging by the less than intelligent antics of Sportacus and Ms. Primple, the gods clearly aren't the sharpest tools in the shed. Yet maybe they know enough. They know the rules, they see the layers, they know there's a deeper reality than what meets the eye, and that knowledge, in itself, is power ... tremendous power. It's as if the world is trapped in a cave, and a god is nothing more than someone who's stepped out of that cave. You don't have to be good, you don't have to be evil, you just have to get out of the cave.

Gideon looks deep into the eyes of his reflection on the floor. *How could I know what they know?*

He still wonders this while chewing pasta primavera in the cafeteria; for prison food, it's not bad — in fact, it puts Eastward's cuisine to shame.

Dwight, wolfing down a second cup of cream-topped, green jello, asks, "Figured it out yet?"

Outside voices are annoying. Don't they know Gideon's trying to concentrate? "Figured what out?"

"How to get out of here."

"I have realized one thing."

"And that is?"

"I was wrong. I didn't think there was a way out of here, and that was exactly what the gods wanted me to think. Of course there's a way. There's always a way."

"Excellent. And that is?"

"I don't know, but I think believing is the first step."

"Do you *really* believe there's a way?"

"No, but I'm trying."

The next thing Gideon knows, he's scrubbing the char out of an oven. With each stroke he peels away a layer of corrosion, gradually revealing the clear metal below. *Layers.*

Let go of the cruft, Gideon. Find your center.

Next he's in a classroom, where an old woman is giving a lecture on social etiquette. Pointing to a projection of a sad-looking rabbit, she says, "You're never too old or too cool to say you're sorry."

She's right. Suddenly feeling an overwhelming desire to let go of his burdens, Gideon stands up and announces before the class, "I'm sorry."

The instructor gives him a sideways stare. "You have something you want to say?"

"Wanda was right," says Gideon. "I was rude and inconsiderate."

"Thank you for sharing."

Gideon resumes his seat as Dwight rolls his eyes.

While brushing his teeth, Gideon scrubs harder than ever before. The plaque must go. Even while lying in bed, his work is far from over. He sifts through thoughts, dreams, memories, everything that makes him Gideon Greenwich. He remembers the time he made a disparaging comment about his sister's braces.

I'm sorry.

He remembers the time he called the new boy at school a poo-poo head.

I'm sorry.

He sees himself putting on a trench coat and sunglasses, hoping, in some crazy way, that girls will notice him. But it was a lie, a fa-cade. The true Gideon ran deeper than eccentric fashion and bad hygiene, deeper than video games and comic books, deeper than every label and boundary. The true Gideon has something to do with hitting Kyle Slater.

I actually like football.

Basketball, he's still warming up to, though he's up for the challenge. He wants to be so much more than a nerd. He wants to conquer the world. Suddenly he's never felt more Gideon Greenwich, and none of this would have happened if it weren't for the gray lady. However bizarre, he finds himself … *loving* her.

He knows that, in reality, he's lying in bed. He knows it's just his imagination — perhaps he's already dreaming — but for a moment it's as if he's back at the vent cover, which is barely visible in the dim light. No more a mystery or an exertion, he simply wills it to grow larger, and it does. The wall bows outward, expanding, and the vent nearly doubles in size. For a moment he feels the atoms pushing back, resisting the change, but he holds them in place until the resistance fades away.

I'm in control.

The second part of his dream is a make out session with Cynthia McDaniels. Then, inexplicably, he's kissing Wanda, and somehow he's okay with that.

WARP

His eyes snap open to the sound of a rattling bell. It's so loud, so cruel. A second later, bright lights flip on, intensifying the torture.

Springs creak overhead, and Bula — all of him — falls to his feet. "Clyde will come in five minutes," he announces, banging the posts of their beds. "If you're not ready, you'll be sorry."

Gideon rolls out of bed. Dwight, however, just rolls over, moaning.

Gideon feels Dwight's pain. Yet he also feels … peace. Somehow, though he's locked up, though Wanda is in trouble, and though the forces of evil are pitted against him, however crazy, he knows everything will be okay. He doesn't know *how* he knows this; he just knows it. Maybe it has something to do with that lingering sensation in the back of his mind, an abstract memory of something wonderful. Whatever it was, he wants to hold on to the feeling.

And yet, as the memories of yesterday come back, the wild ride that got him where he is, it all seems thoroughly insane. As if blowing up a god wasn't enough, there were those crazy thoughts about parallel universes, inner spirits, and chi. Somehow he thought it all connected. Now he can't make heads or tails of it.

Donning another bright, orange shirt, he looks in a mirror. There's something different in those eyes. Whereas yesterday they were weary, frightened, and overwhelmed, now they're confident. They *know* something.

"*What* do you know?" Gideon asks himself.

"Huh?" says Bula.

"Nothing." Then Gideon notices something else in the mirror. The vent is much large than it was before. The wall behind him is …

warped.

He goes to the vent and falls to his knees. He feels the impossibly huge, metal slits. And from the mere touch of his hand, misshapen screws slide out of skewed holes, and the cover falls and clatters on the floor. "Umm, guys, you may want to look at this."

Bula joins him, his face lighting up. "My friend, you did it."

"*I* did it?"

"Who else?"

"I … uh …"

Bula takes Gideon's arm and embraces him. "*Mahalo nui loa*. I help you. You help me."

Gideon pats his back.

"Now let's go." Bula goes to Dwight and snaps the blanket off of him.

"Hey!" Dwight protests. "What —" Then he sees what's drawing their attention. "Oh …"

"Clyde will be here any moment," says Bula. "Come on!" Always the escape artist, Bula dives right into the rectangular hole in the wall and, notwithstanding his size, slips out of sight. *The man is a marvel.*

Gideon nods at Dwight. "You're next. Hurry."

Dwight has no words, a rare phenomenon. With wide eyes, he slips on his shoes, goes to the vent, and follows Bula into the dark, unknown. It's a tight squeeze.

As Gideon is about to take his turn, the automatic door slides open, and in steps Clyde.

TUNNEL

The burly guard is grinning, perhaps looking forward to inflicting torture on the greenies. Then he notices Gideon on the floor, and the mirth drains from his fat face.

Gideon offers a friendly wave before making his exit. Crawling as fast as human possibly, he's engulfed in a world of metal and darkness. He frantically pulls himself through this claustrophobic nightmare, fearing that a lunging hand could grab his ankle. Thankfully, if Dwight could barely fit through this, there's no way the extra-heavy Clyde could.

Soon there's no more light from behind, and everything is pitch black. Now and then Gideon runs into the shoes of Dwight. Dwight shouts something, but there's so much reverberation in the tight space, it's unintelligible.

Time goes by in a blur. There's nothing to observe. There's nothing to do but think. It's as if his mind — not just his body — has been freed. And the *power* he feels! Yesterday he was searching for his core, but what he sought wasn't within him, it was *above* him. He just needed to let go of the things that were weighing him down. Then, like a balloon cut from its string, transcendence was effortless.

Though he's literally trapped in a tight, dark space, he feels free from the cave, and he's never seen more clearly. Time, space, matter … they're all connected. The universe is wonderful and crazy. It's also finite and comprehensible, and somehow it's all subject to the fifth, irreducible interaction: mind. It's all so exciting, he wants to stand up and fight the forces of evil. If only he wasn't trapped in a two-foot, metal duct.

He imagines the beautiful Ishtar — Ms. Primple — on her golden throne. *No.* He imagines her true form: the human boar with too many horns and arms. Prostrated before her are her loyal priests, dressed in drag.

In his mind's eyes, Gideon walks right into their Babylonian temple. *Can't you see*, he shouts to the priests, *she's a monster?* Then, with his new-found power, he tips the throne right over, and the beast, squealing with hoggish horror, flees for its pitiful life.

"Gideon," comes the voice of Dwight from ahead. It's strange, but there's no more reverberation.

"Yeah?" Gideon responds, surprised by the clarity of his own voice.

"Where are we going?"

"No idea. Does Bula know?"

"No."

Gideon's hands and knees are in pain. Something feels off. The duct is rougher and harder than before. It feels like *stone*.

Dwight hollers, "I think we're in a cave."

Gideon has no words. He can only crawl and observe, wondering if this is a complex hallucination.

Though it's hard to make out anything with the large bodies of Dwight and Bula in front of him, there's a dim light in the distance, and it's growing brighter. The next thing he knows, Dwight and Bula have climbed out of the tunnel, and now it's his turn.

Seconds later, Gideon is standing on his feet. The light is soft and beautiful. The place, with stony, brick walls is big and open. At last he can stand up, arching his aching back. Freedom never felt so good. "Where are we?" he asks.

Getting a better look around, he notices the flaming torches — *torches?* — the pillars, the colored tiles, the stepped patterns, and the ceiling high above. The room is gigantic. There are murals depicting bearded soldiers, lions, unicorns, and strange animals.

Though it sounds inane, he says it anyway. "I don't think we're in the juvenile detention center anymore." As his eyes adjust, he realizes that they're not alone, and his heart skips a beat. Not too far off, a crowd of people are lying prostrate on the marble floor. Long hair, jewels, red robes … they're all women.

There's something familiar about this. Gideon's eyes follow the direction of the women's bodies to a gold-plated throne. And sitting atop the dazzling throne is a woman — a beautiful woman — in a flowing, red gown. Gideon knows that face all too well.

Oh no. The woman looks at him, and Gideon steps back.

A stuttering Dwight says, "Is that —" Then the woman looks at Dwight, and his question is answered. The realization is as heavy as the stone around them. *Of course you can't kill a god.*

It's the very scene Gideon played out in his mind, his abstract musing now an intricate reality. Without time to question how or why, he knows his role. He already rehearsed it. "Fasha!" he shouts, remembering her true name from the secret meeting with the gray lady. The expansive chamber echoes with the obtrusive sound.

The prostrated women are startled. They rise to their feet.

Dwight tugs Gideon's arm. "What are you doing?"

Ignoring him, Gideon shouts, "Can't you see she's a …"

But the women look less than receptive. They throw off their robes, remove their wigs, and reveal their bald heads. They're not women at all.

The goddess maintains her stately posture. She raises a single finger, pointing straight at Gideon. "*Aiqtalhum,*" she says in some guttural language.

The meaning of the word is clear enough when the men unsheathe long knives from their sides.

Only Bula has the presence of mind to cry, "Run!"

BABYLON

Gideon, Dwight, and Bula press against the brass handles of giant doors. As the heavy wood creeks open, blinding light streams into the dark temple. They push harder until, at last, they can squeeze into the outside world. The day is hot and arid. Though they can barely see, they stumble down a wide, brick staircase. The stairs go on and on.

Squinting, Gideon takes in the blocky architecture. "It's a *ziggurat*," he announces. "I learned about these in Ancient World History."

Dwight, very much out of shape, is already panting. "What the heck … is going on?"

The world around them is a colorful metropolis: yellow stone, green palm trees, blue rivers. The roofs are flat, the scene waving in the heat of the day. "I think we're in ancient Babylon."

At last they reach the bottom of the ziggurat. They stand on a dirt road. It must be rush hour, because the road is filled with horse-drawn carts and pedestrians in colorful robes. The men have long, braided beards. The women are draped in ornate fabrics. Just about everyone is staring at the three outsiders and their bright, orange t-shirts.

"Where do we go?" Dwight cries.

Gideon looks back. The murderous priests are half-way down the stairs. He's got nothing. "Bula?"

"We keep running," says the wise Hawaiian. He darts down one of the wide, dirt roads, and Gideon and Dwight follow.

Bula leads them through a busy market. All around them are wooden tables, wicker baskets, ceramic pots, tied goats, the shouts of an exotic language, the smells of smoke and barbecued meat. A man is playing a small harp while another man beats a drum and a girl with jewels on her ears and nose dances.

A woman waves a beaded necklace in front of the running boys. Another woman tries to catch their attention with a squawking chicken. But despite the tempting distractions, the thought of not being stabbed to death is more appealing than the wonders of ancient Babylon.

Following Bula's lead, they take a left, then a right. Many times they just avoid colliding with the chaos around them. They run across a street, down a hill, over a stream, and into a thicket of palm trees. Soon, deep in the heart of a jungle, they're hunched over, catching their breaths. They look back, but there's no priests in sight.

A pink-faced Dwight is the first to speak. "So back to the subject of what the heck is going on …"

Gideon has a theory. "I …" It almost feels like a confession. "I was thinking about Babylon when we were crawling through the duct, and … I guess I let my thoughts get out of control."

"You're saying you *thought* us here?"

Gideon shrugs.

Bula is smiling. "*Oe i ke ano akamai.* You are a genius."

"Yeah," says Dwight. "Why didn't *I* think of escaping to an ancient Bablyonian temple with bloodthirsty priests?"

Bula ignores him. "You did what I tried to do at the library. You traveled between layers."

Dwight adds, "And forced your friends to come with you."

Also ignoring Dwight, Gideon asks, "What do you mean by layers? Time … space?"

"Aren't they the same thing?" asks Bula.

Gideon shakes his head. "We're talking thousands of miles and thousands of years. How many *layers* did we travel?"

"When your mind is in control, moving a thousand miles is as simple as thinking a thought and taking a step."

"How do you know all this?"

"I don't. I'm making it up as we go along."

Dwight is hunched over, still catching his breath. "Well then, Gideon, think us back home."

Gideon throws up his arms. "I don't know how."

Bula thinks for a moment and asks, "Do you know how to jump?"

"Of course I know how to jump."

"Let's see."

"What's your point?"

"Just do it."

Rolling his eyes, Gideon jumps.

"You just pushed against gravity and moved through space and time."

"My *body* did."

Bula bends down and picks up a fallen coconut. He tosses it between hands. "The physical layer is subjected to the spiritual layer. You just need to tell your lower self to let go so your higher self can take control. You did it last night. You did it today. You can do it again."

"What you refer to as today is thousands of years in the future."

"It's only a step away, and we can get there together. Now let us concentrate." Bula extends open hands. Though Gideon and Dwight have never touched hands in their lives, given the circumstances, neither is about to make a snide remark. The three of them join hands and close their eyes.

Gideon imagines the green grass of Eastward high, the pavilion in the park, the gum on the street. Then, allowing his imagination to run deeper, he connects to the chi in the air, takes hold of the atoms, and pulls. The world around them warps, stretches, and whizzes past. Gravity, space, time, these are not insurmountable barriers, only dimensions to be measured, scaled, and transcended. Whether a millimeter or a mega parsec, a second or a thousand years, it can be expanded or contracted like flipping through pages of a book. And somehow his mind knows its way through it all. He need only think the destination, and he's there.

He opens his eyes and sees … palm trees. "Well, I tried."

There's a howl in the distance.

Dwight looks around. "What was that?"

There it is again, louder. There's rummaging bushes and snapping branches.

"Look!" Dwight shouts, pointing to the multi-armed, multi-horned, boar from hell. Fasha. With supernatural strength, the monster is pushing trees out of her way, charging straight for them.

RUN

They run.

Being pursued by cross-dressing guys with knives was bad. Being pursued by a demonic pig-woman is an entirely different matter. Gideon sprints as never before, the breeze beating against him, the palm trees whizzing past. Everything is a blur as he finds himself, more than ever, longing for home.

He runs so fast that he barely notices the approaching fence. First he skids in the dirt, then he crashes into the springy metal and finds himself lying on his back. As the pain creeps in, he's confused by the green leaves of the aspen trees. Overhead, gently swaying in the breeze, the leaves look positively un-Babylonian.

Seconds later, Bula, then Dwight also slam into the fence.

Dwight cries, "Where are we now?"

Bula points through the chain link fence. "Look."

There's a sloping hill, a large field, and … a football stadium. They're looking at *Eastward High*.

Bula leads the way in hopping the fence. Gideon follows, scraping and tearing his pants on the brittle wire tops, which he's grateful for, as there's now a fence between him and ancient Babylon. For Dwight, large and clumsy, scaling the fence is even harder, but with Bula's and Gideon's help, Dwight eventually thuds onto the grassy hill. Then they continue their sprint, never looking back until reaching a side door of the school. Gideon runs his hands along the orange bricks, so real and wonderful.

There, catching their breaths, they look for any sign of the pig-woman, but everything is still. There's no one on the football field. There's houses on the hills, puffy clouds in the sky.

Bula clasps Gideon's shoulder. "You did it, my friend."

Gideon shakes his head. "I think we all must have done it."

"That's right," says Dwight, gasping for breath, "you couldn't have done it … without me."

Gideon notices a bright sparkle in the corner of his eye. A ways off, a police car is pulling into the parking lot, the sun reflecting off its windshield. "Guys, maybe we shouldn't —"

"Hey!" someone shouts. Stepping out of the school through the side doors are two members of the football team: Matt Wilson and Joe Munson. Matt is holding a baseball bat. Joe is wearing brass knuckles.

"It's them," says Matt.

Joe pounds his fist into his palm. "Ow."

As the doors swing shut behind the boys, Gideon gets a quick glance into the hallway, but what he sees makes no sense: a green *fog*.

Joe says, "Should we tell master?"

Matt nods, a grin stretching across his face. "Populous!" he shouts.

"Populous!" Joe repeats.

Dwight and Bula turn to Gideon, the same question on their faces: *who's Populous?*

But Gideon doesn't care to find out.

"All this running is killing me," exclaims a red-faced Dwight.

Gideon is just as exhausted. "We must … find … Wanda."

All three of them ditched their bright-orange t-shirts from the *Bright Horizons Juvenile Correction Facility* long ago, leaving them half-naked. However vulnerable it feels, at least they're no longer advertising themselves as runaways.

They're forced to stop at an intersection. As the cars whiz past, Bula says, "Well, my friends, this is where our paths part."

"Why?" asks Gideon.

Bula points to a Seven-eleven gas station on the corner. "As I told you, I need a Slurpee."

Gideon is at a loss. "But … aren't you going to help us rescue Wanda?"

Bula shakes his head. "You don't understand. I *need* a Slurpee. You'll have to go on without me." He seizes them both in a group hug. "I believe in you." Then he runs to the Seven-eleven, though not before turning back and shouting, "*Ola ka po'e akamai!*"

"What does that mean?"

"Long live the nerds!"

Dwight leans toward Gideon and says, "I'm pretty sure Seven-eleven doesn't serve people without shirts on."

"He's Bula," says Gideon, "he can do anything."

At last, Gideon and Dwight arrive at Fifth West by the old farmer's market. The train tracks are nearby. The houses are old and run down.

"There," says a sweat-soaked Dwight, pointing to a railroad crossing sign. "Those were the bells I heard over the phone. They gotta be."

Gideon nods. "Then she must be close." But where to go from here? He closes his eyes. *Where are you, Wanda?* He's never wanted anything more than he wants to see her face. Somehow he knows she's close. He can feel it as surely as he can feel the beating of his heart.

He opens his eyes. That's *not* his heart. "Do you hear that?"

"Hear what?"

"That pulsing. Someone's playing music." Gideon looks around. There's a brown shack at the end of the street. "There."

"So?"

"Remember the phone call? I think I recognized the voice of the woman. They call her Muza, goddess of music."

"Oh."

"So-called music, anyway."

"Right."

They run to the end of the street, where the pulsing — the base-line of a beat — grows louder. Sure enough, as evidenced by the vibrating boards, the sound is coming from the beat-up shack. A relic from a past century, the shack's nails are rusted, the paint long-since peeled off, the boards barely holding together. And blasting through the cracks, threatening to topple the whole thing, are the brutal shouts of hardcore rap music.

For a moment the boys just stand there as the vibrations pound against their bodies. It's worse than the pep rally, worse than the homecoming dance. The relentless noise is so angry, so powerful, they can only dread what awaits them on the other side of the walls. Another monster, perhaps?

For Wanda.

With cautious steps, Gideon leads the way up the wooden stairs. Though the boards bend beneath him, the music is so loud that no one's the wiser. When he reaches the front door — or what's left of it — he gently turns the rusted doorknob. It's open.

What seems like a miracle, Wanda is sitting in the middle of the small, abandoned house. She's wrapped in ropes, which hold her to a wooden chair. And she's not alone. Standing in front of her is none other than Muza. The goddess of music is dressed in tight, black leather. Her curled hair is practically dripping with oil. Her nails are long, red claws. Her whole body is adorned with chains, spikes, and gold ... lots of gold. Earrings, necklaces, bracelets, teeth ...

There's also some boys — Muza's minions. Gideon recognizes them from school. Backward hats, baggy pants, gang symbols ... those guys. Altogether they're doing a kind of ... dance. At least that's the best word Gideon can think of to describe it. Circling around Wanda with taunting, outstretched arms, their heads are bobbing in and out like pigeons as the terrible beat goes on and on. It looks perfectly insane.

Meanwhile poor Wanda looks on in silent agony. How long has she been subjected to this cruelty?

Dwight, standing at the bottom of the staircase, asks, "What's going on?"

Trying to keep his voice down, Gideon replies, "She's in there, and so is Muza and her gang. They're doing ... rap stuff. You know, with the head bobbing and the arms."

"Poor Wanda."

"I know."

"What are we going to do?"

"I say we barge in there and rescue her."

"That's not a very good plan."

"Do you have a better idea?"

"Point taken, but only if you use your magic."

"I don't have magic."

"You know, your mind stuff. You brought us to ancient Babylon and back. Now do something heroic."

"You know as well as I do that I can't …" Suddenly Gideon is aware of a new feeling within him. Actually, it's all around him. There's something in the air, a positive charge causing the hairs on his arms to stand on end. *Chi?* Whatever it is, he feels it with every breath. "Maybe I can."

But where is this sensation coming from? Is it the presence of the goddess? Or is it …

His eyes meet the metal cell phone tower on the corner of the street. *Of course.*

And then there's the voice of Kyle: *How else? With a tower.*

There's one at the school, and there was one at the juvenile detention center. Maybe there was even one in ancient Babylon: the ziggurat. What if these towers are secretly housing some godly technology? Maybe the big, heavy things are like weights on a trampoline, bending space, time, and other dimensions. And perhaps that bending causes the layers to cross, making a trip to ancient Babylon just a step away, just as Bula said. It could even put the gods' otherworldly powers within reach. Perhaps what he's feeling is the very *dark energy* that fills the universe.

Gideon closes his eyes, clenching a fist. Maybe it's just his imagination, but it feels as if he's squeezing the very fabric of space-time, the atoms stretching toward him. He releases his fist, and it feels as if the atoms spring back to their places.

Dwight says, "Gideon? Are you there?"

"Sorry, I just realized something."

"And that is?"

"Muza's going down. We'll burst through the doors on three."

With wide eyes, Dwight joins Gideon at the top of the stairs. "Are you're sure about this?"

"As long as you use *your* magic," says Gideon.

"Of course." Dwight looks less than assured.

Gideon looks up at the blue sky. Somehow he feels quite certain that they're not fighting these battles alone. "One … two … three."

SO-CALLED MUSIC

They kick open the door and charge, swat-team style. The music is so loud, the vibrations so powerful, it's like hitting a brick wall.

Muza and her gang turn to them with startled expressions.

Within Gideon is a blazing fire. *How dare you do this to my friend!* He feels the otherworldly energy. Locking eyes with Muza, he breathes in and gathers his chi. He concentrates the power in his hands and throws a blast of fury.

Muza flinches as if hit in the face by a gnat. Then she raises a hand, and Gideon feels a crash like a tidal wave. The next thing he knows, his back slams against a wall, and he slides to the floor.

Hasn't this happened before?

A second later, Dwight also impacts against the wall, crunching the boards behind him.

The beat goes on, only now there's three prisoners tied to chairs. The ropes dig into their flesh as Muza's gang continues their insane dance, chests puffed, arms extended, heads bobbing. They circle around their prey like a pack of wolves. All the while Muza stands in a corner, watching with approval.

Gideon wonders what his captors want from them. But with such loud music, communication is only possible over extremely short distances. So he shouts the question into Wanda's ear.

Wanda turns to him, a vague recognition in her face, but she can't speak. She's somewhere else.

So Gideon turns to Dwight, shouting, "Dude, we gotta get out of here."

But even Dwight's eyes are beginning to glaze over, the fight draining away. He replies, "We can't win this one. She's too powerful."

Muza is now tapping on a phone, perhaps messaging the other gods over their supernatural cellular network. It's surely only a matter of time before the gray lady shows up; she always does. And then what? Execution? Eaten alive by the pig-woman? Banishment to some dungeon for the enemies of the gods? There's no saying what spectacular punishments these sadistic beings could concoct. Though could it possibly be worse than this?

Gideon turns back to Dwight. "I think she's telling the others about us. We gotta find our power again."

Dwight is fading fast. "We can't beat them. They're gods." Ever so slightly, his head begins to bob to the beat. "Better to join them."

"No, Dwight!"

"But they're so … cool."

"They're trying to break you."

"So cool," Dwight repeats.

Gideon turns to Wanda. "I know you're still in there somewhere. Listen to me. You're in control of your mind, not the music, not the gods, not anything else. Come back, Wanda. I need you."

Wanda blinks. She blinks again. Though her eyes are still distant, she wheezes, "You came for me."

"Of course we did."

With every blink, she seems a little closer. "How did you find us?"

"The gods aren't the only ones with power. We just have to find ourselves. Then we can do what they do. Then we can fight back."

"But they're so cool."

"Look at them. They're bullies. They're insecure. They depend on each other, because they have no idea who they are. They demand our respect, but that's the one thing they'll never get. You, on the other hand, are cool."

"Me?" Wanda shakes her head. "I don't have any cool clothes."

"Wake up, Wanda!"

Something dark steps in front of them. Muza. She waves a hand, and the music stops. The relief is overwhelming, leaving a painful ringing in the ears.

Gideon looks around. There are no speakers in the shack. It's as if the music was vibrating out of the very walls.

Her black leather stretching with every step, Muza comes much too close for comfort, crouching to stare into Gideon's eyes. There's mockery in her lips. "What's going on, Gideon?"

Gideon is silent.

"If you and your girlfriend have something to say, why not tell the whole class?"

He meets her dark eyes. Running isn't an option. Fighting isn't an option. *Logic* isn't an option. This one's going to be hard, though suddenly he has an idea. "Wanda and I were just talking about how cool your music is."

"I'll bet."

"In fact, we were wondering if we could perform our own rap."

Muza narrows her eyes. "*You* want to perform a rap?"

"Yes."

"How dumb do you think I am?"

"It's a really cool rap."

"Uh-huh."

"If nothing else, it will give you an opportunity to make fun of us."

Muza considers this last selling point. Her mocking lips stretch into a grin, then she bursts into laughter. "What do you say boys, are you up for a little entertainment?" Then she says to Gideon, "All right, do your thing."

"I can't do it while tied up."

"Oh yes you will."

"It's just that … we wanted to show you our break dancing moves; you'll really enjoy making fun of them."

This is a very persuasive selling point. Muza nods to her goons. While one guy brandishes his pistol, a reminder not to try any funny business, the five others work on untying Gideon and Wanda.

The ropes were so tight, they cut off circulation. Only now does the pain creep in, and it creeps hard. Gideon nearly faints as he rises to his feet. He can only imagine how Wanda feels. He helps her up.

Muza folds her arms. "What are you gonna do?"

A wide-eyed Wanda turns to Gideon, clearly wondering the same thing.

"Just a moment," Gideon announces to the audience. Then he whispers to Wanda, "Remember when we were at the Karaoke club, and we did that cowboy line dance?"

"The Hat Scat Boogie?" Wanda whispers back.

"That's the one."

"They'll kill us!"

"Trust me."

From the other side of the room comes the sound of a cocking gun, another reminder from the guy with the pistol to move along.

"We're waiting," says Muza.

Gideon clears his throat and places his hands on his hips. Though he's never felt stupider, it's a noble stupid. "One, two, three, four." He sings:

> *Out in the country*
> *Where the jackrabbits hop,*
> *Was a little, old cowboy,*
> *A plantin' his crop.*

As the line dance dictates, he hops in place, elbowing Wanda until she does the same. Though Gideon is much louder, together they sing:

> *When who came along*
> *But pretty, old Sue,*
> *Saying, "Working too hard*
> *Ain't good fer you.*
>
> *"It's time to put on*
> *Yer Sunday pants*
> *And come with me to the*
> *Barnyard dance."*

At first the gang looks stunned, then horrified.

Dwight, who has awoken from his trance, looks just as horrified.

As the chorus of the song begins, Gideon slaps Wanda on the back, and together they jump into full heel kicks.

> *Kick yer heels and shake yer hips.*
> *Pucker out those pretty lips.*
> *Give my tappin' boots*
> *A little lookie!*

Horror turns to anger.

> *Button down and toss yer hat.*
> *Nothin's gonna hold ya back*
> *When ya do the hat scattin' boogie!*

Anger gives way to violence. Following the wave of Muza's hand, every gang member charges at the performers.

Wanda recoils.

Gideon grabs her arm. "Stay with me!" he shouts. Then, in complete disregard of those who are about to maul him, he resumes his smile, raises an imaginary lasso, and sings:

> *Kick yer heels and shake yer hips.*
> *Pucker out those pretty lips ...*

Though frightened, Wanda also continues the dance.

The gang members lunge forward, but nothing happens. As if trapped by some invisible barrier, they just stand there.

"Seize them!" Muza orders.

Again the boys extend their arms, but no contact is made. All they can do is stare at the performers, their expressions ... stupid.

There's that positive charge again. Gideon turns to Wanda. "Do you feel it?"

Now Wanda is smiling. "Yes."

Together they kick up their heels even higher.

Button down and toss yer hat.
Nothin's gonna hold ya back
When ya do the hat scattin' boogie!

Wanda's really getting into it. With a beaming realization, she exclaims, "Uncoolness is just as powerful as coolness!"

At this, Muza thrusts out both hands, and the walls blast a new wave of rap music.

The onslaught of vibrations, even louder than before, throws off the dance, scattering the energy.

The spell is broken. Once again, the gang lunges forward, only this time they seize their targets.

It takes three of the six boys to subdue a struggling Wanda.

That leaves three on Gideon. He struggles, but there's no contest. This is no game. As the boys grip his arms, a wave of fear comes over him.

Muza is grinning at him. And maybe it's his imagination, but despite the noise and chaos, he can almost hear her thoughts. *Stupid boy, did you honestly think you could beat us?*

Gideon throws his body, only to receive a hard punch to the gut. With nothing to protect his skin, it hurts … a lot.

It's time for you to learn some respect.

As if there's a gaping pit before him, Gideon feels a sickly sense of vertigo. The energy is draining away, taking hope with it. There is no light, only suffocating darkness.

We are your gods. You will worship us and us alone.

His frail struggles end with a knee to the gut and a punch to the temple. He hits the hard, wood, floor. Strength fading, he desperately tries to hold on to something — a hope, a dream, anything — but the outside forces are overpowering.

Why fight us? Deep down, you know you want to be cool.

He attempts to climb to his feet but receives another kick in the gut. He collapses, his strength gone, his body shot.

Let go, Gideon. Let us control you.

That leaves only his mind.

You have nothing.

It's a lie. As hard as they try to pound their way into his skull, he's still in control of his thoughts. They can't take his will away, not without his consent. And he does *not* consent.

Mind — the fifth irreducible interaction, stronger than the gravity and nuclear forces that hold the universe together. It is the power of the gods, and it is his.

He looks at the vibrating walls. With a frail wave of his hand, he thinks, *Stop.*

The music stops.

Then he opens his mouth. Though it takes all his strength, he forces the words out. *"Kick yer heels and shake yer hips. Pucker out those pretty lips …"*

An enraged Muza waves a hand, and the rap music resumes, this time so loud that the floor boards start shaking.

But Gideon stops it again. Clutching his aching middle, he climbs to his hands and knees. *"Button down and toss yer hat. Nothin's gonna hold ya back …"*

The gang members step back in confusion. No one dares touch him.

Muza extends both hands, and the music resumes. The floor shakes so much, it's like an earthquake. Two boys fall over from the force.

Gideon climbs to his feet. Like Moses parting the red sea, he thrusts both hands outward, and not only does the music stop, but both vibrating walls blow to pieces. Boards snap, the ceiling shifts, and debris falls from above, crashing all around.

Once again, the gang is stupefied.

Gideon puts one hand on his hip and twirls his imaginary lasso. *"When ya do the hat scattin' boogie!"*

A guy on the floor gets to his feet and runs for the door. One of his friends follows. Then the other four follow.

Then it's only Gideon, Wanda, a tied-up Dwight, and Muza.

Muza takes a step back, her high-heeled boots clopping against the dusty, wooden floor.

Gideon takes a step forward. "Why don't you run like the others?"

Muza laughs. "Those idiots will be dealt with. As for you …"

"Yes?"

"You have no idea what you're up against."

"What are you going to do, reason with me? I'm all ears."

"What do *you* know of reason?"

"I know it doesn't take a group. It happens in solitude, in quiet, when one can hear himself think."

"You deceive yourself. True knowledge comes from the outside-in. It drives your emotions, telling you how to think and act. Don't fight the beat, Gideon. It's more powerful than you'll ever be. Embrace it. Let it fill you. Then you will know true power."

"Hypothetically speaking, suppose the music were to end, your friends were to abandon you, and yesterday's hip song becomes uncool. Then what?"

"You move with the trend. You follow the *new* cool."

"And who decides what's cool?"

"The majority, you idiot."

"And suppose the majority were to decide that *uncool* is the new cool. What, then, would be left of you?"

Her face in a panic, Muza looks at Gideon, then at Wanda, then at Dwight. She takes another step back and explodes.

UNCOOLNESS

They shield themselves from the shower of sparks. For Gideon, it's become a familiar routine.

Warm daylight streams in through the missing walls. There's a gentle breeze. Birds chirp.

Wanda is the first to speak. "Wow."

"Pretty cool, huh?" says Gideon. He's startled as Wanda seizes him in a hug.

"You came for me," she says, squeezing tighter.

"Of course." Gideon pats her back. "What are friends for?"

"Of course." Finally she lets go and looks away. "Why are you half naked?"

Gideon examines the roof of the neighbor's house. Without trying to look obvious, he flexes his arms and sucks in his gut. "It's a long story."

"I'll bet."

Dwight, still tied up, exclaims, "Guys, we defeated another god! How many are left?"

Gideon counts his fingers. "Only the fat guy and the gray lady. Three down, two to go."

"You can't count Ms. Primple. She came back."

Wanda's eyes widen. "She *did*?"

"In *monster* form," says Dwight. "I mean, she was always a monster, but believe it or not, she got worse."

An exhausted Gideon has to lean against one of the remaining walls. "All right, *two* down. The point is, we can do this."

Wanda looks unsettled. "Where is the monster now?"

Gideon shrugs. "We lost her in ancient Babylon."

"What?"

"That's an even longer story."

Dwight says, "We *think* we lost her. Maybe she followed us to the school."

"Speaking of which," says Gideon, "what's *happening* at the school? Last I talked to Doug, something crazy was going on."

Wanda shakes her head. "After you guys ran off, things got ugly. They forced everyone to line up in the commons. Then they started taking some of the students away … like me."

Gideon asks, "What about the *good* teachers like Mr. Periwinkle and Ms. Fitzwater? Surely they wouldn't stand for that."

"They were also taken away," says Wanda.

Struggling to free himself, Dwight exclaims, "How are they getting away with this?"

Gideon replies, "They own the police, remember?"

Wanda adds, "And no matter how crazy things get, they've got the goddess of normality on their side. Never mind the disappearing people, she'll make everything seem fine. In fact, everyone but me went willingly."

Gaining marginal progress with the ropes, Dwight says, "But this was all yesterday, right? If the students have any sense, they'll stay home today."

Wanda says, "I doubt it. No matter how hellish things get, as long as everything *seems* normal, they'll just keep coming back."

Gideon adds, "Like dogs to their vomit."

Dwight has successfully freed a shoulder. "Why are the gods doing this?"

Gideon says, "Because some of the students have started thinking for themselves. What would happen if the movement caught on?"

Wanda nods. "The gods might lose their power."

Gideon kicks the wall in frustration. More debris falls from the ceiling. "This isn't right. We have to do something about it."

Dwight says, "Yes, indeed. And when it comes to dealing with the gods, I think Bula has the best strategy: pick your battles. Who's up for a *Slurpee*?"

"Dwight," says Gideon, "we have to go back."

"Why?"

"Our friends need us."

"You mean *your* friends … your jocks and cheerleaders."

"They're not that bad once you get to know them."

"How are we going to rescue the entire student body?"

Wanda smiles. "Isn't it obvious? With *uncoolness*. I have a plan. We need to go to my grandma's house."

"I don't like where this is going," says Dwight.

"Believe me," says Wanda, "it's going to be fun."

"I *don't* believe you. Now are you guys going to untie me or what?"

Sweaty and exhausted, their long run ends at the Biggles' residence, where Dwight collapses on the grass. While Wanda's grandma, Mrs. Biggles, reclines on a couch, eating frosted cookies and watching *I Love Lucy* on an ancient television set, Wanda opens the garage, and she and Gideon search through dusty, cardboard boxes.

"A denim jacket?" Wanda asks, holding up the well-worn garment from decades passed.

Gideon shakes his head. "That's arguably cool."

"Plastic pearls?"

"Think eye sores."

Eye sores prove easy to come by in Mrs. Biggles' garage, and within minutes, they're equipped for battle.

Gideon wears bright, green soccer socks, orange swimming trunks, a brown turtle neck, a plaid suit-coat from the seventies, and a fancy sombrero. All eye sores aside, it beats being half-naked.

Wanda wears gray sweat pants, a *Rainbow Bright* belt, an "I *heart* Wisconsin" t-shirt, and a Cub Scout baseball cap covered in plastic sequins … pretty much her standard wardrobe.

Dwight wears moon boots, blue scrubs, safety goggles, a bike helmet, a purple fanny pack, and four slap bracelets.

As the three of them stare at their puke-worthy images in a mirror, Wanda says, "The gods don't stand a chance."

The motley crew packs into Mrs. Biggles' pink Cadillac, which grinds and rattles, spewing a cloud of black smoke before lurching into gear.

"Sorry," says Wanda at the steering wheel, "I'm still learning how to drive a manual."

Dwight asks, "Why don't we just teleport there with our magic?"

Gideon adjusts his terrible turtle neck. "Even if we knew how to do that, there's the towers, remember? The farther away we get, the less power we have. Right now I don't feel anything."

"You're saying we're out of coverage?"

"At least until we get closer to the school."

Dwight thinks for a moment. "What would happen if we destroyed the tower?"

Gideon smiles. "Of course. That's how we'll defeat them once and for all."

But Wanda looks less than impressed. "How are you going to *destroy* one-hundred-fifty feet of steel?"

She has a point. "Umm …" says Gideon, "maybe we'll just have to play this by ear."

The car is so loud, they park a street away from the school. Then, sombrero, sequins, and slap bracelets in place, they make their stealthy advance to the southern entrance.

"Get down!" Dwight whispers, and like clockwork, all three of them fall to the grass. They hide behind a bush in someone's front yard, and Dwight points to the school. "There, do you see them? Matt and Joe. They're still guarding the entrance."

Gideon looks around. "If we go through a neighborhood street, we could hop a fence and cut through the football field. That's where the tower is."

"Even if we can get that far, what are we gonna do?"

"Maybe we just need to unplug the panels. There's gotta be a way to the top, a ladder or something."

"Let's hope you're right."

Wanda shakes her head. "We gotta help our friends first."

"You mean *Gideon's* friends," says Dwight.

Gideon says, "I wanna help them too, and that's why we gotta destroy the tower."

Wanda says, "It's not gonna work. It takes special machinery to get someone up there. Even if we find a way, everyone would see. We can come back at night. As for right now, people need us."

Gideon remembers his brief glimpse of the hallway and the weird, green mist. For all they know, the pig-woman is waiting for them. Even if they can get past the guards, surely it's a suicide mission. And yet, thinking of Cynthia locked in a dungeon, tortured and longing for a hero … that changes things. Perhaps this will finally convince her to rethink her affections. "Wanda's right."

Dwight sighs. "All right, but we need a plan."

To their surprise, Wanda stands up, raising her pink *Barbie* boom box. "We already have a plan," she says.

"No, Wanda!" Gideon and Dwight cry together, but she walks on, fully exposed and undeterred.

In no time, the jocks spot her. So much for stealth. With nothing else to do, Gideon and Dwight walk behind their friend in the Kamikaze mission.

Joe says, "Who are those weirdos?"

"It's Gid!" says Matt, his voice echoing off the school. Then he shouts, "You're not allowed here."

Wanda presses the play button on the boom box, starting a nineteen-eighties cassette of the Mormon Tabernacle Choir. The gentle, harmonious voices sing:

> *Have I done any good in the world today?*
> *Have I helped anyone in need?*

"What is that?" demands Joe.

Still the three friends march on.

> *Have I cheered up the sad*
> *Or made someone feel glad?*

If not I have failed indeed.

With horror in his voice, Matt shouts, "Turn it off!"

Wanda does not turn it off. As she, Gideon, and Dwight get closer, it's clear that the green socks, rainbow belt, and bike helmet are having an effect on the recoiling jocks.

> *Has anyone's burden been lightened today*
> *Because I was willing to share?*

"We'll call Populous!" Matt warns, raising his fists.

> *Have the sick and the weary*
> *Been helped on their way?*
> *When they needed my help, was I there?*

In desperation, Joe shouts, "This is not cool!"

Still the three motley nerds march on. When they're within touching distance of the jocks, Matt and Joe have fallen to their hands and knees.

"This music is making me sad," says Joe.

Gideon opens a door, and they enter the school.

MIST

The long hallway is empty. They walk slowly, cautiously. The air smells of burning, the florescent lights seem dimmer, and green mist is everywhere. There's an ominous sound in the distance.

Dwight whispers, "Do you hear that?"

Wanda nods. "It sounds like chanting."

This can't be good. From previous experience, chanting means guys who want to hurt them or scary things coming out of bonfires.

Gideon closes his eyes and tries to focus on the unseen world around him, but it's all noise, pulsing, and static. There's definitely power here, but it's not clean like before. It's foreign, chaotic, unusable.

Quietly, carefully, they peer around a corner into the commons, and their jaws drop. True to Wanda's description, a large portion of the student body is assembled in lines. Only they're on their *knees*, prostrated like the priests of Ishtar. At the front of it all is the fat guy, but no longer as Mr. Phillips the drama teacher. Now, dressed in a white toga and sitting atop a marble throne, he reigns in godly glory. Four girls, also in togas, fan him with palm leaves.

"Populous," the students chant. "Populous …"

So he's *Populous*, Gideon thinks, *god of popularity.*

Standing at the head of the prostrated students is Kyle Slater, dressed in a red robe. Apparently he's the high priest of Populous. With his hands behind his back, he walks through the lines, making sure that each knee is properly bent.

Dwight whispers, "Have we traveled through time again?"

"Sure seems like it," whispers Gideon, "but I don't think so." He searches the room for Cynthia, but he doesn't see her. His stomach sinks at the possibility that she was also taken away.

"So what's the plan?"

"We gotta take out this Populous guy. That's all there is to it."

"How?"

"We turn on the music and charge."

Dwight rolls his eyes. "Yeah, charging worked really well at the shack."

"We rescued Wanda, didn't we?"

"You've assaulted this guy before. He's powerful, remember?"

"That was before we learned their weakness. Look at how uncool we are."

"He'll crush us before we even get close."

Wanda places her hands on their shoulders. "We gotta believe in ourselves. It's the only way."

After a silent stare, Dwight finally nods.

"On three," Wanda whispers. Silently, she raises a finger for each number, then presses the play button on the boom box. With pounding hearts, they charge into the commons as the choir resumes its sweet song.

> *Then wake up and do something more*
> *Than dream of your mansion above.*

They run right through the columns of prostrated students. Not a single head turns. The fanning girls don't even seem to notice. Only one person acknowledges their presence: Populous. With a subtle raise of his finger, the boom box explodes. He raises another finger and Gideon, Dwight, and Wanda are stopped in their tracks and thrown to the floor. He raises a third finger, and the hundreds of students rise to their feet.

CAPTURED

Dwight and Wanda are seized by the crowd of zombie-like students.

Through some primal reflex, Gideon finds himself leaping into the air ... high into the air. Somehow he's tapped into the foreign energy, and it's flowing through him. He just had to stop thinking and start doing, and there's nothing like a dire situation to make that happen.

He's still rising, air rushing against him. Fearing he'll slam into the ceiling, he pushes against it with his hands before gravity reverses the ascent. Then it's down, down ... down. *Man, this room is big!* His shoes slam against the floor, and he crouches to absorb the impact.

Ouch.

He just cleared the crowd. His feet screaming, he grabs his fallen sombrero and springs into a sprint, down a hallway, up a flight of stairs, and around two corners. It all goes by in an instant.

When he ventures to look back, his heart pounding, there's nothing to see but swirling mist filling an empty hallway. There's nothing to hear but the distant murmurs of "Populous ... Populous ..." It's as if the zombie-students are too brain-dead to put up a chase.

The hallway grows darker, then lighter. The florescent lights are pulsing and crackling as if something's draining their energy. He closes his eyes and tries to connect to the chi around him, but he's met with a forbidding shock. There's confusion and static in the air. It must be coming from the tower, a broadcast of dark, raw power. Whatever it is, he can feel it growing stronger.

There's another sound.

Cheering?

Unsure of what else to do, he lets his curiosity guide the way as he darts from hallway to hallway. The noise is coming from the basketball gym. He opens a door, just a crack, and sees ... burning. In the center of the gym is a huge bonfire, surrounded by crowds of cheering students.

The master of ceremony is none other than the pig-woman. With one of her many hands, she holds up a pair of blue jeans. With one of her other hands, she holds a microphone. She shouts with a deep, monstrous voice — no longer the sweet, breathy voice of Ms. Primple — "Generic brand pants!"

The crowd boos their disapproval.

The pig-woman tosses the pants into the bonfire, and the crowd cheers.

Standing nearby are some of the cheerleaders: Joan Cooper, Kimberly Fenner, and Monica Hawley. Like Kyle, they're wearing red robes, not unlike the priests of Ishtar in ancient Babylon.

Joan hands the pig-woman more articles of clothing, who shouts, "A purple turtleneck over red leggings!"

Again the crowd boos until the turtleneck and leggings meet their fiery fates. Then it's all cheers.

The bonfire is so dazzling that Gideon overlooked the cages. Hanging from the ceiling, suspended by long chains, are human-sized bird cages. And protruding through the iron bars are the naked limbs of languishing students, who have been stripped down to their underwear. Apparently this is their just-desserts for dressing unfashionably.

Gideon searches the crowd, but there's still no sign of Cynthia or Doug. He gently closes the door.

He feels a movement in the threads of energy ... whispers and voices. They're searching for him; somehow he just knows it. He has to hide, but where?

The tunnels.

No sooner does the thought enter his mind than he springs into action, heading for the only way he knows how to get there: through the auditorium. Within minutes he's groping his way through a dark aisle, feeling seat after seat. The room is pitch black, though he dares not turn on a light. At last he reaches the stage, where he slips into the orchestra pit. From there, though he can't see a thing, it's all familiar territory, as if, just minutes ago, he was holding Cynthia's warm hand, feeling her breath on his face.

Where are you, Cynthia?

Feeling his way along walls, down stairs, and through doors, in no time he enters the "steam tunnels," where assuring lights dot the walls. Though he has no destination, he moves quickly. *Something* is drawing him forward. He runs his hands along the pipes, looking for … whatever it is he's looking for.

"Gideon!" someone shouts.

His heart leaping, Gideon turns to run. Then he registers the voice. It was gentle and familiar. He looks back to see none other than Cynthia McDaniels.

She smiles. "I thought I'd find you down here."

"How did you …" He's even more amazed when she lunges forward, wrapping her arms around him and pressing her body against his.

"Oh Gideon" — her voice quivers — "I'm so scared. I don't know what to do."

Gideon squeezes her back. He's not about to let go. "I'm here" is all he can think to say. Despite all his new-found power in mind and body, he's still just as paralyzed in the presence of beautiful women.

"When they started ordering us around," she says into his ear, "and everyone started acting like zombies, I knew something was wrong. I tried to tell my friends, but they just called me a weirdo. As if *I* was the one acting weird. I totally didn't know how to take it. But then I thought …"

She pulls away to look him in the eyes. "I thought of *you*, Gideon, the weirdest guy I know. And then I thought" — she looks contemplative — "maybe the weirdos are the normal ones and the normal ones are the weirdos." Again she smiles.

Should I kiss her?

"And *then* I thought, why do I care what these psychos think? So I *stopped* caring." She snaps her fingers. "And like that, everything changed."

Oh man, I want to kiss her.

"I just had to get away. So I ran, and … here I am, free … awake … alive. And all because of you."

The timing will never be better. Gideon closes his eyes, puckers his lips, and goes for the gold.

"What are you doing?"

Gideon stops, mortified. "Nothing."

She grabs his hand, then looks at him with imploring eyes. "Will you help me?"

"Of course."

"Then come on."

Without further explanation, she leads him to the end of a tunnel, then points to a vent cover at the top of the wall.

Gideon obediently peers through the metal slits and sees …

A conference room, the same one where the gods held their secret meeting.

Only this time the lights are dim, and there's only two people in the room: the gray lady and Doug Rock. The poor guy is tied to a chair.

Cynthia whispers, "We need to help him."

Gideon can hardly bear the sadness in her face. *I know. I love him too.*

Meanwhile the gray lady is saying in her cold voice, "Are you listening to me, Mister Rock?"

"Eat bantha fodder," Doug responds, his voice weak and tortured.

"I'm trying to have a serious conversation. The school board and I are concerned about your education."

Gideon rolls his eyes. *The act is up, lady.*

She continues. "The way you've been dressing, your peculiar expressions, the dubious company you've been entertaining … it's not proper for a bright, young man of your upbringing. You, Mister

Rock, are an athlete, not a nerd."

Though he struggles to even speak, Doug says, "You will refer to me as *Sir* Douglas, mystical knight of Arathor."

"Will you please!" shouts the gray lady. "We're not going to get anywhere if you keep talking like an imbecile." She taps a remote control, and a screen on the wall displays coverage of a college football game. Men are hitting each other. "There, you see? This is how young men of your clique are *supposed* to act. You do not read comic books. You do not think. You hit."

Doug's eyes are distant. "I am Sir Douglas, friend of the dark elves, defender of the crystal sphere. You can torture me, but you'll never break me."

Though Cynthia looks weirded out, Gideon can't help but smile, proud of his disciple. If only there were some way to help him.

Suddenly Cynthia's eyes light up. She whispers, "Remember that big on and off switch?"

Gideon *does* remember. Together, they run through the tunnels until finding the place. And there it is, that great, big, metal lever protruding from a green, electrical box, practically begging to be pulled. Just days ago, the thought of such delinquent behavior was paralyzing. Now they proceed in a heartbeat.

Hand upon hand, they pull. The metal grinds and clanks, and suddenly everything turns black. The lever was, indeed, the master power switch for the school. From above and all-over come the muffled cries of startled students.

Still hand in hand, Gideon and Cynthia feel their way through the darkness, led only by the dim light streaming through the vents.

Gideon feels it again, those chaotic pulses of energy. He hears whispers and voices. He can feel the very minds of the gods. They're searching for him with a new intensity, and this time they find him. A voice screams:

Gideon Greenwich!

Suddenly the ceiling bursts into pieces as flames spill everywhere. Through a massive hole, the gray lady is staring down at them, her hands flaming, her eyes just as deadly.

WATER

Gideon tugs Cynthia's hand in the opposite direction, and they run through the darkness.

From behind, there's a clanking thud. The gray lady has leaped into the tunnels, crouching like a professional gymnast. So much for the stiff, proper woman. In fact, she's turning into something else altogether. Her clothing is ripping and falling apart as she grows larger and uglier. She's a spiky, scaly, gray monster that resembles a tyrannosaurus rex.

Her clawed hands tighten, then ignite with raging flames. She hurls a massive fireball.

Just before being incinerated, Gideon and Cynthia dash around a corner.

As they run, the monster calls after them with a gravelly bass voice. "If I can't burn you, I'll drown you."

Their only light comes from the distant glow of the monster's hands. They feel their way along the pipes. They're at a dead end. Cynthia exclaims, "How do we get out of here?"

"There was an exit sign somewhere," Gideon replies, trying to stay calm, "but now that everything's dark …" It's a dire situation. Dire situations are good. If only he wasn't thinking so hard, he might pull off something amazing. He closes his eyes and tries to focus on the energy.

Gideon Greenwich! shrieks the mind of the gray lady. This isn't going to work.

Meanwhile Cynthia asks, "Do you feel … water?"

Before Gideon can ask what she means, he feels a drop on his face. And then another. From a distance comes the muffled sound of cracking thunder. *Rain ... in the school?*

As Gideon and Cynthia grope through the darkness, they're soaked by spurts of water from above. The spurts grow into torrents, pouring through the vents. They're running through puddles, then sloshing through a stream, then wading through a river.

Cynthia cries, "We can't beat them. They're *gods*!"

"You saw her," Gideon responds. "They're *monsters*."

"I don't care what they are. We're going to die!"

In no time the cold water is up to their waists ... their chests ... their necks. Then they're treading to stay afloat. When their heads are forced against the metal pipes of the ceiling, Cynthia screams.

POWER

As for Gideon, the old adage proves true. His life *does* flash before his eyes.

First Grade, Mrs. Schneider's class. He sees the new boy with the funny accent, the one he called a poo-poo head. Will this tormenting memory never leave him?

I'm sorry!

And who's this standing in the background, that large man who was always just ... there? Someone's dad? A teacher? Gideon grew so accustomed to the face that he tuned it out ... for years. Though every now and then, the man would make eye contact, sometimes smiling with approval. Gideon would always look away, pretending nothing had happened. But now he knows the man's name, and that changes everything.

Populous.

Third Grade, Mrs. Vlam's class. He sees the "I love you" note colored by Tonya Crawford and dropped on his desk. How he relished the thought of her affection and how he, in turn, showed his mutual interest: by finding her after school and insulting her for ten minutes straight ... because, so he thought, that's what boys were supposed to do.

I'm sorry!

And who's this woman in the background? A gray skirt suit? He didn't meet her in high school. The goddess of normality was *always* there, supervising his life.

Sixth Grade, Mrs. Beckstead's class, the end-of-school dance. How he desperately wanted to fit in with the cool kids, putting on his first pair of black shades and bopping his head to the beat. And who's this disk jockey, a dark woman with well-manicured hair? Come to think of it, she was at every party, every assembly. From the moment his friends started blasting beats and stopped using their imaginations, she was there.

They were there all along, controlling him. Controlling *him*.

The fury starts in his chest, then extends to his hands. His clenched fists grow hotter and hotter until the water boils around him. Then, having to release his consuming anger, he thrusts his hands upward.

Something explodes overhead, and the next thing he knows, he and Cynthia are bobbing into sweet, life-giving air. Their heads are poking out of a steaming crater. They pull themselves onto the wet, tiled floor. They're in one of the hallways. Heavy rain is falling from the ceiling, which is obscured by dark mist.

Gasping for air, Cynthia asks, "How did you do that?"

"I … don't … know," Gideon replies, his heart pounding. It's tempting to just lie there.

"Are you one of them?"

"No."

They help each other to their feet, which proves difficult over the sleek floor. It's hard not to stare at the impossible rain clouds over-head, surging with tendrils of electricity.

"How is this possible?" Cynthia asks.

"You haven't seen anything yet. Come on, we're too vulnerable here." Gideon takes her hand, and together they run through the hallway, stomping through the water. They turn at the first corner, then come to a crashing halt.

Up ahead is the pig-woman, standing in front of the school li-brary. She's conversing with Populous.

Gideon and Cynthia hide behind the corner, watching.

Without any effort, the gods are generating light from their hands and sending glowing balls into the air. The dazzling balls are like stars, illuminating the dark, stormy, school.

Someone else is walking through the hallway: a wolf-man. He's tall and muscular, fanged, and clawed. Even weirder, something is *crawling* through the hallway, a dark, hideous … *spider* woman.

The pig-woman acknowledges the newcomers. "Well it's about time."

The wolf-man says — that is, growls — "This better be important." Though deep and gruff, there's something familiar about that voice.

"Sportacus," Gideon whispers, his heart sinking. "He's back."

Sportacus — the wolf-man — snorts. "She's not *my* master."

"Nor mine," says the spider woman.

Gideon knows that voice too. *Muza.* Nothing Gideon has done has had any lasting effect. If anything, he's made the problem worse … much worse.

The pig-woman — Fasha — says, "It *is* important. The dissidents are getting out of hand."

Populous — the only humanoid — pulls aside his toga and scratches his hairy chest. "That may be true, but I've had enough of this." He waves a lazy hand, and the rain stops pouring. "While we've practically got the entire student body, we can't enslave every soul. Now I say we count our losses and clean up before this mess gets out of hand."

A fifth being stomps and splashes into the scene, the gray … lizard. "Is this treachery I hear?" booms the reptilian monster — Normalia.

Fasha, Sportacus, and Muza bow their monstrous heads. Only Populous dares speak. "Of course not, good goddess. We're simply concerned."

"No one leaves the school until the dissidents are taken care of," says Normalia. "They have seen too much, and their minds cannot be controlled like the others. They are an infectious disease. If left alone, they will undo all of our work. They must be annihilated."

Populous raises an eyebrow. "Are we allowed to do that? I thought —"

"We are the gods of this world. We can do whatever we want, so long as we make it look natural. We'll create an *accident*."

"My lady, perhaps the situation is more than we can tackle alone.

Should we not call upon our master?"

"And suffer his wrath? No. We simply need a specialist, some-one who knows how to deal with these … weirdos. Where is our other brother? Should he not be here?"

Fasha nods. "I called for him, but he wouldn't respond."

Normalia closes her reptilian eyes and shouts, "Nerdacus!"

The others look around in apprehension.

"Nerdacus!" she shrieks.

Then, as in Ms. Primple's classroom, the walls of the hallway warp. A man steps into their world. He's overweight, balding, and wearing thick glasses, sweat pants, and a t-shirt thxat reads *Cthulhu Fears Me*.

The man frowns at the others. "I was in the *last* room of the *final* dungeon of level *nine*. I would have gained over a *thousand* experi-ence points." He waits for the gravity of his words to sink in. "Well?"

Normalia stares him down, baring her teeth a little. "In your careless absence, your subjects have run amok."

"*My* subjects?" Nerdacus looks around with disbelief.

"Find them," Normalia orders. "Destroy them."

Nerdacus pushes up his glasses. "But —"

"Now!" Normalia roars.

Nerdacus steps back in alarm. "As you wish." For a moment he just takes in the school. Then he pulls out a device that looks like an extra-large calculator. He taps a few buttons, studies the screen, then decides on a direction. He's coming straight for Gideon and Cyn-thia.

Again the two run through the hallways, splashing. When they're a safe distance, Gideon says, "I didn't think there was a god of *nerds*."

"Of course you didn't," says Cynthia. "You thought you and your friends were the only ones with brains. You nerds are just as prejudiced as the rest of us."

They approach the end of a hallway, where bright daylight streams through the doors. *Deliverance.* Cynthia throws her weight against one of the handles. At least she tries to. She and Gideon shove with all their might, but they can't make contact. An unseen force is pushing back.

"No!" Cynthia screams, trying again and again.

"It's no use," says Gideon, wishing they went for the tower when they had a chance. "They won't let anyone out until they get what they want."

"And that is?"

"You heard them. They want us dead."

Cynthia punches at the invisible force field. "I should have followed the crowd. What was I thinking?"

"Let's stay calm."

"Stay calm?" She punches again, screaming. "There's nothing calm about this. Look around you, Gideon. Our world has gone nuts! What are we supposed to do?"

"We can fight."

A new voice joins the conversation. "I wouldn't recommend that."

Turning a corner, with a big smile, is the god of nerds.

NERDACUS

Nerdacus walks toward them, tapping his thumbs on his huge calculator. "I suppose you think I used my *mathemagical* genius to track you down." He looks up from the calculator. "Nope. You guys just talk too loud. I could tell from the get-go that this job would be boring, so I brought a video game." He tosses the calculator into the water.

Gideon and Cynthia back up against the doors until the invisible force presses against them.

Nerdacus looks Gideon up and down. "So you're the kid who's been taking on the gods. Pretty cool, if you ask me. But then, what do *I* know of cool? I'm just the god of nerds, and no one ever invites me to their parties." He looks between Gideon's and Cynthia's paralyzed expressions. "You think I'm going to hurt you, don't you? Whatever my idiotic associates want, I have nothing against a fellow nerd, especially one of such … promise." He smiles from ear to ear. "Is it true that you made a fool of Sportacus in front of the entire student body?"

Gideon makes no reply.

"Brilliant," Nerdacus continues. "I hate that guy, so full of himself, always picking on me. Then there's those air heads, Fasha and Muza. I hear you got them good, and for that, I will forever be in your debt. But how did you do it? Last I heard, they locked you up in the detention center."

Still Gideon is silent.

"Don't care to elaborate? That's all right. I already know the answer, of course. I'm a god, after all. You extended your mind and discovered the extra-dimensional universe. You learned how to warp time, space, and possibility. You learned that you *too* are a god … of sorts."

Finally, Gideon speaks. "What do you want?"

"I don't mean to be rude, but beginner's luck will only get you so far, and now that my associates have rallied against you, you really don't stand a chance. But forget about those losers. What you need is a mentor to help you develop your gift. Accept *me* as your god, and I will teach you *true* power. Worship me, and I will give you the life you were meant for. Gideon, you're a genius."

Cynthia cries, "Don't listen to him, Gideon! You're cool, but you're not *that* cool. He's a demon, just like the rest."

Nerdacus chuckles. "Don't tell me you're gonna listen to this bimbo. She's a cheerleader, for crying out loud. She's never read a single Tolkien novel. Gideon, it's the mind that matters, not the body. With the mind, I can give you anything. Books, movies, video games, virtual reality as you've never seen it."

Nerdacus waves his hand, and everything changes. Instead of storm clouds and a dark corridor, there's a bright, blue sky and white, puffy clouds. Gideon is startled to find himself high in the air, wind beating against him. His legs are straddled around something large, green, and scaly. He's riding atop a *dragon*.

Overcome with vertigo, he clings on to the dragon's tough neck. For a while he can only stare at its huge, bat-like wings as they beat up and down. Then he ventures to look at the world below. Whizzing past them are the tops of pine trees. Up ahead is a clear river, a white waterfall, a dazzling rainbow, a stony castle, a purple mountain. It's all so beautiful.

"Any illusion you want," comes the voice of Nerdacus, "is yours."

It's all too much. The wind is too hard, the force too great. Gideon starts to slip.

His fear is quelled as he falls onto a soft seat. Again, everything has changed. Now he's in the bridge of a spaceship. In front of him is a huge screen with a dazzling starscape, a green planet in front of a glimmering galaxy. Surrounding him, standing at attention, is a uniformed crew.

Gideon looks down at his own uniform, at the chevrons and medals. He's their *captain*.

"You want muscles?" Nerdacus continues. "I'll give you muscles."

Gideon's body inflates, ripping his red uniform. He sees his massive biceps, his huge chest.

"You want chicks? No problem."

When Gideon looks up, his crew is composed entirely of beautiful women, their lovely, brown eyes fixated on him.

Wow.

"It's not real!" comes a distant voice. *Cynthia.* Part of Gideon wants to listen, but another part doesn't care. Such glorious stars, such massive muscles, so much female attention … what could possibly be better than this?

"Yes," continues that warm assuring voice, "this is where you belong, respected, adored, empowered. This is the *real* world, the world of the mind. Athletics, fashion, hygiene, those are for the unenlightened. Hate them. They're worthless. If they can't control their own minds, they deserve to be enslaved by the gods … gods like you."

There's another distant voice. "Snap out of it, Gid!"

He knows that voice. He loves it. "Doug?" he asks.

"There's no Doug here," says a female attendant. With perfect hands, she massages Gideon's scalp. It feels good. So what if it's not real?

"Remember who you are," says the voice of Doug. Gideon looks around, but his friend is nowhere to be seen.

Then there's that calming voice. "You're a nerd."

"No, you're a running back. No one could catch you at the fight. You outran the entire team at the pep rally. Gid, you and I are gonna take state this year."

It's a beautiful thought. Gideon wants it to be true. He sits up, but his female attendant pushes him back down, saying, "Relax, captain. You've been through a lot of stress." It's true. As her gentle fingers work their blissful touch into his scalp, Gideon finds himself sinking lower and lower, unable to resist.

"There," says the assuring voice, "Let go."

"Let go," Gideon repeats.

"I am your god."

"You are my god."

HYDRA

Suddenly his female attendant punches him in the temple. The hard slam sends him right off the chair and into the water.

Water?

Climbing to his hands and knees, Gideon opens his eyes. As the pain creeps in, he sees stars. He also sees blurry figures coming into focus. Cynthia. Nerdacus. Doug. The bright, dazzling world is gone. Back are the gloomy clouds and dim hallway of the school.

Doug helps Gideon to his feet, saying, "Sorry, man, but sometimes we all need a punch in the face."

Gideon nods, rubbing the bruise. "You're the best friend anyone could ask for."

Nerdacus claps his hands in mockery. "Touching. Who would have foreseen such an unlikely friendship?"

Doug turns to Nerdacus. "You, sir, can leave."

Nerdacus laughs. "You think I'm gonna let a *jock* tell me what to do?"

Doug lifts his chest. "For your information, I am Sir Douglas, mystical knight of Arathor."

"I've seen you. You're a meat head, the lead crony for Sportacus."

"That Doug is dead, like you'll soon be."

Nerdacus steps forward, having to crane his head back to meet Doug's eyes. "Is that a threat?"

"I'll give you two choices, fatso: beat it" — Doug smacks his fist into his palm — "or eat it."

Nerdacus nods, rubbing his chin. "It *is* a threat. Interesting. Well it just so happens that I have some options for you too: worship me"

— he waves a hand — "or be torn to pieces by a seven-headed hydra!"

Suddenly everyone is sprayed by an explosion of water. They turn to see an awesome sight. Rising out of the water — the several *inches* of water — are snapping, snake-like heads with savage eyes and deadly fangs. The heads, hissing and roaring, rise higher, revealing long necks and a single, reptilian body.

While Nerdacus watches with amusement, the friends try to get away, but they're cornered at the end of the hallway. The unseen force field is relentless.

The hydra is drawing nearer.

Cynthia cries, "It's got to be another illusion."

Doug looks around. Spotting a floating textbook in the shallow water, he picks it up and hurls it at the hydra. Two of the monsters' heads catch the book in their teeth and tear it apart, sending pages everywhere.

"I don't think that's an illusion," says Doug.

Cynthia is having a nervous breakdown. "This can't be happening; it's illogical!"

Nerdacus laughs. "As Mr. Spock put it in Star Trek Five, *Logic is the beginning, not the end.*"

Gideon and Doug crowd each other as they both try to shield Cynthia.

As the hydra draws within snapping distance of its helpless prey, an exuberant Nerdacus shouts, "Nerds will always triumph over jocks, because nerds dream bigger."

Gideon, Doug, and Cynthia huddle together. Gideon tries to make his hands burn again, but he feels no anger, only fear. He's got nothing.

Waiting for their impending doom, it's strange to notice something even bigger than the hydra: a colossal set of sharp teeth. Barely fitting within the rectangular hallway, the teeth are creeping up behind the hydra, wrapping around the writhing heads. Then the teeth chomp down, and the hydra is no more. In its place is a giant fish. The fish swallows its huge mouthful, then makes an impossible dive into the inches of water.

The hallway suddenly cleared, the friends see two figures in the background. A purple fanny pack, a Cub Scout baseball cap … Dwight and Wanda.

Wanda shouts, "But some nerds can dream bigger than others." She lowers her outstretched hands.

At first Nerdacus is livid. He stomps toward Wanda. "Did you …" But his red face lightens from anger and turns to wonder. "Was that … yours?"

Wanda cracks her knuckles. "Guilty as charged."

Dwight adds, "And I helped. I have magic too."

Nerdacus gets a closer look at Wanda. "Never in my life have I seen such power in a mortal. How did you do it?"

"Well," says Wanda, enjoying the attention, "it started with a question. Why do you guys try so hard to control us? And the answer was obvious. You're afraid we'll discover that we're as powerful as you are."

Nerdacus scoffs.

Wanda continues. "I watched Populous pull grapes out of nowhere as he stuffed his face. But the grapes must have come from *somewhere*. And then it clicked. To a god, every dimension must be within reach. Time, space, and …"

"Possibility."

"Yes. Then I watched you pull a monster out of some parallel universe, and I thought, I could do that too."

Again Nerdacus claps. "Well done. You all have come to the right man. I will teach you how to develop your talents further. Let me show you the true power of the nerd."

Wanda looks down at the grimy water, thinking. "There's only one problem."

"And that is?"

"This discussion has given me another realization."

"Well?"

She looks up, smiling. "I'm not a nerd. I'm Wanda."

Doug takes a step forward. "And I'm more than a jock."

Now Gideon takes a step forward. "And we are *not* your subjects."

Dwight says, "And that quote comes from Star Trek Six, not Five."

Cynthia adds, "And I totally read *The Lord of the Rings*."

Nerdacus looks around in horror, then explodes.

The friends shield themselves as sparks fall to the ground and fizz in the water. For a moment, the five of them just take in the sweet silence. Then Doug and Cynthia fall into each other's arms.

Gideon forces himself to look away. Instead, he takes a good look at Wanda. Somehow he never noticed how blue her eyes were. "That was … something else."

Wanda smiles. "Thanks."

Has she always looked at him like that? "How did you escape from Populous?"

It's Dwight who answers. "Well, first they locked Wanda and I in cages. You wouldn't believe it."

"I believe it," says Gideon.

"Then Kyle Slater, who was wearing this red robe, ordered everyone to talk about the latest TV shows."

Wanda adds, "He's now the high priest of Populous."

Dwight continues. "When the mic was passed to Wanda, things got really tense, because, as you know, Wanda's grandma doesn't believe in watching anything made after the nineteen-seventies. So she …"

"So I started reciting Emily Dickinson," says Wanda. With dreamy eyes, she recites the poem:

> *That I did always love,*
> *I bring thee proof:*
> *That till I loved*
> *I did not love enough.*

"Kyle got really mad," says Dwight. "He told her to shut up."

"But the more I spoke of love," says Wanda, "the more I felt it for my fellow students, despite clique or class … even for Kyle. The thought was so empowering that I … I …"

"She made the cage explode," says Dwight.

As a demonstration, Wanda points a finger at a nearby locker. It explodes.

Gideon nods his approval. "You're awesome, Wanda." He surveys his four friends. He couldn't have gotten this far without them. He wants to tell them how much he loves them.

There's commotion at the other end of the hallway. Coming their way is a large crowd of students: boys, girls, freshmen, sophomores, juniors, seniors … everyone. They're wielding baseball bats and hockey sticks.

Leading the parade is Populous and his high priest, Kyle Slater. Kyle has murder in his eyes. Raising a hockey stick, he shouts, "Destroy them!"

The army charges forward, shouting one heck of a war cry.

POPULOUS

Gideon turns to Wanda. "Do something amazing!"

With only a moment's hesitation, Wanda raises her hands, and the water rises from the floor, spreading high and wide, forming a wall between them and the charging army. Wanda claps her hands, and the water turns to ice.

Doug says, "Nice!"

An awe-inspired Cynthia mutters, *"Logic is the beginning of wisdom, not the end."*

Gideon looks around. Between the wall of ice and the force field blocking the doors, they're even more trapped than they were before. "If we all work together, I'm sure we can think of a way —"

Suddenly the wall of ice bursts apart and crashes to the floor. In its place stands Populous with flaming fists. Looking at Gideon, he lowers his brow, and the flames burn brighter. The walls bend inward as his body convulses and distorts. Then he's no longer Populous but a grotesque, elephantine monster with too many tusks.

Cynthia screams at the sight of the monster's green eyes.

Gideon turns to Wanda. "Do something else."

Wanda throws up her arms. "That's all I've got."

The elephant is making ready to charge.

Gideon racks his mind. They're unarmed, outnumbered, and trapped. The only available directions are blocked off.

Unless ...

He looks up at the stormy clouds. It's a crazy idea, but that's exactly what they need right now. "Join hands!" he orders.

Though the request is strange, no one hesitates to obey. Within seconds, Gideon, Wanda, Dwight, Doug, and Cynthia have formed a circle.

Gideon shouts, "Step on each other's feet!"

Meanwhile the mob resumes its charge, an onslaught of elephant monster, Kyle Slater, and zombie students. The floor rumbles, the water shakes. They fill the hallway with noise.

Gideon cries, "Now think force field!" Squeezing the hands of Wanda and Dwight, he shuts his eyes and imagines a burning sphere around them. He can feel the presence of something stronger than his own force. He's connected to a network of gentle, beautiful, minds ... *powerful* minds. Together they warp the universe around them, and the field grows brighter and brighter.

When he opens his eyes, there's a warm glow around them. Zombie students are crashing into it and falling to the ground. Kyle beats at the bubble with his hockey stick, but the wood shatters.

Doug watches this with pleasure. "You'll have to do better than that, dude!"

The elephant-man extends his front hands, his green eyes squinting with concentration. A small hole tears into the bubble. The hole expands.

Again Gideon turns to his friends, saying the first thing that comes to his mind. "Think rocket blast!" Still squeezing their hands, he closes his eyes and imagines a blast of red flames. Again he feels the minds of his friends beside him. They imagine the flames growing hotter and brighter. They imagine the force pushing them upward. Together they hold on to the dream, and together they rise.

When Gideon looks down, the floor is dropping fast, the mob looking up in wonder. The flying bubble passes through the rain clouds, then crashes through the ceiling. It breaks through everything: plastered tiles, metal frames, pipes, and concrete.

The next thing they know, they're ascending into a bright, blue sky, and panic kicks in. At once the magic is broken, the flame fizzles out, and the bubble vanishes. Then gravity kicks in. Five disjointed bodies crash onto the hard roof of the school, just clear of the hole they created.

Scuffed but alive, the friends rise to their feet. For a moment they just breathe, feeling the warm sun and gentle breeze. They take in the vast, flat roof of the school and the exalted view of the surrounding neighborhoods. Peaceful streets, green trees, the carefree chirps of birds ... suddenly the hell below seems like a dream.

Doug points to the cell phone tower at the edge of the football field. "There it is, the source of their power." The weird, green energy surrounding it is as clear as anything else in the daylight.

Gideon says, "We must destroy it. Now." He runs to the other side of the roof, and his friends follow. "Wanda, you summoned the fish. Can you summon ... dynamite?"

Wanda closes her eyes, her hands together. "I'll try."

Meanwhile Cynthia screams, pointing to something in the distance. Black, spindly legs — eight of them — are climbing up the side of the building and onto the roof. Muza.

Gideon says to Wanda, "Is there any way you can hurry?"

A frustrated Wanda shakes her head. "I tried, but —" Then she notices the stick of dynamite in her hands. The fuse is sparkling. Wanda screams and tosses the stick to Gideon.

Gideon is just as horrified. "*I* can't throw." He tosses the stick to Doug.

Doug receives the stick without protestation. The wick is growing short. He takes the stance of a baseball pitcher and hurls the stick at the cell phone tower. Notwithstanding the distance, the throw is dead on. The stick detonates with a fiery blast.

But the tower is virtually unscathed.

Gideon turns back to Wanda. "Laser cannon?"

Again Wanda closes her eyes.

Muza is crawling toward them. Suddenly the air warps beside her, and the wolf-man — Sportacus — appears. There's another warp, and the pig-woman — Fasha — appears. Then comes the tyrannosaurus — Normalia — the elephant, Populous — and a new edition — a deranged-looking cat-man with the face of Nerdacus. Together the motley army advances, six demonic beings.

Gideon turns back to Wanda, but there's no need for words. In her hands is a fantastic gun from some future time and place, and this time she has no reservations. She pulls the trigger, and a power-ful beam of light shoots out. The beam sears into the surface of the steel tower, but the effect is still negligible, the process too slow.

With the monsters getting close, Gideon shouts the next thought that comes to his mind. "Godzilla!"

Instead of a look of *what's wrong with you* — the look Gideon has been conditioned to expect when he makes outlandish remarks, Wanda has a look of *why didn't I think of that?*

I could love such a girl, Gideon thinks. If only they weren't about to be destroyed by monsters, he would happily explore this thought further.

Wanda grabs Gideon's and Dwight's hands. "I can't do this alone. Help me."

Dwight says, "Don't worry, I've got magic."

Wanda turns to Doug and Cynthia, shouting, "We need every-one's help."

Cynthia shakes her head. "I'm not … I can't …"

Doug takes her hand. "It's okay to be weird. In fact, it's fun." He tugs her, and together they join the circle.

Wanda closes her eyes, saying, "Think big. Think powerful. Think —" She's interrupted by a blasting roar. "That was fast."

The friends open their eyes to an awe-inspiring sight. Standing even taller than the one-hundred-fifty-foot cell phone tower is a green lizard-man. Covered in spikes, plates, and claws, his massive body lumbers toward the tower.

Dwight asks, "How did we do that so fast?"

Gideon has a ready answer. "Impending doom has a way of bringing out one's abilities."

Meanwhile their impending doom — the army of monsters — has stopped its charge, their attention drawn to the much bigger monster. They just stand there.

Dwight says, "Look, they're intimidated."

Gideon gets a better look at the monsters. Their eyes are closed, their lips murmuring. He feels a wave of dread. "I don't think so."

Cynthia shouts, "Look!"

Materializing in the air, not far from the tower, is an even more colossal creature. Actually, it's a machine, a silver recreation of the lizard-man. It's covered in cannons. At once the robot releases an arsenal of smoking rockets, which impact against the lizard. The lizard, thrown back by the blasts, falls to the ground. The crash is so intense, it causes the entire school to quake, knocking both humans and monsters to the ground and cracking the concrete beneath them.

The cat-man shouts, "Haha! Mechagodzilla wins!"

A terrified Dwight turns to his friends. "Do something."

But what can be done? Exhausted, defeated, they can only watch as the triumphant robot continues its carnage. With the lizard-man out of its way, it proceeds to unleash its fury … on the cell phone tower. Because, apparently, that's what *Mechagodzilla* does; it destroys things.

The monsters cry out in shock at this sudden turn of events.

As for Gideon, he can't help but smile. "You forget, Dwight, that the gods are stupid."

It all happens so quickly, no one can stop it. The robot pushes against the tower with all its strength. At the base, concrete crumbles, bolts are broken, metal screeches, and the entire structure leans, then falls … straight toward the school.

"Run!" everyone seems to cry at once.

MELTING

When Gideon comes to, he finds himself lying in a pile of dust and rubble. His body aches all over. His ears are ringing, his head throbbing. Everything is dark.

Overhead are unearthly rainclouds. Were it not for the orange carpet beneath him, he would have never guessed he was lying in the commons of the school. As the clouds dissipate, he makes out a big, bright spot in the ceiling, the hole through which they fell from the roof.

"Wanda?" he says.

"I'm here." She reaches out, and their hands touch.

Gideon has never felt anything more wonderful. "Dwight?"

"Yo," comes the weakened voice of his friend.

"Doug, Cynthia?"

For a moment there's silence, and Gideon's heart sinks. Then he feels a strong hand grip his own, lifting him to his feet.

Doug and Cynthia stand before him, beat up, bleeding, but alive. Gideon looks around at his friends, overcome with joy. He opens his mouth, but shame gets the best of him. Of course he can't just *tell* them how he's feeling. That wouldn't be cool.

There's voices in the distance, silhouettes in the settling dust. It's their fellow students, surrounding them on all sides. Gideon recoils, clenching his fists. Then he notices the eyes of Joan Cooper. Her zombie stare is gone; in its place is something much more human. She looks confused.

Others have the same look. The students aren't coming to kill them. They're lost souls, searching for something to fill a void.

Joan even goes so far as to smile at Gideon. "Hey," she says.

"Hey," replies a confused Gideon. Joan Cooper is not only looking at him but talking to him. This doesn't happen.

Suddenly the chatter dies down, and the crowd parts. They make a path for a parade of charging figures: the tyrannosaurus, the elephant, the pig, the wolf, the spider, and the cat.

The students gasp at the monstrous spectacle.

Gideon instinctively throws out his hands, intending to send a fiery blast at his foes, but nothing happens. There's no energy in the air. None at all.

Staring at Gideon, the pig-woman raises her many arms, ready to strike with the indignation of an angry goddess. But nothing happens. She can barely hold up the weight of her arms. She falls to her knees, gasping.

Meanwhile Joan Cooper walks right up to her.

"Joan, no!" cries Gideon.

But Joan doesn't listen. Taking a good look at the pig-woman, she says, "You're ugly."

Fasha's eyes open wide. Her jaw, with all of its terrible teeth, falls open — wider and wider — until it falls right off her face.

Joan screams.

Next, a horn falls off, then another. But instead of hitting the floor, the horns just vanish, as if, all along, they were nothing but illusions. The pig woman's skin tears and peels open, her guts oozing out. There goes an arm … and a leg. There goes her head. What's left of the dilapidated beast falls apart until nothing is left.

Nothing but a ghost.

It's a woman, or at least the shadow of one. If the crowd wasn't already staring, they would probably look through her frail image. Misshapen nose, googly eyes, jutting chin, balding hair.

Joan speaks again. "You *are* ugly."

The wisp of a woman steps back, horrified. She looks around, then darts for the nearest wall. She runs right into it … and is gone.

The tyrannosaurs cries, "Fasha, come back here!" Then she sees what's happening to the rest of the monsters. The elephant has fallen to all fours. His legs break beneath the weight. The wolf has also fallen over, his eyes glazing. The spider is shriveling up. The cat is clutching his belly.

The tyrannosaurus roars with fury. She turns to the students. "Fall to your knees," she orders. "Worship your gods."

But no one budges.

"Can't you see you're killing them? They cannot live without your power!" She charges at a group of students, who step back in alarm, but none of them run. As they hold their ground, it becomes obvious that the threat was empty.

The tyrannosaurus recoils. Then even she falls to her knees.

The elephant has vanished. In its place stands the ghost of a scrawny, little man, just as ugly as the woman. The man also runs for the wall and vanishes.

"Populous," the tyrannosaurus wheezes, reaching in vain.

The demise of the wolf, spider, and cat don't take long. Soon there's nothing left but three homely wisps of human beings. They don't hesitate to escape into the wall.

"Don't leave me," moans the tyrannosaurus. But her words are too late. She looks around but gains no sympathy from the crowd. Finally, her eyes meet Gideon's. She squints, she groans, the space around her warps, and then the tyrannosaurs is no more; in its place is the gray lady. She looks beaten up, exhausted.

Still on her knees, she whispers, "Well played, Mister Greenwich. Perhaps there's hope for you yet." She gasps for air. She swallows in anguish. "There's just one thing you lack."

"And that is?" Gideon asks.

"A second opinion. I'm afraid I'm going to have to refer you to my supervisor." Her voice is barely audible when, in a dying whisper, she adds, "Coolar."

"Who?"

"Coolar," she repeats, a little louder than before. With the word comes power. Gideon feels it. The gray lady is no longer sinking but rising to her feet. "Coolar," she says loud and clear. "Coolar!" she screams.

The floor rumbles.

COOLAR

The walls shake. Tiles fall from what's left of the broken ceiling. The rumbling grows louder, an earthquake beneath their feet. Students scream and shout, sloshing through the shallow water, looking for cover.

The gray lady, growing ever stronger, shouts, "Did you really think you could defeat us by knocking over a tower?" Her voice booms with power. "We are gods. We are forces of nature."

In the center of the commons, the floor cracks open, draining the water. The crack grows into a massive hole, and from it spurts a pillar of raging fire.

From nowhere comes music: a pounding beat, a thumping bass, and a guitar solo so amazing, it sounds heavenly.

Then, rising from the midst of the burning glory, is a man. He has black shades, golden necklaces, a jewel in each ear, a ring on each finger … a shiny vest, a bare chest, tattoos on each arm … baggy pants, and high-top basketball shoes.

"Coolar!" comes the cry of an unseen choir.

The spectacle is so awe-inspiring, some students can't help but fall to their knees.

Meanwhile Coolar, sitting in a throne of fire, elevated over the dark pit, takes in his frightened audience. He waves a hand, and the music stops.

For a moment the massive room is dead silent. Then Coolar takes off his glasses, clears his throat, and shouts:

> *Break down the door, big dawg, big dawg.*
> *Break down the door, big dawg!*

His voice fills the room, and the beat from nowhere returns. He leaps from his fiery throne, which vanishes behind him, and he lands on the floor. Busting some hip hop moves, he continues to sing:

> *Break down the door, big dawg, big dawg.*
> *Break down the door, big dawg!*

He struts and jumps with such enthusiasm, few can resist the temptation to bop their heads. Kyle Slater and his friends are the first to join in, shouting:

> *Have another shot, then tumble to the floor.*
> *Scramble to your feet. You're gonna take more.*

Every second, more students join in. It's so catchy.

> *Break down the door, big dawg, big dawg.*
> *Break down the door, big dawg!*

When the song ends, half the student body cheers.

Meanwhile Coolar struts to the gray lady, gesturing the question, *what's going on?*

Without hesitation, the gray lady points a bony finger at Gideon.

Coolar whips around and gives Gideon a good look. "Now what have we here?"

Dwight, Wanda, Doug, and Cynthia step closer to Gideon as Coolar struts toward them, throwing in a spin and some Michael Jackson moves on the way.

From the crowd, Monica Hawley shouts, "He's so cool!"

"So cool," others repeat.

Coolar stops in front of the huddled friends. He takes in the slap bracelets, the orange swimming trunks, the excess cellulose. Then he speaks. "I couldn't help but notice that *awesome* ends with *me*, and *ugly* begins with *U*."

Well over half the student body bursts into laughter.

When they quiet down, Coolar continues. "Can I take your picture? I love to collect photos of natural disasters." The laughter is growing louder. "Oh, and speaking of which, the zoo called. The baboons want their butts back, so you'll have to find new faces." Still more laughter. "I'm sorry, do your faces hurt? 'Cause they're killin' me!"

He gets a good look at Cynthia. "Except for this one. Dang, she is fine. Yo, girl, do you work at the coffee shop? Because I like you a latte."

Doug steps forward, raising his fists. "Don't talk to my girl like that."

A hush falls over the crowd as Coolar, puffing up his chest, struts — almost waddles — up to Doug. He puts his face uncomfortably close. "What you say, boy?"

"I said —" But before Doug can finish, Coolar raises his chin, and an unseen force sends Doug flying to the other end of the room, slamming into a soda machine.

Coolar turns to Gideon and Dwight. "Anyone else have something to say?"

A white-faced Wanda begins to sing:

> *Out in the country*
> *Where the jackrabbits hop,*
> *Was a little, old cowboy,*
> *A plantin' his crop.*

She looks to Gideon for support, but Gideon, hating himself for it, holds his peace. *This isn't going to work.* Wanda's voice quivers as she continues:

> *When who came along*
> *But pretty, old Sue,*
> *Saying —*

Coolar lifts his chain, and Wanda goes flying, slamming into the other soda machine. He turns to Dwight. "Anyone else?"

Dwight is quick to shake his head.

"Are you sure, chunks?" Coolar practically sticks his nose into Dwight's face. "You look like you're *dying* to say something."

A bead of sweat dripping down Dwight's face, he shouts:

Break down the door, big dawg, big dawg.
Break down the door, big —

Coolar lifts his chain, and Dwight is sent flying, smacking into a brick wall. "You're still ugly," Coolar announces, which is met by the laughing approval of the audience.

Meanwhile the gray lady folds her arms, watching with satisfaction.

Coolar approaches Gideon. "And what's your problem, poindexter?"

A frightened Cynthia grips Gideon's arms.

Gideon holds her back. He knows he must choose his words wisely. In fact, he chooses to say nothing at all. Instead, he yawns.

This takes Coolar off-guard. "Did you just —"

"The whole bully routine," says Gideon, " … lame. Anyone can memorize a few lines from funny-insults-dot-com. And throwing your opponents against a wall only flaunts your insecurity."

Coolar lowers his chin, and something sends Gideon downward, slamming onto his hands and knees. "Would you prefer the floor?"

The audience laughs, to which a troubled Joan Cooper shouts, "What's wrong with you people?"

Kyle Slater, however, starts pounding his fist in the air, chanting, "Coolar, Coolar …" His friends join in, and the chant catches like a wildfire.

Gideon rises to his feet, undeterred. In fact, this time he's the one to stick his nose uncomfortably close. "The fact that you have an audience doesn't make you any less despicable."

"You think so?" Coolar asks. "Let's put it to the vote." He turns to the chanting crowd. "Who here thinks I'm hot stuff?" The crowd voices their enthusiastic approval. "And who out there is a fan of white and nerdy?"

A sea of boos is directed at Gideon. Only Joan Cooper ventures a, "Me!"

Gideon runs his hands through his hair. "Are you even listening to me?"

"Listening to *you*?" Coolar throws up his arms in exasperation. "I'm your *god*. You listen to *me*."

Gideon continues. "Crowds make everyone stupider. You can listen to them all you want, but at the end of the day, you still have to live with yourself. And we both know that no one hates you more than you do."

"Enough!" Coolar shouts. "Boy, I think it's time you gain a little education." He raises both fists into the air, and the entire school lurches, sending everyone falling to the floor. As the school continues to shake, a force holds the students down. They're unable to move. Hundreds of voices cry out in terror.

The rainclouds are gone. Bright light shines through the hole in the ceiling and the hole in the floor. When Gideon looks down, he sees houses, streets, trees … the entire city growing smaller and smaller. A second later, the frightful view is obscured by clouds. Then the clouds grow smaller, and the entire scene wraps at the edges, squeezing into a blue globe. Even the globe shrinks into the distance, surrounded by blackness, before, finally, the school stops shaking.

Traumatized students climb to their hands and knees, looking through the windows at the black, empty space and shining, white stars. No one — not even Gideon — climbs to his feet. Instead, many prostrate themselves lower, their eyes glazing over.

"You see that?" asks Coolar, pointing down at the blue Earth. "A little real estate of mine. And you know what makes it go round?" He waits for the question to sink in. "Me."

"Coolar … Coolar …" the students chant.

Coolar flexes an arm and shows off his manly physique. "I am the look." Then he shouts, "I am the sound!" He spins three hundred-sixty degrees, ending with another Michael Jackson pose. "I am sports. I am fashion. I am music. I am your entertainment, your desire, your idol. I am worshiped in one-hundred-ninety-five countries in over one-thousand languages. If you ain't got me, no one's gonna listen to you. 'Cause when I say the brand is *Girbout*, the brand is *Girbout*."

Coolar lifts his hands, and, impossibly, the small Earth rises from the black pit. It's like a giant beach ball. Coolar extends his hands, and the Earth is no longer a planet at all but a spherical screen.

The image of land, clouds, and ocean zooms into a single city, into a single building, into a dance club. A crowd of stylish people move their bodies to a beat. Every last one of them is wearing pants with a *Girbout* label.

"If I say the word is *yo*, the word is *yo*."

Suddenly everyone in the dance club is saying *yo*.

"If I say the thing is mullets, the thing is mullets."

Suddenly everyone in the dance club has a well-manicured mullet, business in the front, party in the back.

"My missionaries are in every field, preaching from my bibles." The earth zooms out, then into another part of the world … a high school. Teenage girls are huddled around magazines, gushing over an attractive, male model.

"My soldiers are on every front, enforcing my law."

The scene moves to another part of the school, where a gang of jocks are dumping the contents of a trash can over a nerd.

"I am judgment. I am the final word. You are either cool or not. And you, Mister Greenwich …" Again he turns to Gideon.

Gideon instinctively rises to his feet, stepping back.

" … are not."

"So what are you going to do?" Gideon asks. "Murder me? Yeah, that's real cool."

"It is if *I* do it."

"So you're infallible."

"Of course. I'm God."

"You're not *my* God."

"You'd better show some respect." Again Coolar puffs up his chest and extends his arms in gangster fashion.

"Respect?" Gideon laughs. "You can throw as many tantrums as you want. You can cover yourself with gold. You can surround yourself with girls." Gideon imitates Coolar's gangster moves. "But *respect* is the one thing you'll never get. Because in spite of all the lip service, everyone knows you're nothing but an overgrown —"

Coolar lifts his chin, and Gideon is sent flying toward the hole in the floor. But before falling in, Gideon grabs onto some jutting rebar, holding on for dear life. His legs dangle into the black abyss.

"Gideon!" Cynthia screams, running to his aid.

Meanwhile Coolar lifts his chin again, and a force slams down onto Gideon.

Gideon loses his grip.

DARKNESS

He knows he's falling because, when he looks up, the bottom of the school is growing ever smaller; but other than that, there's no frame of reference. It's just him, the silent void, and the distant stars.

So much for the laws of physics. He must be in some parallel universe, or else how is he surviving the vacuum of space?

"Even now," comes an ethereal voice, "your blasphemies can be forgiven. I'll restore the school. I'll restore your former life. I'll even give you that fine girl."

"I don't want your illusions," says Gideon.

"I'm the real thing, kid. Anything in this world can be yours. You wanna be a football star? Wanna be handsome? Popular? Done and done. All I ask is that you worship me, and this nightmare will end."

Gideon slaps himself in the face. It hurts. *Yep, definitely not dreaming.*

He thinks of his soft bed, a green park, ancient Babylon, any-where but here. He wills himself away, but of course it doesn't work. There's no energy around him. Without a tower, he's just Gideon Greenwich, a powerless mortal.

"I'm your only hope!" booms Coolar.

"Will you be quiet?" Gideon shouts. "I'm trying to think."

The voice remains silent. Apparently even Coolar knows when to pick his battles.

Speaking of Coolar ... how does he *still have power?*

The gods must harness another source of energy, a secret source.

But then, it's no secret at all. The gray lady announced before the entire school that without their *worship*, the gods would die. That would explain why even mighty Coolar is begging him for it.

Worship? But what does that even mean?

Would Gideon somehow be stronger if people worshiped *him*? That might make him *feel* powerful, but that's not *real* power.

Is it?

What if belief is power in itself? He thinks back to the little prison cell in the detention center, of his first leap through time and space. How did he do it? By drawing energy from some metal contraption, or did the energy come from within him? Perhaps there *was* no energy, only belief.

If he believed I couldn't do it ... I was right.

But when Bula believed in him and Gideon believed in himself, it seemed that anything was possible. If only he could feel that confidence now. If only he wasn't alone, cut off, forsaken.

"Time is running out!" booms Coolar.

"Shut up," Gideon replies.

Why didn't Coolar just kill him as the gray lady tried to? Surely the guy has the power, so why this pathetic pandering to a teenager? Especially when Coolar has so many devoted subjects, does he really *need* Gideon's worship?

There must be something else, but what? Gideon asks out loud, "Do you want me to be your prophet?"

Coolar has no reply. The silence is telling.

"Or do you *fear* me?" Though the thought is gratifying, it's not entirely logical, as there was no contest between Gideon and the powerful god. With a mere flick of the guy's wrist, the fight was over.

"And yet I still exist. Why?" If Coolar is really a god, destroying Gideon should be a piece of cake ... unless even gods have limits.

Which they do. Gideon has learned beyond question that the so-called gods are neither all-knowing nor all-powerful. They're especially vulnerable to logic. Yet logic has gotten him nowhere with Coolar.

What do I have that he fears?

He would like to think it's an iron will, though he proved with

Nerdacus that he's just as corruptible as everyone else. He's far from some chosen hero.

Maybe it's not about me.

If Doug hadn't rescued him … if Wanda didn't have such a brilliant imagination … if Dwight hadn't known his Star Trek trivia and Cynthia hadn't read *The Lord of the Rings*, there's no saying what would have happened.

It's funny, but until now, the thought that Gideon isn't special never occurred to him. For so long it's felt like an uphill battle that he was destined to fight alone.

Maybe that's what the gods wanted me to think.

Since first grade, when he called that poor boy a poo-poo head, to high school basketball with Kyle Slater, the gods taught him to resent. *It's all about you*, they whispered into his ear. *No one else understands.* They flattered him, and he believed them.

Trying to sort his thoughts, he says to the darkness around him, "Instead of turning to each other, we turn inward. We put our time and energy into illusions: clothes, music, games, virtual reality. And when these things turn out to be empty, we nevertheless beg for more, because we can't bear the empty silence. We fear we might hear our consciences. But the more we delude ourselves, the more we lose control."

This is beautiful. Gideon wishes there was someone to write it down.

"On the other hand, the more we look beyond ourselves, the stronger the network. Instead of isolated neurons, we become part of a great brain." He felt it when joining hands with his friends, that warm energy, that amplified, super mind, so much more powerful than what he was capable of alone.

There's a word for this, but what? He knows it flies in the face of everything the gods stand for, but he can't quite put his finger on it.

What's the one thing the laws of coolness absolutely forbid?

"Ohh …"

It's so painfully obvious, how didn't he see it before? Not only is it what everyone secretly wants, it's what the *gods* want. "They want us to give it to them so that we can't give it to each other. They know that our possession of it would shake the very foundations of their kingdom."

Love.

His friends love him, and he loves *them*, and somehow that makes anything and everything seem possible.

Suddenly he feels more energy than ever before. He looks into the stars. "If there's anyone out there who's on my side … I could sure use some help right now."

Again he extends his hands and closes his eyes. He grips the fabric of the universe around him and holds tight … tighter … until he knows he's at a standstill. Then, still gripping the fabric, he flings it downward.

When he looks up, the tiny school is growing larger.

CONFRONTATION

This time it's Gideon who rises from the hole in the floor. Air rushing against him, he lands on the wet carpet, crouching from the impact.

This must look awesome.

He hears some students cheering at his triumphant reentry, though he can hardly see a thing. He's dazed, squinting from the new addition of burning torches on the walls.

Also within the last few minutes, Coolar has willed himself an ivory throne. Like Populous was, he's surrounded by a throng of female admirers, including Monica Hawley and Kimberly Fenner. Thankfully, the pretty girls seem to have diverted Coolar's attention from Cynthia.

Then Coolar turns to Gideon, his eyes deadly. Without saying a word, he extends another blast of energy.

But Gideon is ready, throwing a blast of his own. As the powers clash between them, something like electricity rips through the air, blowing debris everywhere. Frightened students cower and flee from the chaos.

Coolar pushes harder, but so does Gideon. The raging clash grows brighter and fiercer.

Wanda runs to Gideon and shouts over the mayhem, "You can't fight fire with fire!"

Gideon knows she's right. Ever so slightly, he lowers his defense. In turn, Coolar does the same. Gradually, the clash ceases, and the room falls silent.

Finally Coolar speaks. "Back for more? I thought nerds had brains. You must be as dumb as yo mama, who's so stupid, she brought a spoon to the super bowl."

As Coolar turns to receive the laughter from his loyal fans, Gideon feels rage kindling within him. Then he sees Wanda's gentle face. He knows what she's thinking.

Let it go.

As if that's not enough, Wanda takes his hand and whispers, "Compliment him."

"What?" Gideon whispers back, incredulous.

"He wants you to play his game. Don't do it."

Gideon nods, squeezing her hand. Though this is perhaps the hardest thing he's ever done, he shouts, "You are … handsome."

Coolar is taken off-guard. "What?"

"You … you have a nice physique."

The students look at each other, no doubt wondering if they heard correctly.

Finally Coolar turns to Wanda. "Did you know your boyfriend's a homo?"

As the audience laughs, Gideon feels the heat of a flushing face. This is, without a doubt, the hardest thing he's ever done. "You're also … funny."

Dwight smacks his face, murmuring, "He's lost it."

Coolar frowns. "I don't know what you're getting at, poindexter, but if you think —"

"And courageous. No wonder girls swoon over you. Just looking at you, it's obvious that you're not afraid of anyone or anything. You're willing to speak your mind and fight for what you believe in."

Coolar opens his mouth, but nothing comes out. He rubs the back of his head and finally turns away.

Kyle Slater steps forward. "Come on, Coolar, put him in his place."

But Coolar says nothing, so Kyle takes matters into his own hands. Turning to Gideon, he shouts, "You're a brainless turd, and your mom is so stupid, she tripped over a cordless phone." He turns to the audience for validation. He gets some laughs, but not as many as Coolar did.

Gideon takes a deep breath. "And you, Kyle … are an incredible athlete."

Kyle rolls his eyes. "Will you shut up?"

"You are a leader. You're the life of the party. Your friends look up to you. Heck, to be totally honest, *I* look up to you. I admire your discipline, your stamina, you drive. Kyle, you are … cool."

Kyle shrugs. He looks around. He shrugs again. "Thanks, Gid." He's unable to hold back a smile.

Still holding Gideon's hand, Wanda shouts, "Joan, Monica, Kimberly … you are beautiful. I signed up for Fashion Merchandising because I hoped to look more like you."

Joan places her hands over her chest. "That is so sweet."

Next, Doug catches the vision. He shouts, "And you … guy in my fifth period math class. What's your name?"

A scrawny boy shifts awkwardly. "Bernard," he says.

"Bernard." Doug smiles. "You are really smart. I want to be like you."

Then Bernard smiles. "Thanks."

Cynthia takes Doug's hand and steps forward. "I just want to say … I love all of you guys. Thanks for being my peers."

The audience voices their appreciation of the sentiment.

Then Coolar turns around. "Enough!" The torches burn brighter on the walls. His fists start to burn. "This is *not* how it works. I, God, placed you into cliques for a reason. Jocks do *not* associate with nerds. We do not express our love to our peers."

Gideon and Wanda walk toward him, as do Doug and Cynthia.

Coolar continues. "You keep your mouths shut and go with the crowd. Anything else is positively *uncool*."

Dwight and Joan approach him. Other students follow.

Coolar stares them down. "Don't look at me like that. I am *cool*." His eyes widen as the surrounding students start folding their arms. "I am …"

He looks down at his hands. The fire is gone. He looks up … and explodes.

As the fireworks clear, the room bursts into cheers. Some students try to lift Gideon onto their shoulders, but he declines. Rather, he hugs them, and the action goes viral. Wanda hugs Joan Cooper. Dwight hugs a pair of Freshman girls, who may or may not welcome it. Doug and Cynthia hug each other, then those around them. Gideon even attempts to hug Kyle, though he's met with a punch to the shoulder.

It's okay. Not everyone needs to be on hugging terms. Though he does succeed at hugging two other members of the football team, including …

"Bula?"

Bula smiles as he presents Gideon with a large Slurpee. "I hope you like sour cherry."

"I do." Gideon takes a sip from the red straw, the tart flavor forcing a frown. "It's melted."

Bula places a hand on his shoulder. "You did good, Gid." Then Bula runs off, because he's mysterious like that.

For a moment, Gideon is left to himself. He looks through the windows at the glistening stars. "Thank you," he whispers. Somehow, despite all the craziness, the journey was worth it. Then he looks for the next person in the hugging line and sees …

The gray lady.

Her face as stern as ever, she waves a hand, and everything turns black.

NORMAL

Gideon impacts against a hard floor. "Ouch!" He didn't even know he was falling. He's still in the commons, but everything's different. No more rain clouds, burning torches, holes, or cracks. Bright sunlight streams through the windows.

He looks around for the gray lady, but she's gone too. Except for his friends — all lying on the floor — the commons are empty.

Wanda's rubbing her eyes. "What happened?"

Cynthia looks utterly confused. "Did I dream the whole thing?"

Doug climbs to his feet. "I remember something about *Godzilla* and space … no, that can't be right."

Suddenly Gideon feels sick. "Hold on to your memories. You must hold on!" He climbs to his feet and runs to the nearest hallway.

Dwight shouts, "Where are you going?"

But Gideon doesn't reply. He runs until he comes to the picture of the cowboy on the wall. He opens the door to the gray lady's office. He knows this is the one. But sure enough, it's the teachers' lounge.

"No!" he cries as confused teachers look up from their lunches. He slams the door. He closes his eyes and wills the staircase to return. *I will defeat you, yet, Normalia.* He opens the door again. It's still the teachers' lounge. Again he slams the door.

Wanda catches up with him, placing a hand on his shoulder.

Gideon exclaims, "We can't let her get away!"

"She's the goddess of normality," Wanda says calmly. "Perhaps we should look somewhere … *normal.*"

The bell rings. Students usher into the hallways. It's just an ordinary day at Eastward High. Hand in hand, Gideon and Wanda step into the traffic. They look around, but everything is just … normal.

Gideon says, "She undid everything we worked so hard for."

"I don't know about that," says Wanda. "We still have each other."

Dwight catches up with them. "How does she still have power? We turned everyone against her, and we defeated her master."

Wanda says, "Perhaps she's more powerful than we thought. And perhaps she's the *true* master. How can we defeat normality?"

Dwight smashes his fist into a locker. "We were so close! There must be a way."

Then Doug and Cynthia catch up, also hand-in-hand. "I have an idea," says Doug. He gets down onto his hands and knees, then extends an arm in front of his nose.

A disturbed Cynthia asks, "What are you doing?"

"I'm an elephant," says Doug. He then proceeds to crawl through the hallway as an elephant, raising his trunk and making trumpet calls with his lips.

A passing boy demands, "What are you doing?" Another boy goes so far as to throw a book at him, shouting "Get up!" Two girls move to the far side of the hallway to steer clear of this impropriety.

Meanwhile an embarrassed Cynthia tugs at Doug's arm, whispering, "This is not normal."

"That's the idea," says Doug. "Are you gonna join me or what?"

Cynthia looks around in horror. But in the end, her resolve wins out. She also gets on her hands and knees and joins Doug as an elephant.

Gideon can't help but smile. He turns to Wanda. "Cynthia must really love Doug."

"Yeah," says Wanda, squeezing his hand.

Dwight is enjoying the entertainment. He shrugs. "Why not?" Then he also becomes an elephant.

Suddenly Gideon feels a disturbing change in the air, and he notices a reflection on one of the doors.

The gray lady.

Whipping around, he sees her standing in front of the teachers' lounge. She's frowning at the unseemly sight of elephants in the hallway. Then she sees Gideon, and she runs.

"Come on!" Gideon cries. Together he and Wanda run down the hallway and around a corner.

The gray lady is trapped. For a moment she looks frightened. Then she smiles. "As I said, Mister Greenwich, I am impressed. But you must know, the game ends here."

"No," says Gideon, his fury returning. He lets go of Wanda's hand. "You have no right to control us."

"Try as you might, you'll never out-think me as you did the others. I am not some fickle trend or false appearance. I am reality. The world depends on normalized, predictable behavior. If it weren't for me, chaos would reign." She takes a step forward. "You must think yourself some sort of hero, but the sad truth is, your efforts were in vain. You and your friends are mere drops in an ocean. The protectors of the status quo will always outnumber the weirdos. These are the facts of life, Mister Greenwich. Now I suggest you get back to class."

Gideon reaches down and pulls off one of his shoes, the only thing he can think of to throw. He hurls it at the gray lady, but the shoe only impacts against the wall behind her, then falls to the floor.

She's gone.

Gideon groans with anger.

Wanda places a hand on his cheek. "We can't stop evil from existing. What matters is that we do good." She looks him in the eyes. "Whether or not anyone remembers why, I know the students of this school are better off because of you. You are *cool*, Gideon Greenwich."

Gideon can't help but mirror her smile. "You're pretty cool, yourself, Wanda." Then, like no power he's ever felt, something pulls him toward her. Their lips touch, and life is amazing.

Much too soon, Wanda withdraws as someone else enters the hallway.

Joan Cooper. She must have a class in this hallway, but looking disgusted at the sight before her, she turns to leave.

Gideon shouts, "Joan, wait!"

Now Joan looks disturbed. "How do you know my name?"

"Do you remember anything? The gods, the clouds, the stars?"

Joan shakes her head. "You guys are seriously creeping me out." Again she turns to leave, though she doesn't take a step. Then, in a quiet voice, she adds, "I do remember something."

"What is it?"

Joan looks around, perhaps to make sure that no one else is listening. "I have this weird feeling that in some alternative universe … we were all friends. I know it sounds crazy."

Wanda smiles. "It doesn't sound crazy at all." She struggles to get the words out. "You know, I really enjoyed your report in Fashion Merchandising. And you and I are in the same chemistry class. Maybe sometime … we could study together."

Then Joan smiles. "I would like that."

ABOUT THE AUTHOR

Stephen Gashler has spent his life battling the Gods of Cool. When not adventuring through parallel universes, he makes Youtube videos, performs as a storyteller, and writes rock operas about vikings, bums, and dead people. He also makes spicy curries and does a mediocre back flip.

Other novels by Stephen Gashler include *Prisoner of the Molepeople* and *The Bent Sword*. Follow his latest projects at:

http://stephengashler.com